KELSEY CLAYTON

Editing by Librum Artis
Cover Image by Michelle Lancaster

To Rumi,
For loving toxic men as much as you do.
Love you.

It's all fun and games,
until feelings show up to the
playground.

— ERIC VAN VUREN

1

LENNON

My naked body sinks into the bed beneath me. Kellan softly runs his fingertips up my side. I turn my head to face him, loving the way he smiles as he leans in to kiss me. It's nothing too intense, but gives me a taste of what's to come.

As we break the kiss, a hand comes to rest on my cheek and pulls my head to the other side. Colby bites his lip before coming closer. The way he kisses me is different. More demanding. Less gentle. And I'm enjoying every second of it.

The two of them fight for my attention while both pleasing me at the same time. Between the way Colby rubs circles over my clit and Kellan kisses my neck—I'm in heaven. I can't imagine there is anything better than having the two hottest guys I know in bed, with their only mission being to make me feel good.

"Tell us what you want, babe," Kellan whispers.

I let out a shuddering breath. "I want both of you to finger me, at the same time."

They both glance at each other and smirk, but just as they move to do it, they pause. Their brows furrow and mouths open, only for an ear-piercing pulsing beep to come out.

What the fuck?

I'm pulled out of my dream and into the harsh reality that

I'm not currently in the middle of a hot-ass threesome, and I'm still looking at being a virgin for the next hundred years.

Okay, so maybe I'm being a little overdramatic. But can't a girl just finish a sexy dream without being forced awake? Is that too much to ask?

My door opens, and Melani comes in, holding my breakfast. The housekeeper smiles sweetly at me as she brings the tray over to my bed.

"Good morning, Lennon," she greets me in the English accent that has never seemed to fade. "Happy Birthday."

Right. My birthday. I almost forgot, that's today.

"Thanks, Mel."

She lays my school uniform out on the chair in the corner of my oversized bedroom and heads for the door, leaving me to eat my breakfast in peace. Once I'm done, I take a quick shower—trying not to let the dream I was rudely interrupted from fester in my mind—and pull on my uniform.

My dad is sitting at the kitchen table when I get downstairs, reading the newspaper in his perfectly tailored suit. His dark brown hair is cut short on the sides and longer on the top. It's slicked back with gel, making him look like the well-kept businessman he is.

"Hi, sunshine." He smiles at me. "Happy Birthday."

"Thanks, Dad."

I sit down at the table and start to take out my phone when a small box in silver wrapping paper catches my attention. The pink bow sitting on top tells me exactly who it's for.

"Aren't you going to open it?" my dad asks.

Nodding, I take the box into my hands and gently pull off the paper. Once I get it open, my breath hitches. Sitting inside is a key fob. The Mercedes logo on it immediately brings my attention to the front door. My grin widens as I jump up and head outside, my father hot on my heels.

The second I open the door, I see it. A white Mercedes

Benz, topped with a giant pink bow that matches the smaller one from the box. It's beautiful, and everything I would want in a car, *if* I wasn't terrified to get my license.

"It's beautiful," I breathe.

My dad places his hand on my shoulder. "Beautiful car for my beautiful little girl."

I press the unlock button and check out the inside. The beige interior is gorgeous and makes the car look as light as I feel. I take a moment to admire the sight from the driver's seat, but the bliss quickly dissipates.

The thought of driving this thing down the street makes me more nervous than it does excited. It's not a fear I can explain. You'd think I was involved in a traumatic car accident or lost someone important to me because of one, but that's not the case. I let my friends drive me around, have no problem being in a car, but driving one is a whole different situation.

"So, I was thinking sometime this week we'll get you behind the wheel. Teach you how to drive this baby."

This conversation isn't a new one. My dad has been trying to get me to drive since the day I turned sixteen. While most girls were excited to get their permits, I insisted I was just fine with Francois, the chauffeur, driving me everywhere. It's what we pay him for, right? It worked for a little while, but the longer I go without driving myself everywhere I need to go, the more my dad seems to press the matter. He says that Francois is *his* employee, and he needs him during the day. *Whatever.*

"Sure, Dad. Sounds great."

I'm lying. The thought of getting behind the wheel of any car is enough to send me into a panic, but it's not like he wants to do this right now. I'll pacify him long enough for me to think of an excuse. Until then, I have school.

FRANCOIS PULLS UP TO Haven Grace Prep—my home away from home the last four years. I'm only two weeks from graduation, and trust me when I say, it cannot come soon enough. It's not that I don't love it here—I just have a serious case of senioritis. Summer vacation, here I come.

The front of the school is filled with students, and the public school across the street is no different. I walk through the crowd of people as I head up the stairs and inside. Conversation fills the hallways as I navigate my way toward my locker. The second I turn, however, I stop. A huge smile spreads across my face.

Wrapping paper and balloons cover my locker, with a big "Happy Birthday Lennon" sign hanging above it. The culprit, who also happens to be my best friend, stands beside the display. She's looking down at her phone—probably texting her boyfriend—and her long, brown hair is tied back into a ponytail. It looks like she rushed out the door this morning to make sure she'd get here long before me.

"I take it this was *your* doing?"

Tessa jumps and drops her phone. "Don't scare me like that, brat."

I chuckle and pull her into my arms. "I love you. Thank you."

"Happy birthday!"

Carefully, I rip a little hole in the wrapping paper to reach the lock. I put in the combination and open it up. Confetti streams out, and Tessa laughs as I roll my eyes. Everything inside my locker is covered in glitter. Clearly making the outside of my locker look like a party wasn't enough, so I have to walk around looking like I just came from a strip club.

The feeling of someone pressed against my back grabs my attention and makes me breathe in their scent. I don't have to turn around to know who it is. His hands find my waist, and his face nuzzles into my neck.

"Hey, you."

Kellan hums. "Happy Birthday, babe."

I turn around in his hold and look up at my boyfriend. His chiseled jaw is sharp enough to cut glass, but his smile could melt it. He's the hottest guy in school, and while self-esteem isn't something I struggle with, sometimes I'm surprised he's with me. It took two years of me crushing on him before he finally got a clue and asked me out. Now, it's been two months of being official, and I couldn't be happier.

"Thank you."

Stretching up on my tip-toes, I press my lips to his, and he smiles into the kiss. Tessa mocks disgust with a groan and laughter breaks Kellan and me apart.

"You know," I say to her. "You were a lot more cheery when your boyfriend was our teacher."

Tessa rolls her eyes, but I can see the amusement behind them. "I was a lot more cheery when I didn't have to watch you two suck face all the time."

Little does she know, we were sucking face occasionally then, too, but she was too focused on Asher. The two of them met last summer for what they both thought was just a one night stand. It turned out Asher was our new English teacher, and Tessa wasn't exactly honest about her age. After more drama than a teen soap, he ended up choosing her over everything else, and I've never seen either of them happier.

"Yeah, well, now you know how I feel whenever I come over."

She smirks. "Liar. You and Colby are too busy making fun of us to care what we're doing."

Kellan stiffens at the mention of Colby Hendrix. Famous NFL player, voted Hottest Man Alive two years in a row, and a total ladies' man—Colby is everything a girl would kill to have. Every girl but me, that is. It's not that I don't find him attractive. Anyone with eyes can see that he's gorgeous. I've just been around him enough to see that unless I want to be hit and quit, staying far away from his bed is in my best interest.

"Easy, babe," I tell my boyfriend, fisting my hands in his shirt. "We're just friends, remember?"

He growls deep in his chest, but the second I kiss the bottom of his jaw, he softens. And yeah, I may just love that I have that effect on him.

THE DAY PASSES BY with me receiving more balloons than I can count, since Tessa is such a fucking comedian and had them delivered throughout the day. Enough people wish me happy birthday to last a lifetime. By the time school lets out, I look like the house from *Up*. Tessa chuckles at me, making a comment about me flying away, and I lightly elbow her in the stomach.

I walk out the door with Kellan on one side and Tessa on the other. The second I see the familiar car and the wide shoulders leaning against it, I can't help but smile. Kellan grumbles something under his breath, but I don't pay much attention to it.

Handing Tessa the balloons, I run down the stairs and jump into Colby's arms. He catches me with ease and chuckles. He's been away for training the last couple weeks, and I didn't think he would be back yet, let alone show up at my school.

"What are you doing here?"

He squeezes me tightly and places me firmly back onto the ground. "You didn't honestly think I'd miss your birthday, did you?"

I run my fingers through my platinum blonde hair and stare down at the ground. "I mean..."

He snickers and pulls me in for another hug. "Not a chance, little one."

The sound of Kellan clearing his throat makes me let Colby go and step away. Tessa laughs as she embraces Colby. Kellan wraps an arm around my waist, as if he's reminding everyone who I'm with, and it makes me giggle.

"What's with the balloons?" Colby asks. "Are you trying to fly?"

Tess snorts and I turn to glare at her. "This bitch thought it would be funny to make me carry damn near fifty balloons through the hall all day. More got delivered in each class, and by last period, I could barely see the ceiling."

Colby grins and high-fives Tessa. I pretend to pout and cross my arms over my chest.

"Oh, come on," he argues. "You have to admit that's gold, and it made you feel loved."

"Yeah, yeah."

He puts his hand out. "Give me the balloons, Len."

I pass them to him, and he looks up before letting go, watching as they soar into the sky. Tessa stands there, gaping, and my grin widens.

"There," Colby shrugs. "Problem solved."

"Dick." Tess punches him in the arm. "Do you know how much money I spent on those?"

He side-eyes her playfully. "Oh, please enlighten me, Miss Trust Fund."

Her face scrunches up as she tries not to laugh, but it's no use. "I hate you."

"You can't," he tells her, and focuses his attention on Kellan for the first time since he got here. "Mind if I borrow her for a couple hours?"

Kellan's hand tightens on my waist. "Do I have a choice?"

"No," I answer for Colby and turn to give Kellan a quick peck on the cheek. "I'll call you when I get home. I promise."

He makes a show out of grabbing my face and pulling me in for a heated kiss. It's more PDA than usual, and I have no doubt this is totally for Colby's benefit. I let him dip me back until Tessa speaks up.

"Dear God, Kellan. Let her breathe."

Breaking away, a light pink coats my cheeks, and I smile down at the ground. With one more possessive kiss to the top of my head and a warning glare at Colby, Kellan walks away with Tess and leaves the two of us alone. Colby opens the passenger door and helps me into the car.

"So, where are we going exactly?" I ask once he's seated in the driver's seat.

He smiles, with those dangerous dimples appearing. "I figured I'd take you to dinner for your birthday. That okay?"

"That depends. Is it hibachi?"

Humor graces his expression. "Whatever the princess wants."

After a little bit of convincing, he brings me home to change out of my uniform before we go to dinner. The whole ride there, Colby fills me in on everything that happened at training and how excited he is to have a month off. I don't blame him. Playing professional football has to be anything but easy. The pressure alone could break a person.

Pulling up to my favorite restaurant, my mouth waters at the smell radiating from the place. We head inside, and Colby makes it a point to request a whole hibachi table to ourselves. It's not like he's hard to recognize. We haven't been in here more than two minutes and people are already starting to whisper.

"I can only imagine what people will say this time."

He chuckles. "Haven't you heard? You're my first serious relationship."

I roll my eyes with a smile. "I'm sure Kellan will *love* that."

The waitress leads us over to our table, and the whole way there, Colby keeps a hand on my lower back. "He's a bit of a possessive one, isn't he?"

I shrug. "I think he's just intimidated by you, which is weird because he was never like that before."

Smirking, he takes the seat next to me. "Isn't it obvious? You're eighteen now, and no longer off limits."

Heat floods my body, and I'm suddenly aware of how close we are. *Shit, is he flirting with me?* No. He can't be. Colby has hit on me once, but it was quickly retracted the second I told him I was underage. Since then, we've maintained a strictly platonic relationship, and it's one that's really important to me.

I've never been the kind of girl to have a lot of friends. Kids tend to avoid me ever since we were younger. Whether it be because they're jealous of how wealthy my father is, or their parents are afraid of the power he possesses, they always stayed away. All I had for a long time was dance, which came with Brady and Savannah, but other than that I was alone—until Tessa.

Tessa Callahan is everything a best friend should be. She's loyal, strong, and fierce as hell. When Savannah introduced us last summer, I was honestly afraid of her. She came off as this girl who acted first and thought later. It wasn't until we actually got to know each other that I saw everything that makes her who she is. When you're around her, it's impossible to do anything but love her.

When Tess started pursuing our English teacher, it inevitably led me to Colby. My best friend dragged me to a party at Asher's, and Colby was the first person to make us feel welcome. He later admitted it was to make Asher jealous, since he was denying all feelings toward Tessa, but there was something genuine about the baby-faced heartthrob. From there, our friendship grew drastically.

"Does that freak you out?" I ask. "That I'm finally eighteen?"

He snorts and picks up his menu. "No way. Maybe now I can stop feeling like such a creep for hanging out with you."

I raise a single brow. "You're twenty-six, hanging out with an eighteen-year-old. You're still a creep."

"Touché." He pushes his hair out of his face, and I try not to stare. "So, what does that make Asher?"

"A straight-up victim. Have you seen how Tessa gets when she wants something? He never stood a chance at resisting her."

Chuckling, he agrees with me, and the two of us go quiet as we look over our options. I steal a quick glance over at him and take a deep breath. Colby was never an option for me, and he still isn't. I have a boyfriend. But I can't help but wonder what things would be like if he was. If things were different. If I wasn't seventeen when he told me I looked good at that party. *If only…*

AFTER A DINNER FILLED with jokes, laughter, and easy flowing conversation, Colby and I leave the restaurant and get back into his car. He's barely even backed out of the parking space before my phone rings and Tessa's picture fills the screen.

"Hey, Tess."

"Lennon," she wails.

My brows furrow. "What's wrong?"

"Asher and I had a fight. He got so mad and stormed out."

She muffles another sob, poorly, and I sigh heavily. It's not like them to argue. Hell, for the most part, they're all over each other and leave no room for an argument to form. However, the sound of her distress tells me it must have been bad.

"I'll be right there."

She sniffles. "No. It's your birthday."

I tap Colby on the shoulder and mouth for him to head to Asher's. "Shut up. I'm fifteen minutes away. Stay there."

TURNING INTO THE PARKING garage, I notice all of Asher's cars are here. Either he's back and they're arguing some more, or they're having intense make-up sex. Regardless, I promised her I would be here, and I won't leave until I've checked on her.

Colby and I walk over to the elevator and step inside. As he puts in the code for the penthouse, I look down at my phone to see if I've gotten anything else from Tess, but there's nothing. A part of me is slightly afraid for what real-life porno we're about to walk into, but I don't get much time to overthink it before the doors are opening.

"Surprise!" everyone shouts, scaring the shit out of me.

The room is filled with everyone I love, minus my dad and housekeeper, of course. Tessa laughs at my reaction and comes over to give me a hug.

"You're such a bitch," I tell her, failing at maintaining my anger. "I thought you were really upset!"

She flips her hair over her shoulder. "I know. I should be an actress."

Asher comes up behind her and wraps his arms around her waist. "And have to watch you kiss and grope other men for a living? Not fucking happening."

The corners of her mouth raise as she looks up at him. "Not that kind of actress."

"Yeah, still not happening. The only one who gets to touch you is me."

Kellan comes over, and my grin widens. "You knew about this?"

He shrugs and pulls me into his arms. "I may have had some idea."

"Thanks for letting me take her out," Colby tells him, extending his hand.

My boyfriend looks at it for a second, and I jab my elbow into his stomach lightly. He rolls his eyes as he takes it.

"Don't get used to it."

Colby snickers. "Noted."

I glance back and forth between the two of them, and the dream I had this morning fills my mind. It's no secret that they're both fucking gorgeous, and heat builds between my legs as they both stare back at me. That fantasy may never come true, but a girl can enjoy the idea.

"Lenny!" Skye slurs drunkenly. Her brown hair only goes down to a little below her shoulders, but it's still a mess. She throws her arm around my shoulders, pulling me away from Kellan. "Have a shot with me!"

I can't help but laugh at her. "I don't think you need any more shots, hun."

She scoffs. "Trust me, I do."

Kellan and Colby watch me get led away and into the kitchen, both looking nothing but amused. As I take a shot from the bartender Tessa hired, I glance around the room, and a warmth floods through me. I don't see how life can get any better than this.

2

CADE

I STORM OUT OF THE HOUSE, SLAMMING THE DOOR behind me. No matter how many times they call my name, I don't care to turn back. My teal Jeep Wrangler sits in front of the house and allows me the perfect getaway. It may be old, but it's never let me down before. I hop into the driver's seat and peel away before anyone can stop me.

I glance in the rear-view mirror to see my mom standing on the front lawn. She watches me leave with tears in her eyes, but I don't feel an ounce of regret. She *should* be sad. She *should* feel guilty. All of this is her fault.

This is fucking bullshit. Today was going well, until I came home and my parents told me to sit down. *We have something to tell you,* they said. Based on the dreaded look on my dad's face, I knew it wasn't anything good. My first thought was someone died, but honestly, I think this might be worse.

A divorce. They're getting a goddamn divorce. At nineteen years old, I've had plenty of friends with broken families. I just never thought that mine would be one of them. Not when they've done nothing but love each other since the day I was born. Hell, they barely even fight. It's not like they're those parents who keep me up at night with their shouting at each other.

I tried to fight it, tried to get them to change their minds. *What about Molly,* I asked them, bringing up my little sister. She's only ten and I know this is going to wreck her. But there was nothing I could have said to stop this, especially not when my dad dropped the bomb that changed the situation entirely.

Your mother met someone else.

Someone.

Else.

She's throwing everything away and breaking up our family for some other guy, and yet she has the audacity to try to get me to talk to her. Fuck that. She doesn't deserve my attention, and she sure as hell doesn't get my sympathy. Not when my dad would have done anything for her. For us.

The wind blows through my hair as I pull up to the familiar beach. I slip my wetsuit on and grab my surfboard from the back. Hot sand burns the bottom of my feet as I run across it before diving straight into the water.

I push the nose of the board down to go through the wave rather than over it. As soon as the water cools my heated skin, I start to feel better, but it's not enough. I paddle out and wait for the next swell, taking out my anger and frustrations the best way I know how—by commanding the water. When I'm out here, it's like nothing else matters. No stress. No worries. Just me, my board, and the ocean.

Catching the next wave, I stand up on my board and cut through the water. My moves are a little rougher than normal, and if anyone else were here, they'd for sure be able to tell. Thankfully, I have these waves all to myself.

A WHISTLE SOUNDS FROM the shoreline, and I glance back to see Bryce and Jayden paddling toward me. I should've known my friends would find me here. Whenever I go off the grid, they know where to look. Hell, it's probably the most predictable thing about me.

I run my hand through the water, exhausted from the last few hours. I don't even know how long I've been out here, but if the sunset is anything to go by, it's been a while.

"What's up, fucker?" Bryce greets me.

"My mom told you to find me, didn't she?"

Bryce, Jayden, and I have been friends since we were in diapers. When I was twelve, my parents moved us to Hawaii. It was hard being away from them, since they were closer than most of my family to me, but when we all turned sixteen, they came to live with us for a year.

The time the three of us spent there together was unforgettable. We wore our board shorts to school just so we didn't waste any prime surfing time after school. After learning how to surf together as soon as we knew how to swim, it's no surprise that we all took advantage of the perfect swells Hawaii had to offer.

Jayden sighs. "She's worried about you."

I roll my eyes. "That's rich. She wasn't too worried about me when she was out cheating on my dad, was she?"

Both of them wince, and I can tell she neglected to tell them *why* I'm so pissed off. I take a deep breath and look out at the horizon, loving the way the sun kisses the ocean as it dips below the surface. California surfing doesn't hold a candle to the island, but the view isn't so bad.

"So, they're splitting up," Bryce says, as if it's no big deal. "My parents did. It's not so bad once you get used to the change."

"I don't *want* to get used to it. You should have seen the look on my dad's face. He was fucking devastated."

"He didn't know?" Jayden asks.

I shake my head. "I don't think he found out until she told him that she's leaving."

"That's rough."

There are plenty of words I'd use to describe the current status of my home life, but rough pales in comparison. Crumbling. Chaos. A fucking train wreck even. But rough doesn't do it justice.

"We should've never left Hawaii," I grumble, meaning every word more than ever.

If it were up to me, I would've stayed there for the rest of my life. Between the atmosphere, the surfing, and the people —it was perfect. The best place to be all the time. But whoever makes the fucking decisions for my life had other plans. After spending four years living the island life, my dad's job transferred him back to California.

I tried to look at the bright side. At least living back here, I don't ever have to be away from Bryce and Jayden again, but I was living my best life when we were all there. Together. Happy. Carefree. I'd give anything to go back to that.

"Any idea who the shithead is?" Bryce questions.

I smile at his choice of words, knowing he's on my side. They both are. Always.

"No idea. I'm sure I'll find out eventually though." I swipe my hand through the water, sending some flying. "Honestly, I'd like to punch him straight in the jaw."

Jayden smirks. "You know what you need?"

"A Glock?"

The two of them snicker, but a big part of me isn't kidding. "No, asshole. A party."

Being around a ton of people I can barely stand is probably a bad idea, but going home is an even worse one. Besides, I could use a drink, or nine.

"Yeah, fuck it. Where at?"

Bryce's grin widens. "Josslyn's."

I throw my head back and groan loudly. Josslyn and I have

a shared history—one that begins and ends between the sheets. She's not the worst person to be around, but ever since I broke up with her a couple months ago, things have been weird. To be honest, I got bored, but she doesn't seem to know when to quit. She still throws herself at me every chance she gets. Sometimes I indulge her, if I don't have anyone better to focus my attention on. As long as she isn't super clingy, I should be able to stand her for one night.

"Fuck me."

Jayden chuckles. "I'm sure she'd be happy to."

AFTER GRABBING A SHOWER at Bryce's, I throw on a fresh pair of shorts and white tee with palm trees up the side. Staring at my reflection, I swoop my brown hair out of my face. It's not too out of control, but long enough to get in my eyes. I spray myself with his *I'm trying too hard* cologne and walk out the door. Both of them are ready to go and waiting for me in the living room.

"Okay, let's get this shit-show on the road."

We all head out of the house but Bryce stops to laugh at me. "You know, you didn't have to make *that* big of an attempt. She would have fucked you even if you smelled like B.O."

I roll my eyes and push him forward. "Shut up, douche."

My ex's house isn't far, and it only takes a ten-minute drive before we're pulling up to the house. Her parents must be away for a while, because this is bigger than the usual parties she has when they're expected home anytime soon. There's barely even room to park, so I pull partially onto the front lawn. It'll probably start a trend and ruin the grass, but I don't give a fuck.

I pull the key from the ignition and the three of us pour out of the Jeep. Some familiar faces greet us as we make our way inside, but others just stand there, staring with their jaws dropped. I wink at one girl who may as well be drooling, making her drink fall out of her hand and spill onto the floor. *Sophomores.*

"Look who it is," a sickeningly sweet voice meets my ears. I turn around to see Josslyn. She's wearing a black dress that doesn't leave much to the imagination, and enough makeup to look like a cheap hooker. "Never thought I'd see you here tonight."

I shrug. "What can I say? I could use a drink."

She smirks and wraps her hands around my bicep. "By all means then, let's get you one."

REMEMBER WHEN I HOPED that my ex wouldn't act like a stage-five clinger? Yeah, wishful thinking. I can't seem to figure out if it's because I've been avoiding her for the past few weeks, or because she thinks I came here for her, but she's been trying to dig her talons into me all damn night. Thankfully, Jayden took mercy on me and broke a window, pulling her attention away from me and giving me an escape.

We start to head back to my car when I come face to face with the one asshat I can't stand more than my mother right now. *Kellan Spencer.* He's one of those douchebags from the prep school in North Haven. Rich, entitled, and a royal pain in my ass. He and I actually used to be friends at one point in time, until I beat him at a surfing competition when we were ten. All the lessons his parents bought him, and I was still better. No amount of money could have changed that.

Kellan couldn't seem to accept that I just had more drive and determination than he did. Instead, he insisted I cheated. He stopped talking to me and eventually stopped surfing all together—focusing on football and other sports where he actually stood a chance at winning.

What the fuck is he doing here?

"Out of my way, scumbag," he sneers, his arm draped across the shoulders of some brunette.

I laugh dryly and step directly in his way. "Why don't you make me?"

He looks me up and down, and I'm mentally begging for him to hit me. It wouldn't be the first time him and I have gotten physical, or the second, for that matter. We're about the same size, and both know how to fight, which always makes for an interesting scuffle. However, I'm dying for someone to take my anger out on right now. *Go ahead. Hit me.*

"Not worth it," he decides. "I've got better things to do."

The girl under his arm preens as he drops his head and presses his lips to hers, making it clear what *better things* he's referring to. Bryce pretends to gag, and I laugh at the scowl she gives my friend. If Kellan thinks he's got some kind of prize under his arm, he's got another thing coming. I could throw a rock blindfolded and hit a girl hotter than her.

"Come on, Skye. Let's go."

I roll my eyes as he walks away, wishing he would've done something. I could have used a human punching bag right about now. I'd love nothing more than to beat him bloody.

"I hate that prick."

"We know," Bryce and Jayden answer in unison, and a part of me considers leaving them here.

Taylor, a dude we hang out with from time to time, inserts himself between Jayden and me, pushing us forward. "Enough about him. Let's go camp out on the beach. It's not supposed to rain tonight."

That's the first good idea I've heard all day. We leave the party, clingy ex-girlfriends, and jealous assholes behind us and head to the only place where my worries fade away. My life falling apart can be dealt with tomorrow. Tonight, I'm going to get drunk and sleep in the sand.

3

LENNON

THE BEAT OF "EXHALE" BY KENZIE AND SIA FILLS the room. My body responds to the music, hitting each move with the utmost precision. That's one of the best things about dance—there isn't a single emotion that can't be portrayed with your body and a song.

As the chorus starts for the second time, I watch in the mirror as Brady joins me. It only pushes me harder and makes me strive to be better. Being the son of the studio owner, he's here more than he's not, and since he choreographed this dance, it was hard to keep up at first—but I'm nothing if not determined. With dance. With school. With life. My dad has always taught me to never let anything hold me back.

Sweat rolls down my forehead as I exert all my energy into the final few moves. When the song ends, I collapse onto the floor. Brady chuckles as he walks over and grabs our water bottles and tosses mine to me.

"I love when someone pisses you off," he says.

My brows furrow. "How do you know I'm pissed off?"

"Because you always dance better when you're angry. So, what did Kellan do this time?"

I don't know whether I should be concerned that I'm as easy to read as an open book, or find it amusing that he immediately knows it was Kellan to put me in this mood. Regardless, I don't hold anything back from Brady. He's the older brother I never had.

"He just doesn't get it." I sigh, fixing my ponytail. "He got an attitude with me because I wouldn't skip dance for some party he's going to. I guess he thinks that because the recital is over, that we have no reason to keep dancing, but he plays football after the season ended. So, why is this any different?"

"Because he's a guy."

I level him with a look, and he puts his hands up in surrender and snickers.

"I'm just saying, most straight men, who aren't dancers, don't see the importance of it. Hell, some of them don't even consider it a sport, which is funny because I get a better workout in this room than I ever did out on the field."

"Yeah, well, he can shove that mindset right up his ass."

Brady smirks as he messes around with his phone to choose a new song. "I know what you need."

My head lolls to the side. "An IV of straight caffeine?"

He hits play and "B*tch From Da Souf, The Remix" booms through the speakers. All the feelings I've held onto from the argument with Kellan dissipate, and I can't help but laugh. He comes over and puts out his hand to help me up. We dance around the room with no care about how unprofessional we look.

By the time the song ends, I feel so much better—like a weight was lifted from my chest. My energy level might be a little more lacking, but that's the price you pay for fun sometimes. The room goes quiet aside from the sounds of mine and Brady's labored breathing, yet we both have wide grins on our faces.

"I just have one question."

I hum in response.

"What do you two plan on doing? Like, in September, when you go to New York for Juilliard."

"Honestly, I hadn't thought about it," I murmur, frowning at the concept.

The realization that I hadn't even cared to consider our future slaps me in the face. It's not that I don't like Kellan—I do, or I wouldn't be with him—but I just don't think he's the guy I'm going to end up spending the rest of my life with. Especially not when he can't support one of the most important things in my life, all because he wants me to come to a party. However, the thought of not having him puts an uncomfortable feeling in my chest.

Brady shrugs. "Well, no rush. You still have a few months before you leave."

I'M SITTING ON MY bed, texting Colby about why it wouldn't be wise for him to hire a female publicist, since he has a tendency to screw anything with a hole, when my phone rings, and a picture of Kellan and me graces my screen. It's one from prom. The two of us had been playing cat and mouse for weeks until he finally caved and we became exclusive.

It's crazy how we went from being *that* happy to arguing over something as simple as a party. I take a deep breath and hit answer before bringing the phone to my ear.

"Hello?"

"Hey," he sighs, sounding relieved that I answered.

"Hey."

It goes quiet for a minute, as if the two of us are just enjoying the sound of the other breathing. The corners of my mouth raise involuntarily, and I roll my eyes.

"Are you busy today?" he questions.

I glance at the clock. One in the afternoon. "Not until dinner. My dad said he has something to tell me."

"Can I come pick you up for a bit? I miss you."

My heart aches at the sound of his words, and I know I miss him, too. "Yeah. Are you coming now?"

I can hear as he jumps up. "I'll be there in ten."

Before I can ask for a little more time, he hangs up and leaves me to rush around my room. Knowing Kellan, he probably doesn't have anything fancy planned, so instead of getting dressed in something cute, I keep my T-shirt and sweat shorts on. I run a brush through my hair and add just a little bit of eyeliner.

True to his word, Kellan pulls into my driveway no more than ten minutes later in his black BMW. I run down the stairs, waving goodbye to Melani on my way, and head out the door.

The second I climb into the car, I can feel the tension in the air. Kellan looks so laid-back in his white sweatpants and matching T-shirt, and if we weren't in some sort of argument limbo, I'd kiss him something fierce right now. Instead of greeting me properly, however, he puts the car into drive and pulls away.

It's not a long drive back to his house, but this one feels uncomfortable. A part of me starts to wonder if he's going to break up with me, but I've known him for years. He's not above breaking up with someone over the phone to avoid confrontation. If that was his plan, he wouldn't have picked me up to do it.

He parks the car and shuts it off. I climb out and follow Kellan to the front door, noticing there are no other cars in the driveway. The second we step inside, the level of silence tells me we're alone.

"No one is home?" I ask.

He shakes his head and locks the door behind me. "My

parents are at some charity thing. They won't be home until late."

"Oh."

I'd be lying if I said I'm not nervous. As much as I may joke around that I'll be a virgin forever, it's not like I haven't had the opportunity to lose it. Kellan has tried, more than once, but it's never felt right. The closest we've come is prom night, when he got us a hotel room and sprinkled the bed with rose petals because he saw it in a movie. I had every intention of giving it all up then, but the gesture felt a little too...practiced.

"Do you want anything to drink?"

The two of us make our way through the house and into the kitchen. "Yeah. Water, please."

I sit on the barstool as he grabs a bottle of water from the fridge and hands it to me. An awkward silence fills the air. Kellan must feel it too because he pulls on his hair and groans softly. I watch as he walks around the island and puts his hands on either side of me. He rests his head on mine, sighing heavily.

"I'm sorry I was such an ass last night," he apologizes.

"Why were you?"

He breathes me in. "I just feel like something is constantly taking you away from me. Whether it's dance, or Tessa, or Colby, you never seem to have time for me."

His words hit me where it hurts. I hadn't realized I was making him feel like second choice. I wrap my arms around his neck and hold him close, finally feeling the connection we share. The connection that made me want to be with him in the first place.

"I'm so sorry, Kel," I say sadly. "My life has always been so busy that I don't even see it when I'm not making something a priority."

"I guess I've just had so much free time since baseball

ended that I finally noticed how little we see each other," he explains.

Unable to hold back any longer, I close the gap between our mouths and press my lips to his. It's soft and sweet, just the way I like it. "I'll do better, just promise me something?"

"What?"

"That next time, if there *is* a next time, that you'll talk to me about it instead of snapping at me."

He chuckles and nods. "Deal. That party was a drag anyway. You wouldn't have had much fun."

WITH ALL THE TENSION long gone, Kellan and I cuddle up on the couch and start bingeing the third season of *The Walking Dead*. Halfway through the second episode, I get up to grab some popcorn. The faint sound of his phone dinging echoes through the room. By the time I get back, he's biting his lip as he focuses his attention down on his phone. My brows furrow as I make my way over to the couch.

"Everything okay?"

He startles slightly, clicking off his phone and putting it back in his sweatshirt pocket. "Yeah, why wouldn't it be?"

I sit next to him and cuddle into his side. "You just seemed really into your phone."

"Oh, that." He sounds caught off guard, but he shakes his head. "It was just Oakley. He met some girl at the party last night."

Dread floods through me as I listen to his lie. There is no way Oakley was at that party last night, because he's in Massachusetts, discussing his college options with his dad and the coach at Boston University. A part of me wants to push the subject—find out why he lied and insist he tells me the truth—but we just finished one argument. I'm not sure I want to have another.

I take a softer approach and relax into him. "Did *you* meet any girl last night?"

He sports a grin that melts me into a puddle of mush. "Don't be ridiculous. You know you're the only girl for me."

In one quick move, he flips us around until he's hovering over me. As he drops his mouth down onto mine, all my suspicions go out the window, and the only thing that's left is him and me. He kisses me with a skill born from experience, from the way he grips my waist to the way his tongue tangles with my own. It's so sexy.

It only takes a few minutes of making out before I feel his hand start to slide down to the waistband of my shorts. I hum against his lips and grab his wrist to stop him.

"Kellan," I murmur.

He pulls away and drops his head against my shoulder. "Why not?"

Because I'm scared.

Because I'm not sure about us.

Because I don't want to.

But all of those answers would only cause an argument I'd really rather avoid right now. So, instead, I play it safe.

"I have my period," I lie, and giggle as he jumps off me like I'm going to spurt blood at any second.

"Okay, yeah. That's a good enough reason."

I roll my eyes playfully and smack him with a pillow when he moves to sit five feet away from me. "Relax, dork. Menstruation isn't contagious."

He cringes. "Can we please stop talking about this?"

It's hilarious how he acts like such a manly man, but something as natural as periods can make him so nervous. I lay on the couch with my head in his lap and smile as he runs his fingers through my hair.

"So," he changes the subject. "What do you think your dad wants to tell you tonight?"

Now that's a question I've been asking myself since he

mentioned it in passing this morning. My dad is a serious businessman to just about everyone but me. The last time he told me he had something important to tell me was when he told me a private investigator found my mom. I hadn't even known he hired one. My mom walked out on us when I was three, and I barely remember her. However, when I started to ask about her, my dad had someone find her in case I wanted to reach out. I didn't, and still don't, but the effort he went through to give me the choice made me love him even more.

"I honestly have no idea," I answer. "I just hope it's nothing bad."

WE SPEND THE REST of the afternoon watching TV with sporadic make-out sessions. Once I'm no longer afraid he'll try to have sex with me, it becomes easier to let things go a little further—like his hands finding their way up my shirt.

Kellan drives me home shortly after six, and when we get there, I notice my dad's car is already in the driveway. I kiss my boyfriend goodbye and make my way inside. The second the door closes behind me, an unfamiliar laugh flows from the kitchen.

"Dad?" I call out.

"In here, sweetheart."

I walk through the house and toward the noise, only to find my dad standing there with a woman I've never met before. She's pretty, with short brown hair and plump, pink lips. I'd say she's probably only a few years younger than him. My dad smiles at me and places a hand on her lower back.

"Lennon, I'd like you to meet Nora, my girlfriend."

The air becomes so thick I could choke on it. "Your g-girlfriend?"

I didn't even know my dad was looking for a relationship, let alone dating someone. I look the woman over again, wondering who she is and where she came from. All my life, it's only ever been my dad and me. I'm not sure I'm okay with some random chick becoming a part of us.

"It's nice to meet you, Lennon," she greets me.

Doing my best to fake a polite smile, I look away from her and to my dad. "Is this what you wanted to tell me? The important news?"

A guilty look appears on his face as he glances at Nora and then back to me. "Well, partly. I wanted the two of you to meet and get to know each other."

No thanks. "I mean, I'll try, but I'm super busy with graduation and dance and getting ready for college. I'm just really swamped, Dad."

He gives me the no-bullshit look that he always uses whenever I'm in trouble. "That's okay. I'm sure there will be plenty of time since you'll see so much of each other."

"I'm sorry, what?"

With the little time my dad spends in this house, I don't see how I'll see her at all. However, my dad drops a bomb that very well may destroy the comfortable home life I've always loved.

"Sweetie, Nora is moving in—with her two kids. It's about time we fill this big, empty house."

My vision tunnels, and everything becomes hazy. I can faintly hear my dad mentioning something about her son being my age, but I can't find it in me to care. Everything I've ever known is about to change.

4

CADE

OUT OF EVERYTHING I COULD BE DOING RIGHT now, packing has got to be the worst option. It's bad enough that my parents are splitting up, but to top off this shitty situation, I have to go live with the homewrecker. Sure, I could stay here with my dad. I'm nineteen. It's no one's choice but my own. However, my mom is insisting on taking Molly with her, and I can't leave my little sister—especially not when I don't know who the hell my mom's new boyfriend is or what he's like. Obviously, he's the kind of guy who's okay with breaking up a family, and in my book, that instantly makes him a piece of shit.

I grab the shirts from my closet and toss them into a box. There's definitely a neater way to do this, but I don't want to be doing it in the first place. Why'd she have to go and ruin everything? Why couldn't she just talk to my dad and tell him what was making her so unhappy? They could have worked it out. No one can tell me that my dad wouldn't have done what it takes. He's spent the last twenty years putting her and our family first. He would have done anything.

This past week was probably the most awkward time of my life. My mom hasn't spent too much of her free time at home, claiming she's getting the rooms for Molly and me ready at the new house. Honestly, I think she just can't bring herself to be around my dad. Not when she knows that she's to blame for this. Our perfect family is in shambles, and it's all because of her.

Taking my surfing trophies down from the shelf, I wrap each of them up tightly and lay them inside a box. I write FRAGILE all over it, because if these get ruined, I very well might hurt someone. Surfing is the best thing in my life. My outlet. My favorite hobby. My lifeline. It's the one thing I can always count on, no matter what.

Fighting at home? *Surf.*

Life in shambles? *Surf.*

World burning down around me? *Surf.*

I'm just placing the last trophy inside the box when my bedroom door bursts open and Bryce throws himself onto my bed. He groans in pain, pulling a block of wax from under his back. I roll my eyes and snatch it away from him.

"That's what you get for not looking first."

He frowns. "Well, who would have thought you'd have a random block of wax in your bed?"

I say nothing, instead just looking at him until he chuckles. Anyone who knows me would expect exactly that.

"Okay, touché."

Jayden comes in next with a whole damn sandwich and a can of soda. My brows furrow as he takes a massive bite.

"What?" he asks with his mouth full. "Your mom made it for me."

To be honest, I didn't even know she was here. Then again, I shouldn't be surprised. My dad is at work, meaning there's no reason for her to be avoiding this place. I'm sure she'll leave before he gets home, because God forbid she actually faces the person she broke.

"Anyway—" I shake myself from my thoughts. "What are you guys doing here?"

Bryce gets up, as if he remembers the purpose for them being here. "Oh, right. We're taking you out."

My brows raise, and I look around the room. "Uh, do you not see that I'm packing? We're moving into Casa de Satan tomorrow."

"You've been packing all week," Jayden retorts.

"I have a lot of stuff."

It's not exactly a lie, but I haven't been up for company lately. I've spent most of my time going to a different beach to surf so I could be alone. It's not that I don't love my friends. They're practically my brothers. It's just—sometimes I don't want to talk or fake a smile. Pretending I'm all right gets exhausting, and I haven't had the energy to do it lately.

"Well, we don't care," Bryce tells me. "You're coming, even if we need to drag your ass out by your hair."

They've both got looks on their faces that dare me to go against them. I consider it for a second, but then realize the last time Bryce was this determined, he threw me in a pool—fully clothed, with my cellphone in my pocket. If I try to tell them no, they really will drag me out of here, and there's two of them. I run my fingers through my hair and sigh.

"Fine. What'd you have in mind?"

The two of them smirk, and I immediately wonder what I've gotten myself into.

THE LARGE BONFIRE SITS in the middle of the large crowd. It's easily over seven feet tall, and there has to be more than fifty people here. Everyone is drinking beer and having a good time. My friends were right—this is exactly what I needed. Then again, it also reminds me that I'm being forced to leave all this soon. It may only be a twenty-minute drive to North Haven, but the people there suck compared to the people here.

I grab my board and head for the water, seeing the perfect swells starting to roll in. It may not be the smartest thing to do—go surfing at night—but I can't help it. I need the high I get when I'm riding a wave.

Making quick work of paddling out, I can barely see the waves, but I can feel them. The bonfire provides a small amount of light that lets me see what's coming if I squint really hard. Finally, I paddle into the movement of the water and just as it starts to take me down, I hop up on my board.

My whole body feels lighter as I ride the wave. Like nothing can get to me. Like my problems aren't real. Like everything is going to be okay. And in the water, all of that is true. I'm standing on top of a board but it feels like I'm on top of the world.

A scream pulls me from my euphoria just in time to see my board heading straight for a chick who looks no older than I am. Her eyes are wide with fear. I cut to the side to avoid hitting her, but my balance never stood a chance. The wave takes me over and crashes directly on top of me and my board.

I tumble in the water for a few seconds until I can get to the surface, but no part of me panics. I've been in this situation enough to know what to do. When I manage to stand up, however, my heart drops. The shore break must have been strong enough to snap my board in half because the other part of it is washing up on the beach while the back half is still strapped to my ankle. Fuck.

"Oh my God, are you okay?" the girl shrieks.

Do I fucking look okay? "Are you out of your mind? What the hell were you doing out there?"

I snatch the other half of my board up and turn around. A blonde girl no taller than five foot two stands in front of me. It doesn't take a lot of light to see that her eyes are the kind of blue that reminds me of the water back in Hawaii. If I wasn't so angry at the current condition of my surfboard, I'd probably acknowledge how gorgeous she is.

"I just needed to clear my mind, so I thought I'd go for a swim," she explains shyly, rubbing her arm and looking down.

I roll my eyes. "Didn't your mother ever teach you not to swim in the ocean after dark?"

That seems to strike a nerve, because the sullen look falls right off her face and is replaced by one that threatens to put me in the ground. Her hip juts out to the side, and her eyes rake over my body, as if she's sizing me up. To be honest, I'm not sure I'd stand up in a fight with this chick. She may be little, but she looks scrappy.

"Lennon!" A girl around the same size with long, brown hair comes over and eyes me suspiciously before grabbing her friend's arm. "Come on. Colby's waiting in the car."

The blonde—*Lennon apparently*—hesitates, and a part of me wonders if she really does plan on trying to square up, until she scoffs and walks away. I can't help but watch as they disappear out of sight. Once they're gone, though, I remember my board.

I move closer to the fire and use the light to inspect the damage. It's not even a clean break, meaning there is no fixing it. It's as good as a pile of junk now. Bryce and Jayden come over with fresh beers in their hands, but when Bryce sees the board, he drops his. It spills out into the sand.

"Dude, party foul," Jayden scolds him, until he notices it as well. "Fuck. What happened?"

"Some dumb bitch went swimming in the middle of my path. I managed to swerve out of the way in time, but it fucked up my board."

Bryce sighs and looks at the pieces. "That sucks, man."

"Yeah," I grumble. "You're telling me."

Jayden hands me his beer. "Only thing to ever come close to surfing is getting drunk."

I snort sarcastically, but he may have a point. If I can't surf away the chaos, I may as well drown it in alcohol.

LIGHT SHINES IN THROUGH the window of Jayden's room and lands on my face. As soon as I open my eyes, a sharp, stabbing pain shoots through my head and has me hissing. I pull the pillow over my face in an attempt to drown out the morning, but it's no use. Today, my life changes, and I have a hard time believing it will be for the better.

After getting Jayden's older brother to give me a ride back to my Jeep, I hop inside and head for home. It's only nine in the morning by the time I pull up, but my mom already has the U-Haul here and people packing things up.

Shit. I never finished packing my room.

I slip past a couple movers standing in the doorway and make my way through the house. As I get to my room, however, I find the only thing left in it is my bed, dresser, and nightstand. Everything else has been packed up and moved out. Of course, a few knickknacks are left, being as this is still going to be my room, but everything I need to live is gone. My eyes move to a note sitting on top of my dresser.

Cade,
Hope you had a good time last night. I finished packing your room and instructed the movers on what to take. Molly and I will meet you at the new house.
Love,
Mom

An address for what I can only assume is our new humble abode is written at the bottom. I take a deep breath before folding it up and slipping it inside my pocket.

Once I leave my room, I glance around the house. My

mom didn't decide to take much, probably not finding a need for it all. My room, Molly's room, and my mom's personal belongings are all cleared out for the most part, but everything else is left in place. As I head back into the living room, I find my dad leaning against the wall, watching as the movers finish closing up the truck.

"Hey, Dad."

He jumps, turning away and rubbing his hands over his face to hide the obvious fact that he was just crying. "Cade. I didn't realize you were home."

I nod. "I just got back a few minutes ago. I didn't realize Mom packed up the rest of my room."

'Yeah, I think she finished that last night after you left."

In all the years growing up with my dad, I don't think I've ever seen him this torn apart. He's trying to put on a strong front for my sake, but I can tell he's breaking inside. Having lost the love of his life and now having to live in this house alone, it has me second guessing my choice to stay with Molly.

"Are you sure you're going to be all right?" I question. "Maybe I should just stay with you."

He shakes his head. "No, your sister needs you to be there for her. Hell, *I* need you to be there for her."

I rub the back of my neck to try to dull the pain of not only my hangover, but the reality of the situation. "Well, if you need me, just call. I'll be here within twenty minutes."

That makes him smile. "Are you worried about your old man?"

"A little," I quip. "It's like you just said—you're old."

He chuckles and pulls me in for a hug. "You're a good kid, Cade."

"I learned from the best."

I PULL UP TO the big, white house that could, by any standard, be considered a castle. Massive doesn't even begin to cover it. This place should have its own zip code. There must be at least three floors, and there is literally a tower in the front corner. The two Mercedes sitting in the driveway don't even begin to surprise me, and a part of me wonders what kind of cars are in the oversized garage.

Walking up to the front door, I hesitate. Do I knock or walk right in? I mean, technically I live here now, but I've never been here before. Thankfully, in the middle of my mental debate, the door opens and my mom appears in the doorway.

"I thought I heard your Jeep." She grabs my wrist and pulls me inside. "Come on. I want you to meet Ken."

I let her drag me through the house and into an office that's bigger than my former living room. A man in a suit sits behind the desk with a phone pressed firmly to his ear. When he sees me, however, his expression changes.

"I'll have to call you back, Jay. Nora's son just got here."

With a few more polite words, he gets off the phone and stands up. He's taller than me, maybe three inches above my own height of six feet two, which I didn't expect because I'm the tallest person I know—until now, I guess. He comes toward me with his hand outstretched.

"You must be Cade. I'm Kensington, but you can just call me Ken."

Kensington? What kind of rich-prick name is Kensington?

My mom gives me a look, and I remember I've yet to shake his hand. Honestly, I'd rather not, but I know it will only cause problems if I don't. His hand wraps around my own firmly, as if he's trying to silently assert his dominance—or maybe it's just a habit from being in the business world.

"Your mother has told me so much about you."

I scoff. "I wish I could say the same."

My mom scowls at me, but I couldn't help it. I didn't even

know this guy existed until last week, and I found out at the same time I was being told my parents were splitting up. Forgive me if I'm not the most warm and welcoming.

Ken maintains his composure and shoots my mom a comforting grin. "That's okay. We have all the time in the world to change that."

He leads us out of his office and into the living room. Molly is sitting on the floor, playing a game with a blonde-headed girl. I can only see the back of her, but I can tell she's much older than my ten-year-old sister.

"This is my daughter," Ken tells me, and the girl turns around at the sound of his voice. "Lennon, sweetheart. Come meet Cade, Nora's son."

As her turquoise eyes meet mine, I'm blasted back into last night.

The girl in the water.

My board snapping in half.

The way she looked as if she wanted to throw down right then and there.

Of course this chick is his daughter. She looks as spoiled and stuck-up as I expected, especially after seeing the size of this house.

I watch the realization dawn on her that she's met me before. Something that looks awfully close to sorrow is there for a second, before it's covered with a mask like I've never seen. She plasters on a sickeningly sweet smile and puts out her hand.

"I'm Lennon. It's nice to meet you."

All eyes are on me, giving me no choice but to be equally as kind, and equally as fake.

"Cade."

THE REST OF THE day is spent with the most uncomfortable "family time" I've ever had the displeasure of sitting through. Lennon tries to act polite and involved in the *get-to-know-each-other* game our parents have us playing, but I can tell she would rather be literally anywhere else.

By the grace of God, we're all excused until dinner, and I use the time alone to check on Molly. Her room is right down the hall from mine, and decorated exactly the way she has always described her dream bedroom, with tie-dye everything and her favorite posters on the wall. There is even an aquarium in the corner. Overall, she looks happy.

"Knock, knock," I say, without actually knocking. "Can I come in?"

She nods, flopping herself onto her new bed.

"I just wanted to make sure you're doing okay."

Molly sits up and sighs. "I miss Dad. I like the house and all, but I miss our old house and having our family together."

The pain in her voice twists up my insides. "I'm sorry, Molz. I tried to get them to change their minds."

"I know you did, but they wouldn't listen. I wish we could have made them listen."

"Me too, kid." I pull her into me. "Me too."

After spending a little more time comforting my sister, since our mother is too busy acting like a lovesick trophy wife to realize her own daughter is hurting, I head back to my new room. To my surprise, Lennon is already in there waiting for me.

"What are you doing in here?"

She runs her fingers through her hair. "I just wanted to, uh, thank you, for not mentioning the bonfire last night to my dad."

If I'm being honest, I hadn't realized I wasn't supposed to, but she doesn't know that. "Yeah, well, now you owe me."

"Owe you?"

I cross my arms over my chest and smirk. "Yep."

It's been all of two minutes, and it's clear she's already done with my shit. "And what exactly do I owe you?"

Stepping closer, I hover in her space. The smell of her perfume infiltrates my senses but I force myself to stay focused. She swallows harshly as I glare down at her.

"Stay the fuck out of my room, and out of my way."

I shove past her while she stays in place, and for a second, I wonder why she's still here, until her small yet strong voice sounds again.

"You know, I don't want you here just as much as you don't want to be here."

I snort. "Somehow, I doubt that."

She rolls her eyes, and that attitude I got a taste of last night comes back out in full force. "You think that just because you're the one that had to move means that only your life has changed? You're wrong. Mine's been flipped upside down, too."

At, the sound of her words, a brilliant idea comes to mind. One that could give us all what we want. My sister. My dad. Me. It could work.

"Oh yeah?" I ask, leaning against my dresser. "Prove it. Help me split them up."

Her brows furrow. "Split them up?"

I nod slowly. "It's a win-win for us both. I can put my family back together, and you'll have your precious daddy and big fancy house all to yourself again."

For a moment, it looks like she's actually considering it. My hopes start to build at the possibility of getting my old life back, until she sends it all plummeting back down with a shake of her head.

"I can't."

I don't even attempt to mask my disappointment. "It's not that you can't, it's that you won't."

She stands firm. "Either way, I'm not doing it. Their relationship is none of our business."

That almost pulls a laugh out of me.

"Well, I'm doing it with or without you." I take a step forward, and she takes one back. Like a pattern, I keep it going until she's backed herself into the hallway. "And if I were you, I'd stay far as fuck away from me. I'll do whatever it takes to repair my broken family, and I'll have no sympathy if you're caught in the crossfire."

With that, I swing the door closed right in her shell-shocked face.

5

LENNON

I WALK THROUGH THE HALLWAY, NAVIGATING around all the students hanging out before class. Tessa stays by my side as we dodge the obnoxious amount of make-out sessions. I don't understand why they need to do this shit where everyone can see them. Hasn't anyone taught them to have some class?

"Okay, I have to meet this guy," Tess quips.

I run my fingers through my hair. "You already have. He's the one you saw me standing with on the beach the other night."

Her jaw drops. "The one you wanted to backhand because he mentioned your mom?"

"That's him."

"Damn. Small world."

I sigh. "You're telling me. And for the record, he isn't any less of an asshole during the day either."

She chuckles. "Well, what did you expect? You kind of broke his surfboard."

"It was an accident!" My back rests against the locker next to Tessa's and my head lolls to the side. "And if you really want to pull that, technically he almost killed me."

"Sure, babes. We'll go with that."

The whole incident from last night plays in my mind. That boy has more mood swings than anything I've ever seen in my life. I went into his room to apologize, but that wasn't enough for him. When I refused to help him, his eyes looked like they had actual fire in them. He became a scary version of himself—even worse than on the beach.

His last name may be Knight, but he's far from dressed in shining armor and he's definitely not here to save me.

I explain everything to Tessa, including his little plan of trying to break up our parents. When I'm finished, her brows furrow.

"But wait—why not agree to help him? I thought you didn't want this."

I let out a long exhale. "I don't, but for the first time in a while, my dad looks really happy. I don't want to be the one to take that away from him."

She gives me a sympathetic smile. "You're a good daughter, but enjoy your new step-bro. He sounds like a real prize."

"Ugh, don't remind me. I've never met someone that has made me want to hit them as quickly and as often as he has."

"Who are you hitting?" Kellan asks, coming up next to me and dropping his head down to give me a kiss.

I shake my head. "It's no one."

Tessa snorts. "Sure, if you call a guy who lives in your house no one."

Kellan's brows dip, and I know I need to explain before his mind starts to wander.

"My dad's girlfriend and her two kids moved in. Her son is around our age."

A hint of jealousy sparkles in his eyes. "Oh really?"

I can't help but laugh as I grab the front of his shirt and pull him into me. "Don't even go there. He's practically my step-brother."

Kellan smiles before connecting our lips once more. His hand grips my waist and he hums into me, until Skye's voice pulls us apart.

"Yuck. Get a room," she teases.

Tessa snickers. "Kellan is just claiming his territory after finding out Lennon has a new man in her life. Her dad's girlfriend moved in along with her teenage son."

"Oh," she coos. "Is he hot?"

"You have a one-track mind, you know that?" Tess remarks.

Skye shrugs. "We can't all be dating football royalty. How is Asher these days? Regretting how he threw everything away for some high school chick yet?"

Tessa and I share a look and the two of us roll our eyes in unison. Thankfully, we don't even need to answer that before Tanner does it for us.

"Damn, Skye. Jealousy is not a good look on you."

"I am *not* jealous."

She is, and everyone knows it. Before it became a known thing that Tessa and Asher were dating, he was our English teacher, and Skye had a massive crush on him. I'm surprised there wasn't a puddle of drool around the desk every time she sat there. When she found out about him and Tessa, she was devastated. It's like she actually thought she had a chance—she absolutely didn't. It took Tessa weeks to break him down and get him to admit he wanted her too, and they had already had sex. Skye was never even on his radar.

"Are you still coming over for dinner tonight?" I ask Kellan.

He drapes his arm across my shoulders as we start walking toward first period. "Well, obviously. I have to meet this new beau of yours."

I shake my head and playfully elbow him in the stomach. As if anyone could compare to Kellan Spencer.

WALKING OUT OF THE school, I'm pleasantly surprised when I find Colby parked at the curb. I know Tessa and I have plans with him and Asher today, but I didn't expect for him to pick us up. Kellan groans as soon as he sees him.

"Babe, how many times do I have to tell you? We're just friends."

He sighs. "I know. It just sounds like a double date."

I roll my eyes. "It's not even a date for Tessa and Asher, let alone a double. Tess and I are just planning our graduation party, and being as it's at Colby's house, he kind of needs to be there."

It looks like he wants to fight me on it some more, but instead he gives in and nods. "All right. I'll see you later?"

"Six o'clock. Don't be late."

He presses a soft kiss to my lips. "I won't."

With a warning look at Colby, he walks away and toward his own car. Tessa laughs as she loops her arm with mine and we make our way down the steps. Colby pulls his gaze from my boyfriend and over to us.

"Should I be worried he's going to slit my throat in my sleep?"

I chuckle. "I mean, it's possible."

He holds his hands in front of his body as I go to hug him. "Better not show me any kind of affection. He might cut my balls off."

"And God forbid Colby Hendrix loses his balls."

"They're the most important part of my body."

Tessa and I both give him a look, waiting for him to change his answer. He laughs.

"Okay, second most important part."

My grin widens. "That sounds more accurate."

We all climb inside Colby's car, with me taking shotgun

and Tessa sitting in the back. Colby puts the car in drive and pulls out onto the road.

Halfway through the drive, Tess and I are talking about potentially getting a bounce house like we're a couple of children, but this is the last chance we have to be kids. This summer in general needs to be epic.

"Have you ever had sex in a bounce house?" Colby questions, making Tessa choke on air.

I cock my head in thought. "Why would I have done that? Why have *you* done that?"

He shrugs. "I hooked up with a single mom after her kid's birthday party a couple years ago. It was the only place we didn't risk getting caught."

A small tinge of jealousy settles in my stomach—the same one that always seems to come any time he mentions another girl. I do my best to shove it away, just like I do every time.

"Are you ever not such a pig?"

A wide smile stretches across his face, making his dimples come out to play. "What fun would that be?" He glances over at me and juts his bottom lip out. "Aw, is the Virgin Mary jealous?"

I ball my fist up and punch him directly in the arm, but I think it hurts me more than it does him. I try to shake the pain out of my hand but it's pointless.

"Oh my God, your biceps are like fucking rocks."

Colby switches which hand is holding the wheel and flexes, making his muscles bulge against the confines of his sleeve. "Damn right they are."

He kisses it quickly, like a complete tool. I curl up into a ball in the passenger seat and rest my head on my knees. It only takes a second of my fake pouting before he notices and reaches over to tickle my side.

"Don't," I warn him, but he does it anyway. "Colby, stop."

"Aw, what's wrong?" he mocks. "Is Little Lennon mad she's still a virgin?"

Trying to look mad, I shove him away from me but I can't keep the grin off my face. "Shut up."

"Don't you have a boyfriend to change that for you?"

Yes. "We are not discussing my sex life, or lack thereof."

He bites his lip with his eyes full of amusement. "I mean, I don't blame you for holding out. You don't want some little boy fucking up your first sexual experience."

"Little boy? And what are you, a man?"

Colby parks the car and turns in his seat, looking me up and down. "Through and through, baby. I could show you."

He's teasing, that much is clear, but I'm starting to see how he gets so many girls in bed with him. I'm frozen completely in place as thoughts I really shouldn't have run through my mind, until Tessa scoffs.

"You two have more sexual tension than a porno."

She climbs out of the car, leaving Colby and I alone as she heads for the elevator. I smirk and lean closer into Colby, lowering my lids and parting my lips slightly. When I'm inches away from him, I stop.

"In your dreams, playboy," I murmur, pushing him away by his forehead and climbing out of the car.

He chuckles and follows suit, and the conversation stays where it belongs—far away from me. I have a boyfriend, and as gorgeous as Colby Hendrix may be, Kellan is special. He's a possessive little shit, but he's mine.

AFTER SPENDING HOURS GOING over all the different things we want to have at our graduation party and listening to Colby groan a hundred times about how we're going to destroy his house, I have to get home for family dinner. My dad insisted last night that I be there for it.

Family. It's such a funny word for our household dynamic right now. I mean, I didn't even meet Nora until my dad was telling me she was moving in, and I didn't meet her kids until their stuff was already filling my house. I'd hardly call that a family. It's a foster home at best.

Thankfully, I'm at least allowed to have Kellan there, which shows how badly my dad wants my acceptance of all this. He and Kellan met a couple months ago, right before prom, and my dad put the fear of God into him. He's always scared away any boy I've had the slightest interest in, but Kellan wouldn't budge. I thought maybe that would buy him some respect from *the* Kensington Bradwell, being a man of loyalty and all that, but it didn't. My dad still watches him like a hawk whenever he's around.

"You all right?" Colby asks me from the driver's seat.

I must have been lost in thought, because I hadn't even realized we're almost to my house. "Yeah. I'm just not exactly thrilled about this combined family thing."

"Don't get along with the new fam?"

I shrug. "Nora and Molly aren't so bad. It's Cade I have a problem with. The dude has some serious anger issues."

Colby's grip tightens on the steering wheel. "He hasn't done anything to you, has he?"

"No," I assure him. "Nothing like that. He just got in my face when I wouldn't help him break our parents up."

Turning into my driveway, we're both faced with Cade sitting on the front steps. He's wearing a pair of board shorts and a tank top as he holds a cigarette between his fingers.

"That him?"

I nod. "Yep. My new roommate."

Colby reaches over to pull me into a hug. "If he fucks with you, even a little, call me. I'll teach him a lesson."

I chuckle. "Okay, my big, scary protector."

Going to back away, he stops me and holds my chin between his thumb and index finger, keeping my gaze locked with his.

"I'm serious, Lennon. Even a little."

Unable to speak due to the close proximity, I simply nod and he releases me. I climb out of the car and wave goodbye as I walk toward the house. Cade's gaze meets mine, and he rolls his eyes.

"Of course, you're dating Colby fucking Hendrix. Why am I not surprised?"

I roll my eyes. "I'm not, not that it's any of your business."

He puts the cigarette between his lips and inhales, making his cheeks hollow at the movement. Then, he lets it out in a way that looks way more erotic than it should. All my attention is focused entirely on his lips as he moistens them with his tongue.

"See something you like?"

That manages to pull me from the weird haze I was locked in. My upper lip curls in disgust, and I shake my head. "Get over yourself."

I step by him but stop as soon as I open the front door.

"Also, if my dad sees that cigarette, he's going to lose his shit."

Cade gets up and focuses all his attention on me as he drops the butt onto the step and puts it out with his shoe. He steps by me and into the house, leaving the half-smoked cigarette there for all to see. I run my fingers through my hair and follow behind.

Well, living with him won't be boring.

6

CADE

If I had to pick one person who is pissing me off the most lately, it's Lennon. She's infuriatingly spoiled and walks around like she owns the whole goddamn world. I guess with a dad as rich and powerful as hers is, she kind of does—and that only irks me more.

Seeing her in the car with Colby Hendrix, football extraordinaire and known ladies' man, it sparked some emotions I wasn't expecting.

Curiosity.

Confusion.

Anger.

Jealousy.

I watched her walk toward me like a fucking goddess, with her blonde hair falling to the sides of her face and her turquoise eyes staring into mine. With the sun hitting her just right, even a blind man would admit she's beautiful, and that's part of the problem.

For the first time since the morning, I head up the stairs and into my room. When I get there, however, I practically stop breathing and my eyes double in size. Laying on my bed is a Lost LayZ Toy II surfboard. It's probably the best one on the market right now, and I almost drool at the sight of it.

A note lies on top, and I notice the girly handwriting on it before I even pick it up.

Cade,
Sorry for breaking your other one.
- Lennon

Fuck. I was wondering how I'd pull together the money for a new one. I was even considering trying to get mommy's rich new boyfriend to buy me one, but it looks like now I won't have to. A part of me wonders when she even had time to do this, because it definitely wasn't here this morning, and I left after her.

After admiring my new board for a little longer, I head out of my room and over to the balcony that overlooks the living room. Lennon is down there, sitting next to Molly and helping her with her homework. The way my sister looks at her is enough to make me wonder if I'm going about this the wrong way. Maybe Lennon isn't all that bad, and if Molly likes her, I guess I could get along with her for my sister's sake.

Just as I'm about to walk down the stairs and suggest a do-over, the doorbell rings.

"I got it!" Lennon shouts.

I watch as she jogs over to the door and opens it. She greets whoever is on the other side with a big smile, and when he steps inside, my jaw drops. It's none other than Kellan fucking Spencer. He pulls her into his arms and presses his lips to hers. Lennon laces their fingers and drags him into another room, out of my view.

Every single one of my previous thoughts go flying out the window. Not only is she the daughter of the guy who played a key part in causing my parents' divorce, but she's dating the one person in the world I might hate more than Kensington Bradwell. That, by default, makes her the enemy and at the top of my shit list.

A HALF HOUR OF avoiding being seen later, we're all called to dinner through an obnoxious intercom system in every room of the house. I roll my eyes and force myself off my bed. For a minute, I hope that Kellan isn't here anymore, but that hope dies when I hear his voice echo down the hall. I step out just in time to see them coming from the direction of Lennon's room. The second Kellan's eyes meet mine, his eyes narrow and he swallows hard.

"What's he doing here?"

Lennon sighs. "Kellan, this is Nora's son, Cade."

"I know who he is," Kellan growls, and his anger makes me smirk.

"You do?"

He nods. "And if he knows what's good for him, he'll stay away from you."

His words are spoken to Lennon but fully meant for me. He drapes an arm around her and shoves past me. It's a move to intimidate me, but little does he realize, I now have something to hold over his head. The image of him in the same position with a short haired brunette from only a week ago plays in my mind. Unless they just started dating, I'm sure Lennon would love to know all about what, or rather who, he does when she isn't around.

We make our way into the dining room and take a seat around the oversized table. Lennon and her piece of shit boyfriend sit across from me, while Molly sits to my left. My mom comes in with Ken and slides into the seat to my right while Ken sits at the head of the table. Not surprising.

"Wow. Kellan Spencer, is that you?"

The prick smiles brightly at my mom. "It's nice to see you again, Ms. Knight."

My mom looks pleasantly surprised at our unexpected company. "It's been ages. Look at you! You're all grown up." She turns her attention to Lennon. "Are you two dating?"

The two of them nod, and the way Ken's jaw ticks doesn't go unnoticed. *Good*. I'm not the only one who sees right through Kellan's bullshit.

"That's great. I'm so happy for you two. You make a beautiful couple. Don't they, honey?"

Honey? Vomit.

"Sure," Ken grumbles a half-assed agreement. "Can we eat?"

My mom rolls her eyes with a smile. "Don't be such an overprotective father." She focuses back on the happy couple. "How long have you been together?"

Finally, some information I can use. I watch as Kellan's eyes glance at me quickly. Lennon, however, looks at him dreamily, and it makes me want to punch someone. Him, particularly.

"Only a few months, but it feels like longer," she answers.

A few months, putting that party when he was all over some girl—who was clearly not Lennon—dead smack within a timeframe that makes him guilty. I sit back in my seat and grin widely at Kellan, giving him a look that silently tells him he's fucking busted.

"Are you done inquiring about my daughter's love life?" Ken asks, his tone light but his words serious. "I'm starving."

The chefs, because that's something we have now, like it's fucking normal, bring out the gourmet meals and place them in front of us. The food looks delicious, and I think it's actually one of few things I'll miss once I find something that will send my mom running back to my dad with her tail between her legs.

Though I must admit, today wasn't all bad. I got a badass

new surfboard and leverage over the guy I hate most in the world. I don't see how anything could get better than that, except maybe getting my old life back and never having to see Lennon again for as long as I live.

"So, Lennon," my mom says. "Are you excited for graduation? It's in a few weeks, right?"

She nods. "Yeah, on the fifteenth."

"I was thinking this week we could go shopping for a dress. Every girl needs something special to wear under her gown."

I can see the hesitation all over her face, but with a glance at her dad, she caves and fakes the best smile she can manage. "That sounds great."

"Perfect," my mom cheers. "I'll set it up."

I wonder if she can see the animosity Lennon has toward her. And more so, if the princess is so against their relationship and our being here, why didn't she agree to help me? Does she have her own plan up her sleeve that she didn't want me involved in? What's her game?

"Oh, speaking of graduation," Ken chimes in. "I had the cleaners at the beach house today. It should be all set for you."

Lennon squeals in delight. "Great. Thank you, Daddy."

The fact that they have a beach house shouldn't be appealing to me, but anything about the beach always has my interest. I'm just about to ask about it, when Ken sets his sights on me.

"You should go with them, Cade. It would be good for you to spend time together, and what better way than a couple weeks on the beach in Malibu?"

I hold back my snort. The last thing I want to do is spend time around his demon-spawn daughter. "I was planning on teaching Molly how to surf."

My mother puts on a face that tells me she's done something sneaky. "Didn't I tell you? She's going to that sleep-away camp she's been begging for. Ken was nice enough to set it up for her."

Ken was nice enough. Fucking Ken. Well, it looks like my options are either spending two weeks in this house alone with no one but the two lovebirds, or at a beach house in Malibu with Lennon and her friends. I glance across the table and see the looks on their faces, as if they're praying I turn down the offer. It only makes me want to accept it more.

"Can I bring a couple friends?"

My mom and Ken share a look, and he smiles. "I don't see why not. The house is plenty big enough."

I'm sure it is, Mr. Moneybags.

I nod, and with another look at Lennon, I smirk. "Well then, who am I to deny a couple weeks in Malibu?"

Kellan tenses, and Lennon subtly rolls her eyes. I bask in the fact that I've made them uncomfortable and potentially ruined their little trip. They better get used to it. This is only the beginning of the shit I'll put them through.

OUR PLATES ARE CLEANED up by the housekeeper—Melanie or Melissa or some shit—and all of us are too stuffed for dessert. I get up from the table with everyone else, and we all start going our separate ways. Just as Lennon goes to walk back up the stairs, Kellan stops.

"I'll meet you up there, babe," he tells her.

She gives him a confused look and glances at me before nodding. Once she's gone, Kellan looks around to make sure no one can see us. Then, he drops the polite facade he had going on.

"It's funny," I start. "Lennon looks nothing like the girl you were with at Josslyn's party."

A deep growl rumbles in the back of his throat as he gets up in my face. "You don't know what the fuck you saw."

I smirk. "Oh, I think I do. Does she know you're cheating on her, or did you tell her you were sick so you could spend the night with your side piece?"

"Don't fucking start with me, Knight."

"Or what? You'll tell everyone that I cheat at surfing competitions? That seems to be your usual M.O."

His chest bumps against mine, like it's meant to be intimidating, but I'm not afraid of him. The only reason he's so riled up is because I have something on him. Something that could fuck up the best thing he has going for him, because rumor has it he didn't get into the college he was hoping for—or any, for that matter. Even North Haven University wouldn't take him, and they're a sucker for the locals.

"I'm warning you, Cade," he says threateningly. "You breathe a word of this to Lennon, and I'll make you wish you were never born."

I stick my bottom lip out in a mock pout. "Oh, I'm shaking."

He steps back and looks me up and down. "You think I didn't notice the way you look at her? She's drop-dead gorgeous, and she's mine. I won't let you take this from me, too."

"If I wanted her, there wouldn't be a damn thing you could do about it."

Walking over toward the stairs, he glares at me with a cocky grin. "Try it. See how that goes for you."

7

LENNON

I'M SCROLLING THROUGH MY PHONE WHEN KELLAN comes in after what felt like forever. I don't know what he wanted to talk to Cade about. I had no idea they even knew each other, but it's clear there's some kind of history between them that I'm dying to figure out.

Kellan smiles at me and leaves the door open like my dad requires, even though I'm eighteen. Don't even get me started on that nonsense. Like, hello—if I wanted to have sex, I wouldn't do it with him home. *Duh.*

"Everything okay?" I ask.

He seems unsure as he sits beside me. "I need you to stay away from him, Len."

Uh, okay. "And how exactly do you expect me to do that? He lives in my house."

"I know, but at least as much as you can. He's not a good guy."

It's a broad statement, and one I'm not exactly disagreeing with—especially not after how he's been since I met him. There hasn't been one nice thing that's come out of his mouth. I swear, the only thing he has going for him is his looks.

I sigh. "Okay, I get it, and I'll do my best, but you're going to have to give me more than that. How do you know him?"

He runs his hand over his face and falls back. "We were best friends when we were younger. Our parents were close, so we hung out a lot. We actually learned how to surf together."

Now *that* surprises me. "I didn't know you surf."

"Because I don't. Not anymore at least." He pauses to take a breath. "Cade and I spent every waking moment out there. There were four of us, actually. Cade, Bryce, Jayden, and me. I think I spent more time around them than I did my own family."

"So, how did you go from that to how you are now?"

He shrugs. "Because Cade didn't like that someone was actual competition for him. Bryce and Jayden were good, but they didn't stand a chance against Cade and me. We absolutely destroyed all the competitions. Sometimes he would take the gold, and sometimes I would."

I wrap my arms around my stomach, feeling sorry for Kellan that he lost someone he was obviously very close to. "He hated you because he was jealous?"

"Pretty much. I guess he got tired of coming in second sometimes because one day he wouldn't answer my calls. He managed to turn Bryce and Jayden against me and the three of them cut me out of their lives."

I frown. "That's horrible, Kel. I'm so sorry."

He turns to face me, looking every ounce of the heartthrob I know him to be. The boy I started crushing on at sixteen years old. His expression changes to a pleading one.

"He clearly hasn't gotten over whatever it is he's holding against me, and I'd hate to see him try to get to me through you. So, just promise me you won't let him."

Bending down, I press a lingering kiss to his lips. "You have nothing to worry about. I promise."

Kellan sighs in relief and pulls me close, maneuvering me

so I'm lying down with my head on his chest. His hand brushes against my back, and the two of us cuddle in silence, just enjoying each other's company.

TEN O'CLOCK COMES FASTER than expected, and like clockwork, my dad calls to let me know that it's time for Kellan to leave. I roll my eyes as I yes him to death and hang up. Kellan is already getting his shoes on before I even relay the message.

The two of us walk downstairs and to the front door. I can feel another pair of eyes on me without having to see them. Well, if Cade wants to spy, I might as well give him a show.

I wrap my arms around Kellan's neck and pull him into me. Our mouths collide in a bruising kiss. He grips my waist and moans softly into my mouth. I can feel him harden in his jeans, and if I wasn't so scared, and it wasn't past my ridiculous curfew, I might have even done something about it.

Listening to Kellan open up about his past with Cade felt like a good step for us. He's normally a very secretive person. He doesn't share too much about his personal life, and I'm the kind who yearns for information. Something that can make me feel connected to him. Something that makes me feel like he's more than just the hot guy that managed to catch my eye. His vulnerability tonight helped with that.

We finally break apart, and he winks at me before walking out the door. I stand there for a second and bask in the butterflies. When I turn around to head back upstairs, I stop.

Cade is standing at the top of the steps, watching me with an angry scowl on his face. I take a deep breath and accept the fact that I have no choice but to walk by him. Sure, I could take the elevator, but it's on the opposite side of the house, and he'd probably just meet me over there. With him living here, if there's something he wants to say, I have no choice but to listen.

"I can't believe you're dating him." he sneers. "I thought you had more class than that."

I scoff. "Like you'd know anything about having class."

"I know Kellan Spencer doesn't have an ounce of it."

Trying to ignore him, I walk away and toward my room, but he's hot on my heels. Clearly, he isn't finished. I turn the corner and head up the second set of steps—the ones that go straight up into my bedroom. I can hear him behind me, but he isn't saying anything for once.

I'm about to slam my door shut in his face, but he stops it with his foot. I take a second to breathe and then turn around. He's looking around my room, as if he's taking it all in. His gaze rakes over my bed, my dresser, the wall of dance trophies, and then lands on me.

"Your room is the tower," he says, like it's new information.

"And your point?"

He shakes his head. "I don't have one. I just assumed that was the master bedroom."

"It is," I confess. "But I was six when my dad had this house built, and I had an unhealthy obsession with castles, so he gave me this room."

"Why doesn't that surprise me?"

Fed up with his shit, I cross my arms over my chest. "Is there something you wanted, or can you fuck off now?"

He chuckles, and I hate how I like the sound of it. "I just wanted to say thank you, for the surfboard. You didn't have to do that."

Shit, I forgot about that. To be honest, I felt guilty about breaking his board, and it didn't look like he had another. So, today on my lunch break, I went to the surf shop. I asked the guy behind the counter which one he recommended most, and bought it. It was more than I thought it would be, but not enough to cause any kind of dent in my bank account. Not with the obnoxious allowance my dad gives me every month.

I shrug. "It's no big deal. Your old one broke because of me, so I kinda did."

His eyes meet mine, and there is something brewing behind them. Something I can't decipher. It's alluring, and dangerous. Kellan's words play through my mind and pull me from my stupor.

"Is that all you wanted? Because I just want to shower and go to bed."

Cade grins, and I do my best to look away so I don't get lost in the way it makes him look so much hotter. He's practically my stepbrother, for crying out loud, not to mention a major jerk. Off limits isn't even the word for it. Besides, it's probably all part of some game to mess with Kellan.

He makes no attempt to move, so I walk toward him and press my palm to his chest. I gently press until he backs up onto the steps and stands right outside my doorway. Then, I close the door and lock it.

Kellan was right. I need to stay away from Cade.

A WEEK FLIES BY in what feels like seconds, and I can't believe graduation is on Friday. Cade, thankfully, hasn't tried anything since he stalked me into my bedroom. Then again, I haven't been home enough for him to do much. Family dinners have started becoming more sporadic and less mandatory, thank God, and I've been spending most of my time at Tessa's or Kellan's.

After our talk, I've started making more of an effort to make Kellan feel less like a second choice and more like a priority. However, I'm still not ready to have sex with him. I just don't think we're at that level yet, despite the fact that he's been good to go for weeks. But for him, it isn't as big of a deal.

I walk into the kitchen to see Nora dressed and ready to go. Today, we're going to my favorite boutique to find a dress for graduation. It's something I definitely could've done on my own, but she wanted to take me, and I didn't have the heart to tell her no—especially not with the way my dad was looking at me. His eyes urged me to agree.

"Oh good, you're here," she greets me. "Just let me finish filling out this form for Molly's school and then we'll go."

I sit on one of the bar stools and pull out my phone, texting Tessa. Her anxiety is sky high after finding out that Asher is going to have surgery on his shoulder. Since being taken out of the NFL from an injury, he's been itching to get back to playing and it looks like he may finally get his wish. First, however, they need to repair the nerve damage and see if it works.

"Mom, I need you to take me to Bryce's," Cade demands as he walks in the room.

Nora doesn't even look up from what she's doing. "What's wrong with your car?"

He rolls his eyes. "It's making a weird noise. I dropped it off at the mechanic this morning. So, can you take me?"

She signs her name and then turns to him. "I'm sorry, hun, I can't. I'm taking Lennon dress shopping."

Scowling, he glances at me and his upper lip curls in disgust. "She's like a gazillionaire. Doesn't she have enough dresses?"

"Not the point, Cadence." *Cadence?* "Graduation is a special occasion and deserves a special dress. You'd know that if you hadn't insisted on dropping out and taking your GED."

He scoffs. "I'd rather spend my time surfing."

"Obviously, but that doesn't mean everyone has your views. See if Bryce can just come pick you up."

With that, it's clear the conversation is over by the way she turns away from him and grabs her purse. Cade sighs in frustration and storms out of the room, stomping up the stairs and slamming his bedroom door like a child having a temper tantrum. I can't help but laugh at his antics.

"I'm sorry about my son," Nora apologizes. "He can be a bit of a handful."

I giggle softly and shake my head. "Don't worry about it. He doesn't bother me."

"I didn't think he would. You're tough. I don't think he stands a chance against you."

I smile and shrug. "I don't think anyone does."

We leave through the garage and climb into the new car my dad bought Nora a week ago. As she pulls out of the driveway, I text Francois and let him know that Cade needs a ride to his friend's house. I know Nora wouldn't ask. She hasn't gotten comfortable with the staff yet. He texts me back with a thumbs up and I put my phone away, happy to be the bigger person—even if he doesn't deserve it.

TESSA AND I STAND in the middle of my room, checking ourselves out in my floor-to-ceiling mirror. It may be overkill, but I had a professional hair and makeup artist come to my house so we could look our best. What can I say? You only graduate high school once.

The two of us head downstairs where everyone is waiting. My dad and Cade are having a discussion in the kitchen, and I'm surprised to hear that it sounds relatively friendly. The second we walk into the room, however, everyone goes quiet.

"Wow," Molly says, and it makes me laugh. She's an adorable little kid.

"Molly is right, sweetheart," my dad chimes in. "You look beautiful."

Cade is yet to say a word, but I don't expect him to. What I did expect, however, is for his eyes to be glued on Tessa. With her long brown hair and the way that red dress hangs perfectly on her body, the girl is a knockout. But that's not at all what he's doing. Instead, his gaze is locked on me—unmoving and unashamed.

"Are we ready to go?" I question, suddenly needing to get out of here.

Everyone gets up and heads for the door, except Cade. He made it very well known that he has no intentions of going anywhere near Haven Grace Prep. Not now. Not ever.

ONE OF THE BEST parts of having such a small graduating class is getting to sit with my friends instead of in alphabetical order. Tessa is to my left and Kellan is to my right, both holding my hands as Tess and I tear up at the speech Charleigh is giving. How that girl managed to become valedictorian is something I'll never understand.

"Before we start handing out diplomas," Principal Hyland says, "there is an award that brings me great pleasure to present. This one is for our most improved student. Someone who has been through more than her fair share of struggles and still managed to come out stronger. Give a round of applause to the girl who deserves this most, Miss Tessa Callahan."

Our whole class cheers as Tessa stands and walks up to the podium to accept the plaque, but no one is louder than Asher, Colby, and me—except maybe one. I glance over to the crowd at one particularly loud and familiar scream to see Delaney standing on the bleachers and celebrating her twin sister's successes.

Principal Hyland is right; the stuff she went through was the worst kind of nightmare. At one point, I thought I was going to lose her, but she's fierce. It took a lot for her to admit she needed help, but now, she's thriving, and shining, and I couldn't be prouder.

They call each of our names to come up and get our diplomas, and when we're done, the whole class throws their caps in the air. It's a tradition that everyone does, but no one ever thinks about when they come back down. I shield my head to protect myself from the onslaught of flying graduation caps. Tessa laughs and pulls me into her arms.

"We did it!"

I chuckle. "We did!"

It takes a little bit until we find our families, but we finally manage. They're all standing together, which is strange to see. Asher, being ten years Tessa's senior, is standing next to Tess's dad. I don't think I've ever seen them together, and I never expected to. My best friend's relationship with her dad is a strained one, but they're working on things.

A flash of brown hair flies past me and almost tackles Tessa to the ground. Tess laughs as she hugs her sister. I didn't even know she was in town, and judging by the happy smile on Tessa's face, I don't think she did either.

"Congratulations, Little Lennon," Colby says, giving me a hug.

I cringe. "Okay, that nickname has to go. I'm eighteen now. I'm not so little."

He chuckles and rests his arm on top of my head, showing me how short I am. "You're always going to be Little Lennon. Sorry, babe."

I roll my eyes playfully and shove him away from me. "You're lucky you're my best friend."

"Aye!" Tess glares. "Nuh-uh."

"Okay, other than you."

Colby laughs. "Fake news. You're just using me for my house."

Now that makes me smile. "Damn. You caught me."

THE POOL IS GLOWING from all the lights Colby had put in when he moved into this place. The decorations are set up nicely, and the DJ is playing all the right music. It's the perfect celebration, and our entire class would agree as they mosey around the house. Half of them are just relieved to have graduated, while the other half are excited to be at Colby Hendrix's house.

I'm standing with Colby and Asher, with Kellan's arms wrapped around my waist, listening to Asher make fun of Colby for the time a girl bit his dick. Colby shakes at the memory, smacking Asher in the stomach and telling him it was a very traumatizing time and how he still gets nervous during blow jobs.

"Now this is a party!"

A familiar voice booms across the yard, and Kellan tenses against me. I turn around to find Cade, flanked by the two friends I always see him with. He's looking right at me—strong, determined, and daring.

Of course, he's crashing my graduation party. Why did I expect anything less?

8

CADE

BRYCE BRINGS THE JOINT TO HIS MOUTH, INHALING deeply and holding it in. Jayden is already high as a kite and dancing to music that isn't actually playing. I considered smoking, but I think I have better plans for tonight.

"Are you two morons done?" I ask exasperatedly.

Bryce chuckles and lets out the smoke in the process. "What's got your panties in a twist?"

Not what. More like who. Seeing Lennon before she left for her graduation was the worst kind of torture. She's gorgeous even on her worst day, but the way she looked today was something else. The other people in the room didn't even occur to me. They didn't matter. Just her.

"Fuck off. I just want to get there."

Him and Jayden share a look and try not to laugh. It's Jayden who finally breaks.

"Aw, Cade misses his girlfriend." He goes to pinch my cheeks, but I slap his hands away.

I get up and grab my keys off Bryce's dresser. "One, she's not my girlfriend. And two, I'm not going there for her. I'm going there to get under Kellan's skin."

Okay, so maybe the second part isn't entirely true, and these two assholes know that.

"Because you're pissed he's dating your girlfriend and you're not," Bryce calls me out on my shit.

I roll my eyes and head out of the room. "If you're not in my car in three minutes, I'm leaving without your asses."

WE PULL UP TO the fancy house, and honestly, I'm surprised it's not bigger. You'd think a professional NFL player would live in some big-ass mansion, but Lennon's house could swallow this one whole. I park in front of the driveway, not caring that I'm blocking the cars in the driveway from getting out. You can hear the loud music from a block away. It's only a matter of time before the neighbors call for a noise complaint, unless someone already paid them off.

Bryce and Jayden follow me through the house and into the backyard. Like a gravitational pull, I find Lennon instantly, and my jaw ticks. She's laughing with Colby Hendrix and Asher Hawthorne, but she's comfortably tucked into Kellan's arms as he holds her from behind.

"Now this is a party!" I shout, and all heads whip toward me.

Lennon looks like she wants to kill me. Like if given the chance and the right weapon, she wouldn't hesitate to put me in the ground. They all walk toward me, and Kellan tries to slot himself between me and his girlfriend. Stupid prick. He's really starting to piss me off.

"What the fuck are you doing here?" she growls.

I feign innocence with a boyish grin. "What do you mean? It's a party."

She places one hand on her hip and juts it to the side. "A party *you* weren't invited to."

"Well, I'm here, aren't I?"

Colby looks me up and down, unsure what to make of me, then he turns to Lennon. "I'll kick him out if you want. I'm leaving it up to you."

Lennon goes quiet as she stares back at me. When she doesn't say anything right away, Kellan nudges her.

"Why are you even thinking about it?" he asks. "Get him out of here."

I snort. "Go ahead, princess. Kick me out. I'm sure your dad will love to hear about how you had me thrown out of your graduation party. You know, with how much he wants me to fit in and all."

That gets to her, just like I knew it would. If there's one thing Lennon doesn't like to do, it's upset Daddy Dearest. He can get her to do just about anything he wants with a single look.

She sighs and runs her fingers through her hair. "Just fucking leave him."

Kellan's glare intensifies as she shakes her head and walks away. I smirk triumphantly, winking at Kellan just to piss him off a little more. *Step one, done.*

ONE THING ABOUT RICH pricks—they always get the best alcohol. I'm not a lightweight, but it only took a few drinks to put a good buzz on. Seeing Kellan all over Lennon, I fucking need it. It's like he's claiming his territory. He may as well just piss on her at this point.

"Look who it is." A voice I haven't heard in a while gets my attention.

Knox Vaughn appears in front of me, and it's like a blast from the past. The two of us met a few years ago at the skate park and really hit it off. He's one of the most down to earth people I know, and I always wondered why we lost touch.

"No shit! What's up, man?"

"Not too much," he answers. "What's new with you?"

I shrug and take a sip of my beer. "Eh, you know. Surfing, skating, drinking, and smoking."

He chuckles. "Living the life."

"Exactly."

A girl comes up next to him that looks a lot like Lennon's friend. With no effort on her part, the toughest guy I know becomes soft in an instant. He wraps his arm around her and kisses her cheek.

"Cade, this is my girlfriend, Delaney," he says. "Delaney, Cade Knight."

I smile politely, trying not to show how shocked I am by Knox having a girlfriend. "It's nice to meet you."

"You, too," she says. "I've heard a lot about you."

My brows raise. "Oh really?"

She giggles. "Well, my twin sister is best friends with Lennon."

Twins. That explains a lot. "All good things, I hope."

Knox snorts and Delaney cringes. "I mean..."

I wave them off dismissively with a snicker. "I was kidding. It doesn't take a rocket scientist to know she can't stand me. I just like getting under her skin."

"Under her skin or under her shirt?" Knox claps back.

That's what I always liked best about him—he's never afraid to tell it like it is. Bryce and Jayden may be able to see right through my shit, but Knox isn't afraid to call me out on it. One thing's for sure, I need a better poker face.

"Fuck off, asshole," I tease.

He throws his head back, laughing. Bryce comes up next to me, obviously stoned out of his mind, and shoves another drink into my hand.

"I figured you'd need this."

I turn my head slightly to the side. "What? Why?"

He doesn't need to answer before I see it. Kellan has Lennon pinned up against the wall, practically sucking her face off. Vomit threatens to rise in my throat as I bring the cup to my lips and chug the contents of it. Leave it to Bryce to be right.

THE WHOLE PLACE IS spinning as I keep my eyes on Lennon from across the party. Jayden has some girl I've never met on his lap, and Bryce is passing a blunt back and forth with Knox. Since I started drinking heavily, they've stayed near me like they're my fucking babysitters. Like they aren't just as fucked up as I am.

"He doesn't deserve her," I slur drunkenly.

Bryce rolls his eyes. "So, you've mentioned, like a hundred times."

For the first time all night, I see Kellan standing without Lennon, only he's not alone. The girl from Josslyn's party is talking to him while he glances at his girlfriend every few seconds. My blood starts to boil as I get up and struggle to find my balance. Once it feels like the floor isn't falling out from under me, I storm over to him.

"Are you fucking kidding me?" I sneer.

The brunette's eyes narrow on me, and Kellan groans. He pushes her away from us and stands directly in front of me, trying to look tough.

"What the fuck is your deal? Why can't you lay off me for longer than a minute?"

I step forward and get in his face, the same way he did with me. "Because you're a piece of shit, and you don't deserve that girl to even look your way."

"Is that right? And what does she deserve? You?" The mocking tone to his words has me wanting to punch him in his smug face.

"Eat shit, douchebag," I counter. "One day she's going to wise up and leave you, and I can't fucking wait for it."

That strikes a nerve, and he shoves me backward. Bryce catches me, and I instantly race toward Kellan, clenching my fist and decking him right across the face. Gasps and shrieks sound all around us as we go at it—each of us getting a few good hits in. Unfortunately, it ends too soon, when Bryce and Knox pull me off Kellan and one of his friends stands in front of him to hold him back.

"You're fucking dead, Knight," Kellan threatens, spitting blood out onto the ground.

I smile happily, but it quickly fades when Lennon rushes over to make sure he's all right. With a glare in my direction, she watches as I'm led away and out of the party. Once we're in front of the house, I shove Bryce and Knox off me.

"Goddamn, Cade. What the fuck brought that on?" Knox asks.

I shake my head and look at Bryce as I pace back and forth. "Mark my words: if that shithead is in Malibu, it's going to be an interesting couple of weeks."

I WAKE IN THE morning to someone pounding at my door. My head is killing me and my jaw aches every time I move it. I roll out of bed, not caring to put clothes on, and answer the door in just my boxers. Lennon immediately shoves her way inside. She closes the door behind her and glares at me.

"What the hell is your problem?"

I wince at the shrill of her voice. "Can you keep your voice down?"

That only seems to piss her off more. "No, you lowlife. Not until you tell me why the fuck you felt the need to fight my boyfriend last night."

What the fuck am I supposed to tell her? That I saw him

with the chick he's been cheating on her with? She'll never believe that. Instead, I take a different route.

"That guy is a piece of shit, and he's no fucking good for you."

A dry laugh bubbles out of her, and her eyes roll toward the ceiling. "That's not your call, and it's not a good enough reason to attack him when he did nothing wrong."

Nothing wrong? Do you call him fucking around behind her back nothing wrong? Fuck, what I wouldn't give for her to know the truth right now—not even because I want her, but because she deserves so much fucking better than him.

"Well someone had to do it," I argue. "He deserves a good beating."

Lennon steps forward and shoves her finger into my bare chest. "I swear to God, Cade. I'm not playing this shit with you. Stay away from my boyfriend."

I look down at where she's touching me, feeling the fire that's radiating from her touch. I glance up to find her blatantly checking me out, like she's finally realized I'm in nothing but a pair of boxers. When her eyes meet mine, I smirk, and she snaps her hand back like it's injured. I can't help but notice the pink tint to her cheeks.

Unable to say another word, she turns around and walks out the door—leaving me to wonder why the burn of her touch is still there long after she's gone.

9

LENNON

ASHER DRIVES DOWN THE INTERSTATE AND GROANS to himself when Tessa continues to whine like a child who missed her nap. I swear, if she asks if we're almost there yet one more time, I'm going to smack her. My feet rest on the center console, despite Colby complaining about not wanting them near his arm. I laughed at him, and he left them there. There aren't many times he's able to deny me, and I love that.

"Lennon," Tessa says with a pout. "Stop reading your stupid book and entertain me."

I glance up at her through my lashes. "You're seriously like a five-year-old."

Her jaw drops. "Asher, Lennon called me a five-year-old!"

He snorts in response. "That was generous of her. I would have said three."

She crosses her arms over her chest and pokes her lip out. Tessa never does well with long car rides, which is the main reason none of us wanted to let her drive. She'd be going 100 miles per hour just to get there quicker. Colby turns around in the passenger seat and sticks his tongue out at her. Now I know what Asher means when he calls them immature. Put the two of them together, it's like being back in elementary school.

"I'm going to die of boredom," Tessa presses. "Colby, switch seats with me."

"How would that solve anything?"

She shrugs. "Because at least then I can blow Asher while he's driving."

The water Colby was pouring into his mouth sprays out and all over the dashboard. Asher sighs heavily and punches his best friend in the arm, though I can see the amusement on his face through the rearview mirror.

"Oh, come on," Colby complains. "You can't possibly blame me for that."

Asher chuckles. "Yes, I can. You should have expected it."

He thinks for a second, and then nods. "Touché."

Tess looks utterly satisfied with herself. I smile and shake my head. Asher is right; she's always been bold. Beating around the bush has never been her style. She just goes in for the kill and hopes for the best. I turn off my e-reader and slip it into my purse on the floor.

"All right, you win," I tell her.

She cheers triumphantly and turns so she's lying with her head in my lap. "At least you love me."

"Ay!" The protest comes from the front seat, but Tessa only laughs.

"I'm glad you decided to ride with us," she murmurs. "I thought for sure you were going to go with Kellan."

It was an option, and one I thought I'd choose, especially after that fight with Cade. I hated seeing him all beat up like that. I even tried to get my dad to rescind his offer for Cade to join us in Malibu, but he wasn't having it. Let's just hope they keep their hands to themselves while we're there.

"I thought about it, but he promised Skye he'd bring her with him. I love that girl, but I'd rather eat glass than be stuck in a car with her for six hours."

Tessa quirks a brow. "Why didn't she go with Charleigh?"

"Because Charleigh isn't coming until tomorrow," I answer. "Her, Tanner, and Oakley are leaving at like two in the morning so they'll get there in the morning."

She doesn't sound convinced, but drops the subject anyway. I don't even mention the argument it caused when I told Kellan I was riding with Tessa instead. He insisted I only chose this car because I'd rather spend six hours with Colby instead of him. His jealousy used to be cute, but there's only so many times I can explain that Colby and I are just friends.

HALFWAY THROUGH THE DRIVE, we stop for gas and so Princess Tessa over here can stretch her legs. She and Asher go into the store in search of snacks while Colby fills up the tank. I climb out of the SUV and extend my arms all the way up. The tense feeling in my back is already too much, and we're not nearly there yet.

"You okay?" Colby asks as I wince.

I nod halfheartedly. "It's just my back. It tightens up during long car rides."

He walks away from the gas pump and over to me. "Turn around."

Doing as he says, I cross my arms in front of my chest and he picks me up—bending me just right and making my back crack in multiple places. I sigh in relief as he puts me down. I roll my neck from one side to the other and feel even better when that cracks, too.

"I needed that. Thank you."

He leans against the car next to me. "Don't mention it."

As I'm looking around, I realize I have no idea where we are. Asher must have gotten off at some random rest stop. I just hope we get there before dark. The sunset at the beach house is one of my favorite things. My room has the best view of it.

"So," Colby interrupts my thoughts. "Do you think I'm going to need to play referee to your boyfriend and your new faux-bro?"

"Faux-bro?" I giggle.

He shrugs with a dimpled grin. "Sounds fitting."

I run my fingers through my hair and sigh. The thought of how Kellan and Cade are going to be over the next two weeks is something that has been plaguing my mind since I found out they not only know each other, but would rather die than be in the same room. Kellan seems to mind his own business, but Cade has a habit of pushing all the wrong buttons.

"I don't know. I hope not, but..."

"But you know it's more likely they'll end up trying to beat each other to a pulp," he finishes for me.

I nod, unable to deny it. "Pretty much."

The pump clicks, letting Colby know the tank is full, and he pushes off the car to stand up straight. "Well, if you need me to play bouncer, let me know."

"Thanks."

Tess and Asher come out in perfect timing, carrying three bags filled to the brim with snacks. My best friend smiles at me like she's a child who just suckered someone into buying her a ton of candy. When I glance into the bags, I realize she really is one. Lord help us for this sugar rush.

IT'S EIGHT THIRTY BY the time we reach the house. Luckily, no one else is here yet. It gives me time to lock my bedroom so no one tries claiming it, and for Tessa, Asher, and Colby to have dibs. I unlock the door and go inside, loving the motion sensor lights that come on when I walk in.

My friends aren't poor by any means, but all their jaws drop when they take in the place, including the floor-to-ceiling windows that fill the whole west side of the house. I've always loved being here. I used to beg my dad to let us live here instead of the house in North Haven, but it's just too far from work. One day, this place will be mine, and I'll never leave.

"Come on, babe. Let's go outside. I want to check out the view." Tessa grabs Asher by the wrist and pulls him away.

I go over to the fridge, finding it all stocked up just like my dad said. I grab a bottle of water and pass a beer to Colby. He thanks me quietly and takes a sip. When Tess and Asher come back in a few minutes later, they both have guilty looks on their faces.

"Please don't tell me you've already thought of like eight places you want to have sex," I plead.

Tessa laughs. "You know me so well."

Colby groans and hops up to sit on the counter. "Do you two have to be so coupley all the time? My God, you make me feel lonely."

She comes over and pokes him in the chest. "Well, that could change if you found a girlfriend."

He cringes at her words and looks over to me. "Len, help me out here."

"Sorry," I raise my hands in surrender. "Tessa might have a point. Maybe you should consider settling down."

"Definitely not." He shakes his head.

"Aw, come on. It could be cute!" Tessa leans against Colby with her head back against his chest. "We could double date and have photoshoots." She gasps. "Imagine how great those pictures would look!"

He shoves her forward and off him. "Kill switch. Stop this."

Asher chuckles. "If you keep talking about this, he'll break out in hives and a cold sweat."

Tessa and I find it hilarious, but I don't think he's kidding. Colby jumps down and puts his empty beer bottle in the trash.

"I'm going to find my room before all the good ones are snatched up."

I glance at where the balcony overlooks the kitchen and living room. "The big one on this side of the house is mine."

Colby hums. "Maybe I'll just share a room with you instead."

"Oh yeah, I'm sure Kellan will love that," I roll my eyes playfully. "Besides, I'll be waking up bright and early to dance. Brady will be stopping by in the mornings. He and Jake are staying at a hotel nearby."

Suddenly, his face becomes dull and serious. "That's not a vacation, Lennon."

My shoulders raise as I smile sweetly. "I have to stay in top shape for Juilliard in the fall."

He's clearly unamused, but he drops the subject as he heads for the stairs. When he's halfway up them, he looks out the window facing the front and snickers.

"Your favorite person is here."

Seconds later, the door opens and Cade walks in with his two friends. They look like they're in actual heaven. One of them nudges Cade in the arm.

"Dude," he says in disbelief. "Your mom hit the fucking jackpot."

I consider saying something about how this house has nothing to do with Nora or anyone else but me and my dad, but starting an argument on night one isn't really on my list. Cade doesn't answer him as he comes over to me and leans on the other side of the island.

"Nice house."

I keep my expression neutral. "Thanks."

"So," he looks me up and down, making my eyes narrow. "Which rooms are ours?"

When his eyes linger a little too long on my chest, I reach forward and use my index finger under his chin to lift his head back up. "East wing."

Sure, I could let them pick their own, but having him on the opposite side of the house is probably the best bet. Keep him as far away from Kellan as possible.

He smirks at me and backs away, grabbing his bag off the floor and heading toward the other side of the estate. Now that I think about it, I should have put him in the guest house. Probably would have been safer.

"How's that going?" Tess asks as soon as he's gone.

I huff. "He's infuriating."

She snorts and wraps her arms around me, resting her chin on my shoulder. "Yeah, but you have to admit, he's really hot."

A low whine emits from the back of my throat, but I don't answer her. Not because she's wrong, but because she's right. So fucking right.

MY ALARM GOES OFF at six in the morning. Kellan groans next to me, mumbling something about turning off the siren. I sit up and silence the sound before tying my hair up. Brady should be here any minute, and if I'm not caffeinated by the time he is, it's not going to go well for me.

I turn on the coffee pot and grab the creamer from the fridge. As I turn around, however, I smack directly into something hard. I topple backward until a hand wraps around my lower back and pulls me in. It takes me a minute to realize it's Cade.

Stepping back, I find him standing in front of me half naked, once again, only this time he's in a pair of board shorts. My eyes rake down his body involuntarily, like I'm unable to stop myself. When they linger a little too long on his abs, he grabs my chin and brings my focus back to his face—just like I did to him last night. I swallow harshly.

"You know," he says, caging me in with his hands on the fridge. "If you want me, all you have to do is ask."

What an arrogant prick.

I bite my lip, running the tip of my finger down his perfectly toned stomach. I dip inside his shorts for a second before continuing down the outside. His pupils are blown wide as I lightly brush over his quickly hardening cock.

My palm flattens against him. "Is this what you wanted?"

He moans softly and rests his head against mine, until I grip his balls in a vice grip. He hisses in pain, and it only pleases me more.

"If I wanted you, you'd know it," I growl.

The doorbell rings and I let go, smiling as he falls to the ground and curls into a ball. I let Brady in, pepped up and ready to dance.

"Let's go out back," I tell him. "We can practice there."

At the sound of a whimper, he turns around and sees Cade on the floor but I don't stop walking.

"Uh, is he okay?"

I glance over at the lump of a man and shrug. "Don't know. Don't care."

10

CADE

JEALOUSY ISN'T A THING I DO WELL. IT'S NOT something I've ever really had to deal with—until now. There is something about seeing Kellan's hands on Lennon that sets my blood on fire. It's like every chance he gets, he's rubbing it in my face that he has her and I don't.

I shouldn't want her. Shouldn't want this. But fuck, there's something pulling me to her and not a damn thing I can do about it. Even after damn near ripping off my manhood with her bare hand, I want her. What kind of sick fuck am I?

My board soars across the water, whipping with ease at every turn I make. Lennon's friend Charleigh and Kellan's side piece are sitting on the beach, watching Bryce, Jayden, and me surf. Their desperation is almost comical. Although, I think Jayden may end up actually making a move on Charleigh. Whatever floats his boat.

Out of the corner of my eye, I see Lennon on the balcony of her room. She's watching me, too. That thought alone has me wanting to show off—show her what a real man looks like. I spin the board into the perfect roundhouse cutback and grin to myself as I pull it off. When I look back up at the balcony, however, Kellan has her turned around and pinned against the railing.

Fucking asshole.

"You're such a tool," Bryce teases as I paddle back out.

I mock confusion. "I don't know what you're talking about."

"The fuck you don't. This isn't a competition. Tell me you didn't do that roundhouse cutback for Lennon's sake."

I smirk. "What if I wanted to impress our little entourage over there?"

He glances back at Charleigh and Skye. "Nah. You know Jayden is considering Charleigh, and you wouldn't dip your dick into anything Kellan's been with." He pauses and the two of us share a look. "Except maybe Lennon."

I scoop up a ridiculous amount of water and splash him with it. "You're sick. She's practically my sister."

"Hardly, and your parents aren't even married."

Instead of listening to him and being forced into denying more shit I have no business talking about, I see the next wave coming in and start paddling away. "Sorry, bruh, the water calls."

ONE OF THE THINGS about waking up early every morning to go surfing is that your body develops an internal alarm clock of sorts. It's at the point now where even if I wanted to sleep in, I can't.

I hop out of bed and head for the balcony. I'm instantly disappointed by the fact that there aren't enough waves to boogie board, let alone surf. I'm just about to get back in bed when I see her. Lennon is on the patio, running through a dance routine with her friend.

The way he grips her hips as he lifts her into the air spurs something inside of me. It's like my mind knows he's gay, but with Lennon, I lose all sense of logic. It's dangerous, playing this game, but anyone would admit she's nearly impossible to ignore. Her infectious smile. Her strong willed personality. And her vice grip. I wince at the memory.

"She's gorgeous, isn't she?" an irritating voice says from behind me.

Yeah, like I'd ever admit *that* out loud. "I've seen better."

Kellan steps up next to me. "Good, then focus your eyes on them instead of my girlfriend. I could see you staring from the kitchen windows."

I laugh dryly. "You are one insecure son of a bitch, aren't you?"

"Cut the shit, Knight. I've seen the way you look at her. She isn't single, you know?"

My eyes roll. "Obviously. You've made sure to hump her like a dog in heat every time I'm within fifty feet of you two."

He grins smugly. "Good, then do yourself a favor and find someone else. That one's taken."

Lennon hits every move with professional skill. I don't think I've ever seen someone so talented. When Brady touches her again, I force myself to look away.

"I appreciate your concern, Spence, but I don't think I'm the one you need to worry about."

My head gestures toward the back door, where Colby is leaning. He's watching her, too, only he isn't doing anything to hide his smile. I don't know what's going on between those two, but I don't fucking like it. Kellan Spencer and his cheating ways aren't even a challenge. Colby Hendrix, however, might be.

WE ALL SIT AROUND the fire pit, drinking and having a good time. Jayden and Charleigh are making out on one of the lounge chairs. Bryce is getting along with Tanner and

Oakley. Even Kellan and I have managed to not get into each other's faces tonight.

"Let's play a game," Skye suggests.

Lennon and Tessa share a look, silently communicating before Tessa speaks. "If you suggest spin the bottle again so you can try to kiss my boyfriend, I'm going to punch you in the tit."

She sighs heavily. "That was one time."

Clearly this isn't her first rodeo, being a cheater. It's like one of her requirements for a guy is him having a significant other. I almost want to call her out for being such a bitch, but there's a time and place for everything, and this isn't it.

I glance down at my phone and the picture I managed to capture this morning. Kellan thought he was the only one awake when he snuck across the house and into Skye's room at three in the morning. Little did he know my insomnia just so happened to kick in at the right time.

Telling Lennon about it while we're here wouldn't do much good for anyone. It would ruin her vacation and give Kellan a chance to beg for forgiveness, being as they're stuck in a house together for another week. However, the second we get home, I'm going to figure out how to tell her. He doesn't get to keep doing this shit. Not if I have anything to say about it.

"What about truth or dare?" Lennon asks.

Tessa hums. "Works for me."

Bryce pulls Jayden off of Charleigh and we start the game. It starts off easy, with dares of jumping into the pool with our clothes on, win for me being always in board shorts, and silly questions for truths. When it gets to me, I decide to spice it up a little.

"Kellan, truth or dare?"

Lennon glares at me, but Kellan wraps an arm around her and doesn't shy away. "Dare."

The corner of my mouth raises. "I dare you to go put on one of Lennon's bikinis and wear it for the rest of the night."

He glares at me, but if I know anything about Kellan, it's that he won't shy away from a dare. His pride is too big for that. Instead, he'll do it and then come after me for it later. Sure enough, he gets up and heads inside.

"You're a dick, you know that?" Lennon sneers.

I take a sip of my beer and smile. "Baby, I'm just getting started."

When Kellan gets back, he's wearing Lennon's hot pink bikini. Everyone laughs at his expense as he sits back down next to his girlfriend. Not wanting to talk about it, he focuses his attention on Charleigh.

"Char. Truth or dare?"

She puckers her lips for a second. "Truth."

"What's your biggest regret?"

"That's easy. Losing my virginity to Jace London." Charleigh turns to Lennon. "Lenny, truth or dare?"

Lennon grumbles a quiet fuck. "Truth."

"If you weren't with Kellan and needed to pick a guy here to hook up with, who would it be?"

Kellan tenses next to her, and I'm starting to think Charleigh isn't so bad. I smile at the question and watch as Lennon's gaze meets mine, then she quickly takes it away. Colby looks just as anxious for her answer as I do. Unfortunately, her best friend comes to her rescue.

Tessa nudges Lennon and gives her a soft smile, and I already know what she's going to say.

"Asher," Lennon announces, and Skye spits out her drink.

"Oh sure, so I can't make a couple comments, but Lennon can say she'd fuck your boyfriend and it's fine?"

Tessa sends Skye a fake smile. "I like Lennon."

Skye immediately looks offended. "And you don't like me?"

Tessa just shrugs.

I make a mental note to add Tessa to the list of people who aren't so bad. Meanwhile, my mind goes to how the second the question came out of Charleigh's mouth, the first person Lennon looked at was me. I know the morning of our little rendezvous in the kitchen ended badly, but it couldn't have been completely faked. She felt something. It was written all over her face.

Looking up from my lap, I find her gaze back on me. I can even see a hint of an involuntary smile for a second. She may not have said it out loud, but if I had to guess, I'd say her real answer was me.

I'M STANDING OUTSIDE, SMOKING a cigarette, when Lennon comes out. She wraps her arms around herself as she walks over to me. I take a deep inhale, not knowing what to expect, and then watch as the smoke fills the air around me when I let it out.

"You need something?"

She sighs, giving in to whatever mental debate she was having. "A fresh start. We have to live together, at least until I leave for New York in the fall. I think it would be easier if we weren't hating each other."

Little does she know, I don't hate her. I should, but I don't.

"I don't know. You did almost neuter me."

She giggles behind a closed fist. "You kind of deserved it."

A huff of laughter bubbles out. "Maybe a little. You've got one hell of a grip though."

"My dad has made me take self-defense classes since I was nine."

"Somehow, that doesn't surprise me."

A bright smile appears. "So, are we good?"

I let her sweat it for a minute, and then chuckle and nod. "Yeah. We're good."

"Perfect, so then as your friend, can you do me a small favor?"

I should have known there was a catch. "Depends on what it is."

"Take it easy on Kellan." Her sickeningly sweet tone could cause cavities.

I snort. "That's not a small favor."

She sighs and runs her fingers through her hair. "I just don't understand why you have to be such an ass to him. You two were really good friends when you were younger. If you'd just talk, clear the air, then maybe you two could get that back."

Seriously? Who does this chick think she is, Dr. Phil?

"Listen, princess. That ship sailed eight years ago when he decided he was too good for us."

She looks taken back. "But, he said that you got jealous and cut him out, and then turned Bryce and Jayden against him too."

"That's what he told you?"

She nods.

"Unbelievable," I scoff, shaking my head.

Without a second thought, I put the cigarette out with the bottom of my shoe and march into the house. Kellan is standing with Tanner and Oakley, talking about who knows what, and I go straight over and shove him. He stumbles back for a second before finding his footing.

"The fuck?" he shouts.

"Are you that fucking threatened that you had to go and lie?" I get up in his face, ignoring the way Oakley puts a hand on my chest to try to hold me back. "Were you that afraid that I was going to take her from you that you felt the need to paint me as the villain?"

"I don't know what the hell you're talking about."

"Bullshit!" I roar. "You told her that we cut you out because I was jealous of you."

"Seriously?" Bryce chimes in from across the room.

I shove my finger into Kellan's chest. "That wasn't at all how it went down. *You* got pissed because I kept beating you at competitions. *You* ghosted us. *You* threw away the fact that we were best friends since diapers, so don't you dare try pinning that shit on me."

He knows he's stuck. He can't stick with his story. Not with Bryce and Jayden here to back me up and tell her what really happened. So instead, he squares his shoulders.

"Scream at me all you want. I'll do whatever it takes to keep that girl."

I scoff in disbelief. "Yeah, everything except be fucking faithful. Banging Skye while Lennon is asleep down the hall is low, even for you."

Kellan's eyes double in size, and I don't know why until a soft, yet broken, voice echoes through the now-silent room.

"What?"

11

LENNON

My eyes are locked on Kellan, who only continues to stare at Cade. Everyone in the room is deathly quiet, making it so I can hear the blood rushing through my head. I'm feeling so many different emotions I can't even comprehend them all. My brows furrow as Cade turns around with shock on his face. Clearly, I wasn't meant to hear that.

"Kellan?" I breathe. "Is it true?"

He runs his fingers through his hair and laughs nervously. "What? Of course it's not. I told you, he'd do anything to get to me."

His tone is giving him away, and I turn to the counterpart in this. "Skye?"

She looks like she's on the verge of tears. "I'm so sorry, Lennon. I never meant for it to happen."

I let out a short breath as the truth comes out. "Unbelievable."

"Len, baby. Don't listen to her." Kellan starts to cross the room, but I stop him before he can get too close.

"Stay the fuck away from me before I smack you," I growl.

"Everyone told me I was too good for you. I should have listened."

That seems to strike a nerve. "Too good for me? Why, because you're some innocent little virgin?" My jaw drops, but he doesn't stop. "Maybe if you would have put out, I wouldn't have gone elsewhere."

Everything in me snaps, and I take off toward him, only for Colby to catch me halfway. I kick and scream as he carries me to the other side of the room and pins me to the wall. He's caging me in, with his cologne taking over my senses, but it's not the lustful feeling one would expect. I feel safe.

Kellan scoffs. "You're all on me because I slept with Skye, like you haven't been fucking Colby behind my back this whole time."

I struggle to move again, but Colby pins my wrists to the wall. He whips his head around to look at Kellan.

"Get the fuck out of here, before I let her go."

He mumbles something about this being bullshit as he storms out the door. As soon as he's gone, I feel a little calmer, until Skye tries to talk to me.

"Please don't hate me," she begs.

I scowl at her, unsure if I want to punch her in the face or throw her off a balcony. "How long?"

"What?"

"How long have you been fucking my boyfriend behind my back?" I elaborate.

She sighs and shakes her head. "It doesn't matter."

"You don't get to tell me what matters!"

Her whole body flinches from my tone. "Since the party at Oakley's."

I cross my arms over my chest. "You mean the one I left because I wasn't feeling well?" She nods. "That was over a month ago!"

"I know, and I'm so sorry."

Raising a hand to stop her, I look away. "I don't want to

hear it. Just go. If you hurry, you can get a ride home from Kellan."

She drops her head and walks out the door. Tessa comes over to hug me, and my eyes meet Cade's from over her shoulder.

"You knew."

He rubs the back of his neck. "Uh, yeah."

I leave Tessa's arms and walk over, shoving him in the chest. "You knew, and you didn't tell me!"

"You never gave me a chance!"

"Oh, that's bullshit and you know it," I sneer. "The only reason I'm not kicking your ass out of here is my dad, but don't get it confused. I want nothing to do with you, either."

THE WAVES CRASH AGAINST the shoreline as the breeze blows through my hair. I don't know how long I've been sitting out here, but I'm numb. So many different things are running through my mind, I can barely formulate a coherent thought. The range of emotions is intense.

Anger.

Betrayal.

But the most confusing of all—relief.

It's not that I didn't have feelings for Kellan, but it's like I spent two years painting this picture of him in my head. When he wasn't what I thought he was, I tried to make it work. The fact that I have yet to shed a single tear speaks volumes.

"Are you going to be okay?" Tessa asks. She's been sitting with me since I came out here, just being someone to lean on if I need it.

I nod. "Yeah, they both just better hope I don't see them again. Leaving for New York can't come soon enough."

"Hey," she whines. "Don't say that. I don't want you to leave."

Chuckling, I rest my head on her shoulder. "Oh, shush. You know I'm going to miss you."

Standing up, she brushes the sand off her clothes. "Okay, no more talking about leaving. You need sleep. Brady will be here in like four hours."

The two of us make our way back inside, hand in hand, and I've never been so glad to have her as my best friend. Everyone seems to be asleep except for Colby, who's sitting in the kitchen waiting for us.

"You want me to wait?" Tess questions.

I shake my head. "It's okay. You go to bed."

She gives me one more hug and disappears up the stairs. I let out a heavy sigh as I sit down on the stool next to Colby. He wraps an arm around me for comfort.

"Do you want me to kick his ass?"

Chuckling tiredly, I glance toward him. "Possibly. I'll let you know."

He finishes his beer and the two of us head upstairs together, being as his room is across the hall from mine. As we meet my bedroom door, I realize Kellan's stuff is still scattered. His suitcase is in the corner, and his dirty laundry is in a pile on the chair. Even his computer is still sitting on top of my bed.

My anger takes over, and Colby watches as I open the door to the balcony. I scoop up a handful of his stuff and bring it outside, throwing it off the balcony and into the pool.

"Wow, okay. So this is what we're doing," Colby says, leaning against the wall and not getting in my way.

I grab the suitcase from the floor and watch as it flies through the air and splashes into the water. Finally, I take his computer—a brand new Macbook pro I bought him as a graduation present—and smash it against the railing before tossing it to join the rest of his stuff in the pool.

Colby comes out and stands behind me. The two of us watch as everything sinks to the bottom, just like my relationship. It doesn't do much for my mood, but a small smile graces my lips. Colby chuckles quietly before shaking his head and going back inside. Just as I'm about to follow him, I notice Cade on the opposite balcony. He's leaning forward on the railing and smoking a cigarette, but his eyes are on me.

He may have not had anything to do with Kellan cheating, but the fact that he knew and said nothing hurts. I force my eyes away from him and walk inside, closing the doors behind me.

Tomorrow is a new day.

THE SOUND OF BRADY'S voice meets my ears, but I can hardly force my eyes open enough to see him. He softly rubs my arm, trying to force me awake. I groan as I roll over and pull the blanket up over my head.

"Come on, Len," he presses. "I already gave you an extra two hours to sleep. Any longer and it'll be too hot out to dance."

He has a point. The reason we practice so early isn't because we like the morning. It's because any time past ten or eleven and we're practically drowning in humidity.

I sigh and rub my eyes with the back of my fists. "I'm up. I'm up."

"I heard you had one hell of a night."

"Don't remind me," I grumble.

Kellan's betrayal still burns, but not as much as I thought it would. The fire in my blood is doused by relief. At least I found out now, before I spent all of university being cheated on by someone I never should have taken seriously. I mean, it's not even like we were that serious. Sure, I crushed on him for a couple years, but we only dated for a few months. It's not the end of the world.

Hopping out of bed, I tie my hair up into a ponytail and pull on a leotard. Usually I'd go with a T-shirt and shorts, but it's already close to nine. A leo will keep me cooler.

Brady follows me downstairs and waits while I grab a couple bottles of water out of the fridge. I'd prefer to have coffee, but let's face it—there's no time.

As we walk by the pool, the crew that comes to take care of it are fishing Kellan's things from the bottom. Brady's grin widens as he watches them.

"That's all of Kellan's stuff, isn't it?"

"Yep." I pop the p for emphasis.

He laughs and pats me on the back. "That's my girl."

WE'RE ALL HANGING OUT in the living room. Apparently, throwing Kellan's stuff into the pool made them need to shock it, so we can't go back in until tomorrow. I still don't regret it. When they asked what to do with all the stuff, I told them to shove it in a bag and give it to Tanner—except for the Macbook. That went in the trash.

Thankfully, Oakley, Tanner, and Charleigh haven't tried to defend Skye and Kellan's actions. I'm not sure if it's because they don't want me to kick them out too, or because they realize what they did was wrong. Regardless, Tanner is Kellan's best friend, and Charleigh is Skye's. I have a hard time believing that neither of them had any idea.

"What room was Skye sleeping in?" I ask no one in particular. "I'll need to have the staff deeply sanitize that one."

"I don't know if that'll be enough," Tessa quips. "Might need to just burn the whole house down and rebuild."

A giggle bubbles out of me. "Probably a good idea."

"Well, at least you didn't let this ruin your vacation," Colby chimes in.

I sit up from where I was lying on the kitchen island. "Please. The only thing I'm upset about is the fact that I'm still looking at being a virgin for the rest of my life."

"Hey, I offered to help you out with that."

Tessa and Asher watch our banter, like they're praying I'll take him up on that. Tanner and Oakley exchange a look, but I roll my eyes and bite my lip to conceal my amusement.

"Me and every other girl in California."

He snickers and gives me one of his seductive grins. "Nah. I make it a point to avoid taking v-cards. I'd just make an exception for you."

The sound of glass breaking pulls all of our attention to the other side of the room. The glass Cade was holding has shattered in his hand, with the liquid now a puddle on the floor. Bryce and Jayden laugh at him while Tessa raises her brows at me. I shake my head, refusing to acknowledge him.

"Maybe I'll have to consider it then."

It's obvious Colby is just kidding, or at least he is unless I say yes, but messing with Cade is too much fun to resist. Colby comes over and drapes an arm around my shoulder, then leans in to whisper in my ear.

"Using me to make faux-bro jealous?" he teases.

I smile sweetly up at him, but say nothing. It doesn't require an answer.

THE SUN RAYS BEAT down, warming my skin and making me perfectly bronzed. Tessa's beach chair sits next to mine as the two of us sip on fruity drinks. We're a little way down the beach, but you can see Cade, Bryce, and Jayden surfing in the distance. I've never been more thankful for my sunglasses than I am right now. They allow me to watch without Tessa being able to see where I'm looking.

I'm still so pissed at him, but there's something about him that I can't explain. It's like my eyes are drawn to him whenever he's around, and all I want is to be the center of his attention. At the same time, he infuriates me. From his bipolar mood swings to his stone-cold attitude about practically everything, sometimes I just want to smack him.

"What's got you all lost in thought?" Tessa questions. "Or rather, who?"

I snap my focus back to my drink and the sand in front of me. "Just thinking about dance. Brady told me today that the studio is closing, so we're throwing together another recital. Sort of like a farewell."

"Wow. How does Brady feel about that?"

I shrug. "He seems okay. He's sad because he practically grew up there, but I think he's ready to move on with his life. He might even join Sav and me in New York."

Her lips curl into a smirk. "And what about Cade? Is he going to join you in New York, too?"

My head falls back, and I groan. I should have known better than to think she can't see right through me. Still, saying that I feel something for him out loud only makes it more real, and I'm not even remotely ready for that.

"Please. The sooner I can leave him behind, the better."

She clearly doesn't believe a word I say as she nods toward where they're surfing. "Might be sooner than you think. He just wiped out, hard."

I look over to see the wave tossing his board around as he must be tumbling under water. A part of me panics but I do my best to keep my composure.

"Maybe you should go check on him." She nudges me in the arm.

Sighing, I take another sip of my drink. "That would require me to care, and I don't."

But the truth is I do, and I hate that I do.

12

CADE

I DON'T KNOW WHAT PISSES ME OFF MORE—WHEN she's being an irritating little shit, or when she refuses to acknowledge me at all. No part of me should want any part of her. I should be glad she declared me dead to her or whatever the fuck it was she said, but I'm not. I crave her attention like a goddamn heroin addict, desperate for a fix.

The waves are perfect, but my eyes are glued to the blonde sitting on the beach. She's yet to say a single word to me since I let the bomb slip about Kellan's actions behind closed doors. I can't say I blame her, but that doesn't make it any easier to deal with.

"Why don't you just go talk to her?" Bryce suggests, as if it's the easiest thing in the world.

I roll my eyes. "Because I don't care enough."

"Yeah, okay."

Just the sound of his voice is irritating me, let alone the way he's acting as if he can read my every thought. And don't even get me started on the fact that he's fucking right. The only thing I want is to get him off my case.

"I'm serious, fuckwit. She can do whatever the hell she pleases."

He smirks at Jayden and then back at me. "So, if I wanted to go for her…"

My jaw ticks, but I look away in time to cover it up, making it seem like I'm checking out the incoming waves. "Knock yourself out."

"Sweet. Thanks, bruh."

Bruh.

Fucking bruh.

He uses that word only on rare occasions, and almost all of them are sarcastic. He and I both know this is only a ploy —an attempt at getting to me. And I refuse to let him win. I can't. I'll never hear the end of it.

Instead of making it obvious I'm pissed off, I grab the first wave that comes our way, even though it isn't the neatest of the bunch. The second I stand up on the board, I cut it to the left. My frustration must be a little more than I thought, because I'm not used to how hard I turn into the wave. I lose my balance, and before I know it, I'm being tossed around under water.

Lesson learned: never take your anger out on the ocean. She has no mercy.

THE BONFIRE ASHER AND Colby lit in the middle of the beach is exactly what we need for the last night here. We all sit around in the Adirondack chairs they pulled from the deck. To be honest, Colby and his tendency to hit on Lennon has been getting to me since the second we got here. What's even worse is the fact that she gives it just as well as she takes it.

Jayden plops down into the chair next to me and hands me a beer. I murmur a quiet thank you and take a long swig, until I realize the other part of our trio is MIA. My brows furrow as I look at Jayden.

"Where's Bryce?"

He becomes smug as he nods behind me. The second I turn around, my blood goes from cool to scorching hot in a millisecond. Standing next to Lennon on the beach is none other than my best friend. I can tell from here that he has the charm turned all the way up. Lennon laughs at something he said, looking like she's actually having a great time.

"You all right, Cade?" Jayden questions.

The almost-full can of beer cracks in my hand and liquid spews out. "I'm fine."

He chuckles. "Maybe, but your beer sure as hell says otherwise."

"I said I'm fucking fine."

If it wasn't obvious before that this little scheme is pissing me off, it is now. I toss the can onto the ground and get up. Jayden tries calling my name, but I can't be bothered. He's my best friend. She has to know that if I was aware of Kellan's extracurriculars, Bryce was too. Then again, maybe she just doesn't care.

I walk across the patio and into the kitchen, trying to calm down. My fingers tug at my hair as I groan, until a small giggle pulls my attention to the fact that there's someone else in the room. Tessa leans against the kitchen island with nothing but amusement in her eyes.

"You good, Casanova?"

"I really wish people would stop asking me that," I grumble.

She shrugs. "Then maybe make your emotions a little less obvious."

"Like I haven't tried. Your best friend is fucking infuriating."

The grin that stretches across her face shows nothing but love. "I know. That's exactly why she's my best friend."

A brilliant idea comes to mind, and I smirk. If she wants

to flirt with Bryce, it's only right I do the same. Unfortunately, Tessa notices the second I take a step closer.

"I wouldn't even attempt that if I were you," she warns.

My brows raise. "Oh? And why's that?"

A male voice sounds from right behind me and has me freezing where I stand. "Because I'll break you in half for even thinking about it."

Asher walks around me and over to Tessa, pulling her into his arms. She smiles dreamily up at him.

"You're such a caveman."

He bends down and kisses her quickly. "You love it."

"Ugh," I groan. "You two make me sick."

Turning around, I go to head back outside when Tessa stops me.

"All right, this is the only time I'll take pity on you," she says, and I turn back around to face her. "She's more affected by you than you think, and judging by the way seeing her with Bryce has you, I'd say it goes both ways."

I cross my arms over my chest, unsure if I should deny it or just let it go unmentioned. "What's your point?"

"My point is that you shouldn't let fuckboys take your girl —even if he is your best friend."

"She's not my girl."

Tessa snorts and holds Asher's hand as she slips past me. "Sure she's not."

The two of them leave me alone in the house, and in an instant, I'm completely on edge. Since when do I let some chick get to me like this? She's nothing but a stuck-up, spoiled, trust fund brat with a serious attitude problem. She just also happens to be one that sets my soul on fire.

It means nothing.

It's harmless.

I should ignore it.

However, all of that goes flying out the window the second I step outside to see Bryce tucking a strand of hair behind her ear. A light blush coats Lennon's cheeks as she smiles down at the sand, and I see red.

I storm over to the two of them, grabbing Bryce by the back of his shirt and pull him away. He makes a noise like I'm choking him, but I honestly don't give a shit. Not about that, and not about the fact that Lennon is calling me an asshole as I drag him toward the water.

The second I let Bryce go, he falls to the ground.

"The fuck was that for?" he shouts as he pushes himself back up.

"You fucking know what."

"You said you were cool with it!"

I get up in his face. "Yeah, well, I changed my mind."

The two of us stand chest to chest, staring each other down, until he finally snickers and shakes his head while taking a step back. I didn't just fall for his trap; I fucking threw myself into it. Still, I couldn't stand seeing Lennon with him for one more second.

"You're so screwed," he tells me.

"Fuck off. I am not."

"Sure, bruh."

He walks away and back over to Jayden, leaving me to process what the fuck just happened.

Fucking bruh.

THIS BED VERY WELL may be an actual cloud, but I still can't seem to get comfortable. Thoughts of Lennon have plagued my mind since the bonfire. Even after my very public outrage, she has refused to say a single word to me. I wish it didn't get to me, and I could just let it go, but it does and I can't.

Giving in, I slip out of bed and make my way across the house. Maybe if I can just see her, get close enough to admire her cheekbones and the way her hair falls around her face, maybe then I can get some sleep.

I quietly open the door to her room, but her bed is empty. My first thought is Bryce, but I know he would never do that to me. Colby Hendrix flashes into my mind, and I'm about to lose my shit, until a figure on the balcony catches my eye.

Lennon is looking out at the ocean, with the breeze blowing through her hair, despite it being three in the morning. The way the moonlight hits her just right has me wishing I could commit this sight to memory—lock it away for a day when I don't get the privilege of seeing how breathtakingly beautiful she is.

"It's not nice to stare," she tells me, not even needing to turn around to see that it's me stepping outside behind her.

I can't help but laugh. "Who said I was nice?"

Turning around, she looks me up and down. "You play hard, but I think you're secretly a softie."

"Are you always this wrong?"

She sighs. "Potentially. I thought Kellan was a good guy."

That manages to cut right through me. I don't know if it's the pain in her voice, or the fact that he is even on her mind—because that prick doesn't deserve even an ounce of her attention—but I instantly want to find Kellan and pummel his face in.

"Lennon, that wasn't your fault."

"I know. Or at least I think I know." She runs her fingers through her hair. "Still, it doesn't make it any easier, knowing he cheated with someone who was supposed to be my friend."

I shake my head. "It's their loss. Both of them."

Her bottom lip starts to tremble. "I'm not even that upset about Kellan. He can go fuck himself for all I care. But Skye? I never expected this from her." A dry laugh bubbles out of her mouth. "And I was stupid enough to leave them alone together on the drive down here."

"Hey." I grab her chin and turn her to face me. "You aren't stupid. You trusted them, and they betrayed that trust. That's on them, not you."

The second her eyes narrow on mine, I can practically see all the questions she must be thinking. The most obvious one echoes out.

"How long did you know?"

Fuck. "I saw them together at a party before I met you, but I didn't know you two were together. I connected the dots when he came over for dinner."

She winces, as if the answer pains her. "Why didn't you tell me?"

"Would you have believed me? Kellan made sure to plant all sorts of lies in your head the second he saw me at the house. If I tried telling you he was cheating, you would have told me I was pathetic and kicked me out of your room."

"I would not," she argues, but I just give her a knowing look. "Okay, fine. You're probably right, but you're still a dick."

I chuckle softly. "Tell me something I don't know."

It may be tense, and not exactly how I'd prefer to be spending any time I have alone with her, but having Lennon's attention again feels like coming up for air. The two of us stare out into the darkness, watching the ocean kiss the shore time and time again, until she breaks the silence.

"Okay, one more question."

"You're rather inquisitive tonight, aren't you?"

She turns her head and looks up at me. "Why do you want my dad and your mom to split up so badly?"

A heavy feeling sits on my chest, but I know she deserves the answer. "My parents were happily married, up until a few weeks ago—or at least I thought they were. My mom was having an affair with your father, and she finally decided to leave my dad for him."

"Oh, my God. Did my dad know she was married?"

I shrug. "I have no idea, but my dad had no idea there was anything wrong until she told him she met someone else and was leaving him. I've seen how much divorced parents can fuck up a kid..."

"And you're worried about Molly," she finishes for me.

Nodding, I finally allow my gaze to meet hers again. "I just want what's best for her. That little girl may be a pain in my ass sometimes, but she's the closest family I have."

Lennon looks like she's battling an internal debate before she comes to a resolution and exhales. "Okay, then, I'll help you."

"What?"

She giggles. "If getting between them so you can get your family back together is still what you want, I'll help you."

I open my mouth to speak, but she stops me with a finger on my lips. It takes every ounce of restraint I have not to pull the digit into my mouth.

"But I want you to think on it first, because even if we break them up, there's no guarantee she'll agree to get back with your dad just because she doesn't have mine anymore."

Relief washes over me, and I feel like I finally have someone on board. Someone who might make this easier than I thought. Someone who could get me what I want, or at least part of what I want.

"Deal," I tell her, and pull her in for a hug.

The top of her head comes up to just below my chin, and I subtly burrow my face into her hair—inhaling the smell of it and wishing I could do this every day. But I can't, or at least can't for now. First, I need to do what's best for Molly, and that's mending our broken family.

AFTER SIX HOURS OF driving and having to listen to Bryce and Jayden grill me for half of it, I finally pull into the driveway. The only thing I want to do is fall face first on my bed and sleep for the next day and a half. Lennon and I ended up staying awake until five in the morning, talking about random topics and just enjoying getting along for once. By the time we both went to sleep, we only got a couple hours.

A brand-new Shelby GT sits in the driveway, making my brows furrow. Maybe it's Lennon's graduation present, though I'm not sure she drives. There has been an untouched Mercedes sitting in the garage since I moved in that I'm pretty sure is hers, but I've never seen her behind the wheel.

I walk through the front door and follow the voices into the kitchen. My mom and Ken are sitting at the island. The second Ken sees me, he perks up.

"Oh, good. You're back." He glances behind me. "Where's Lennon?"

I shrug. "She rode with Asher and Colby."

We won't even get into how I hoped she would choose to ride with me, but I'm not surprised she didn't. Besides, Bryce and Jayden would have made shit super awkward and enjoyed every second of it.

"Ah, okay. Well, I have something for you."

He pulls a set of keys out of his pocket and tosses them to me. The new car sitting in the driveway. It's mine.

"You bought me a car?" I ask, confused.

Ken hums and takes a sip of his drink. "Yeah. I figured that way you don't have to drive that hunk of junk around anymore."

My shock slowly turns to anger as his words echo through my head. The sound of my mom's voice barely registers as I stare down at the keys in my hand.

"Cade. Say thank you."

I don't. Instead, I say nothing as I turn around and storm right back out the door. I'm pacing back and forth across the driveway when Asher's Range Rover pulls up and Lennon hops out. The second she sees me, concern etches across her face. She comes closer and drops her bag before putting her hands on my shoulders and stopping me.

"What's wrong? What happened?"

I shake my head and throw the key onto the ground. "He bought me a car."

Her eyes widen. She glances at the GT and then brings her attention back to me. "And you're mad about it?"

I nod. "He called my Jeep a hunk of junk. Lennon, my dad bought me that car. He saved every dime he could manage for over a year."

"And my dad just practically shit all over that by buying you something else without even batting an eye."

The way she understands me should make me want to run away so fucking fast, but instead, it's comforting. I don't need to explain for her to get it, and for her to be there. Maybe I was wrong about her all along. Maybe she's not anything like the girl I thought she was.

"All right," she declares. "I have an idea. Meet me in your room in thirty. I'll explain."

MY MOM LEAVES FOR drinks with a friend, giving Lennon the perfect chance to execute her plan. I have to admit, it's clever, and I'm honestly surprised she came up with it all on her own. I stand at the top of the steps and watch as she turns toward her dad's office. Before going in, she looks back up at me and winks. The corners of my lips raise as she disappears through the door.

"Dad, I need to talk to you," she tells him.

I can't see what's going on, but I walk to the bottom of the stairs so I can hear them.

"What's up, Sunshine?"

"I can't do it—play family with Nora and her kids. I'm sorry. I tried, but I can't do it."

He sighs heavily. "What are you saying?"

"I'm saying it's me or her. There's something about her that rubs me the wrong way, and I can't stay here if she's living here. It's me or her, Dad."

It's quiet for a minute, and I must applaud Lennon on her acting skills. The girl is seriously talented when it comes to faking emotions. Finally, Ken speaks.

"Okay."

"Okay?" Lennon asks.

"Yeah. I love Nora, but you're my daughter. If you really want me to choose between you and her, the answer is and always will be you."

It worked. It actually fucking worked. Every inch of my body is overwhelmed with excitement as I realize something is finally going my way for a change. That is, until it comes crashing right back down.

"I, um...you know what, never mind," she backtracks.

"Never mind?"

"Yeah. Maybe I judged her too quickly. I'll give her another chance."

I can hear as Ken gets up from his desk, I'm guessing to give his daughter a hug. "I really appreciate that, sweetheart. Thank you."

Traitor. She's a fucking traitor. Everything we talked about last night. The time we just spent in my room. It was all for nothing. She's exactly the person I thought she was. Cruel. Selfish. Manipulative. *The enemy.*

Lennon comes around the corner and stops short as she finds me standing there. Her breath hitches, but I'm completely unfazed. Those turquoise eyes don't affect me anymore. Nothing about her causes anything more than rage to spur inside of me.

Now, I have a new mission.

Destroy Lennon *and* her dad.

13

LENNON

Dear Diary,

I have a confession to make. My thoughts about Cade haven't always been as pure as wedding day white. They're more ivory, covered in mud and rubbed in ash. The kind that fill my mind when they're not supposed to. They're wrong. They're dirty. They're forbidden. Maybe it's best that he hates me, because nothing good can come from this.

Melani's voice echoes through the speaker, letting me know dinner should be ready in a few. I close the book and toss it underneath my mattress. Thankfully, "family" dinners have gone from every night to just one night a week. The less time I have to see Cade, the better. He and I have been home for three days, and every time we're in the same room, he mentally shoots daggers into the side of my head.

Okay, so maybe he has a right to be pissed. I told him I'd help, and then right when I had it, I went back on my word. I just couldn't go through with it. The look on my dad's face hit me in all the wrong places. He was making the right decision, but he looked devastated doing it. Nora may not be my favorite person after finding out from Cade what she did to their family, but my dad obviously cares about her.

I can feel the tension in the room the second I walk up to the table. Cade's usual attitude is killing the happy mood of everyone else. I sit down next to Molly and bop her on the nose. She scrunches it up and smiles at me, much to her brother's dismay.

"Molly, come sit next to me," he orders her.

"But I want to sit next to Lennon."

He scoffs. "Why? Traitors don't deserve your attention."

Molly looks confused as she glances up at me.

I roll my eyes. "If you have a problem, take it out with me, not her."

"Oh, I do have a problem, and I haven't even gotten started with you."

I'm about to snap back when my dad and Nora come into the room, looking as smitten as ever with each other. Cade looks disgusted but Molly and I think it's cute. After finding out what really happened, I can understand why he'd be pissed, but shouldn't he just want his mom to be happy?

"So, Lennon, how was dance?"

I finish chewing before answering. "It was good. Nothing exciting. Just keeping in good shape for Juilliard in the fall."

She smiles. "That's right. You'll have so much fun there. When do you leave?"

"Not until the end of August."

The way Cade's grip tightens around his fork does not go unnoticed. He jabs it into his food and it scrapes across the plate. Like nails on a chalkboard, the noise that rings out causes all of us to cringe, him included.

Molly giggles. "Real smooth, bro."

He narrows his eyes on her. "Bro? What are you, thirteen?"

"One day I will be."

"Ugh. Please don't remind me."

Imagine if he knew his precious little sister has her first crush. I would never out her like that, but she came into my room a couple nights ago to ask some questions. I think I answered them pretty well, or at least I hope I did. I'd really hate to give her bad advice on boys, but come on. Is the eighteen-year-old virgin who just got cheated on the right person to ask for dating advice? I didn't think so.

"So, Nora and I have something to tell you," my dad says, and my heart drops. Cade must be thinking the same thing, because all the color drains from his face as he waits for the news. "The two of us are going on a thirty-day cruise."

Cade and I exhale, as if we were both holding our breath. I might want my dad to be happy, but any mention of marriage would have even me rioting. It's bad enough he moved her and her family in the week after he introduced her to me. Holy matrimony should be nowhere in the room, let alone on the table.

"Molly, you'll be staying with your grandparents. Lennon and Cade, I trust you two are responsible enough to stay home alone?"

We both nod, but the tension raises a couple notches at the thought of having to spend a whole month alone with him.

I'm not a very confrontational person. If I'm honest, after Cade caught me going back on our plan, I purposely avoided him for a full twenty-four hours. But, we have to live in this house together, at least until I leave for New York. I'd much rather it be a peaceful experience than having to look over my shoulder every other second. That's why, as soon as we're all done with dinner, I follow him into the kitchen.

"Go away, Lennon," he says without even needing to turn around.

"No."

He glances at me and his eyebrows raise. "No?"

I straighten my shoulders. "You heard me. No. Not until you hear me out."

Chuckling softly, he looks down at the ground for a second, and I'm momentarily stunned by how beautiful he is. The shape of his jawline. His perfect smile. Even the fire in his eyes, as his gaze finally meets mine. It's unfairly gorgeous and could render me defenseless without a moment's notice.

He steps closer and gets in my face. "That's the thing. I don't want to hear anything from you. Not an apology. Not a plea. Not a fucking word."

My chest tightens as he pushes past me and walks away, giving me no choice but to watch him as he goes.

I knew he was going to be pissed, especially after seeing him on the stairs after I left my dad's office, but I never thought he would be this furious. It's like he would rather die than have to even look at me, and I don't know how to fix it.

ONE OF MY FAVORITE parts of this mansion is the ballet studio my dad had built for me in the basement. The whole wing is split in half—one side being my studio and the other being a gym. They're separated by a wide hallway, but both have glass windows filling the upper half of the walls. It was my dad's way of being able to watch me practice as a child while still being able to work out.

I grab my water bottle from the fridge and make my way down. After dealing with Cade's attitude earlier, I need to dance it out. It's the best way I know to relieve stress and let things go. A coping mechanism of sorts.

I walk into the studio when a reflection in the mirror catches my eye. Cade is in the gym, lifting weights and looking like a fucking god while doing it. Droplets of sweat roll down his back as all his muscles tighten. I know I should look away, but I can't. My eyes are glued to him and the way those basketball shorts hang low on his hips.

Change of plans, because I know I won't be able to focus on dance when he's across the hall looking like that. I go into the gym and get on the treadmill. It wasn't exactly how I intended to work out tonight, but I guess I could use a run.

The room is filled with the scent of his body wash and deodorant, but not in a gross way. In an intoxicating way. A pair of AirPods sit inside his ears, telling me he has no idea I'm even here right now. That is, until he catches me staring through the mirror on the back wall. He's in the middle of a rep, and his gaze stays locked with mine as he continues to flex. Thank God I'm only walking, otherwise I'd probably fall flat on my face.

He drops the weights onto the ground and the sound of them clattering makes me jump. I pull my attention away from him and down to the treadmill, pretending to mess with some of the settings. Cade slams his hands on the front of the machine.

"Oh, how the tables have turned. Look who's wanting who now."

My brows furrow, but he doesn't give me a chance to ask him to elaborate before he's walking around to the side and stepping up next to me. He places his mouth by my ear.

"Enjoy the view, Len," he growls, spewing my nickname with venom. "You could have had me in Malibu, but that ship sailed the moment you turned into a traitorous bitch."

I'm stunned completely into silence as he turns around and walks out without giving me a second more of his attention. A part of me wants to call his name, but I know it wouldn't do any good. Besides, the other part of me wants nothing more than to kick him in his junk, but that wouldn't make matters any better either. Instead, I turn up the speed on the treadmill and run until I can't run any more.

AN HOUR LATER, AND I'm no less conflicted than I was when I went down there. Let's face it, as long as Cade is mad at me, I don't stand a chance at feeling any kind of peace—which essentially means the rest of my summer is going to suck. He won't even talk to me, and I have to be alone with him for an entire month.

As I'm walking by his room, I can hear the shower running from his en suite bathroom. It may be ballsy and a little insane, but what else do I have to lose? I twist the knob and cheer internally when I realize it's unlocked.

The whole room smells like him. His cologne fills the air and has me wanting to drown myself in it. I've been in this room before, but it's never looked like this. There's a hole in the one wall where he must have put his fist through it, probably after I ruined everything. Dirty clothes are piled on the chair in the corner, and water bottles fill his nightstand.

Not giving myself time to second guess it, I march into the bathroom and slam the door behind me.

"All right, we need to talk," I demand.

"Lennon?" he asks, confused. "What the fuck are you doing in here?"

"Well, you don't give me a chance to say anything before you walk away. At least in here, you can't walk away."

He groans. "Get out of my room."

"Not until you listen to me." My tone is firm, making it clear I have no intentions of backing down. Not this time. "I'm sorry I betrayed you. It's a shitty feeling, and I didn't mean to hurt you."

"Fuck off."

I ignore him and keep going. "I wanted to help you. I swear I did. It's just, my dad looked so upset. It's been a while since I've seen him as happy as he is with Nora, and I can't be the one who takes that away from him."

Cade's hand hits the wall. "And my happiness doesn't matter?"

"Of course it does, but he's my dad."

"Cade?" Nora's voice comes from the other side of the bathroom door, and I immediately panic.

"In here, Mom!" he calls out.

My eyes widen as I hear her coming toward the bathroom. "What the fuck are you doing?" I whisper-shout.

In a split-second decision, I move the curtain and jump into the shower with Cade. A shocked expression covers his face as the door opens and his mom comes into the bathroom.

"Is everything okay?" Nora questions. "I thought I heard something fall in here."

He smirks at me, and it takes everything in me not to stare at the way the water flows down his body. It's bad enough my clothes are getting soaked just from being in here.

"I'm fine." He looks me up and down. "Just a bug I had to squish."

She shrieks. "Gross. I'll have to let Ken know so he can have the exterminator come."

"Good idea. There are a few pests that need to be gotten rid of."

Without thinking, I go to retort, but he rushes toward me and covers my mouth with his hand. Good move on his part, because I can only imagine what our parents will do if she finds me in this shower right now. Fully clothed or not, it doesn't look good.

"I'm going to take some of these clothes to Melani," his mom says, but I'm too focused on the way his wet body is pressed against mine.

"All right. Thanks."

It feels like an eternity before she leaves and closes the bathroom door behind her. Finally, Cade releases me and steps back. As if I can no longer resist, my eyes rake down his body until they land on his cock, and to my surprise, it's hard. I may not have seen many dicks, but holy fuck he's huge.

"Ahem." He clears his throat, and I immediately know I'm busted. "Either get on your knees and suck it or get out so I can take care of this."

My breath hitches at his words. We aren't even going to talk about how a part of me considers going with option one. I can't. We may not be related, but that doesn't make this any less wrong. Hell, with the way things are going, he's probably going to be my step-brother one day—whether he likes it or not.

I shake myself from the daze I was in and move the curtain to step out of the shower. Just as I'm about to close it again, he grabs my wrist.

"By the way, nice bra."

With a wink that damn near knocks my world off its axis, he slides the curtain between us. I look down and notice my white shirt is now completely see-through and my pink lace sports bra is fully visible. My God, I may as well not be wearing a shirt at all.

I swallow down the humiliation and leave the room, hoping at least my dignity is still intact.

HOPING THINGS WOULD CHANGE a little after seeing Cade naked was stupid. If anything, it's only made my less-than-innocent thoughts about him even more known. Now, he makes it a point to torment me with it.

Looking down at his cock while sitting on the couch.

Adjusting himself when only I can see him.

Biting his lip and winking at me.

Fuck, he's an arrogant son of a bitch.

Why does he have to be so good looking? Why couldn't he be one of those nerdy guys who spent lunch in the library designing robots? Maybe this is just teenage hormones, and the fact that I'm about to go to college with my v-card still firmly attached. My body is just trying to find someone who isn't Kellan—or Colby, for that matter. He'd probably be skilled as hell, but I think my first time should be with someone who doesn't have a body count that resembles an area code.

I'm standing in the kitchen, looking for something to drink, while Nora gets her things together. Cade is sitting at the nook in the corner, eating a bowl of cereal and somehow making it look sexy as he does it. The way his tongue juts out to meet the spoon before it enters his mouth, my mind fills with thoughts I shouldn't have.

"Okay, I'm off to find a new bathing suit for the cruise," Nora announces.

"What's wrong with the bathing suits you have?" Cade questions with his mouth full.

She rolls her eyes. "Nothing. I just want a new one."

He grumbles something under his breath, but she doesn't pay it any attention. She grabs her purse and pulls it up until it rests on her shoulder. Then she smiles warmly at me and leaves the room. Still, Cade's attitude is really starting to strike a nerve.

"What the hell is your problem?" I sneer. "Why do you always have to give your mom a hard time?"

He chuckles, but it lacks humor. "You're going to tell me how to act with my mom now? This isn't her. She was never like this."

"Like what? A nice person?"

"Materialistic," he snaps. "Thirty-day cruises. Shopping for the hell of it. She never gave a shit about any of that stuff until we came here. Now she's turning out just like you. There are bigger things to worry about than debit cards and designer purses. She was better off with my dad. We all were."

His constant judgment and degrading comments finally cause me to break. "What the hell do you want me to do? Apologize for my dad being rich? Get a fucking grip, Cade. The only one paying attention to your lack of wealth is you."

I'M OFFICIALLY DONE WITH everything Cade Knight. If he wants to be a constant asshole, with the mood swings of a teenage boy during puberty, that's on him. This is my last summer at home, and I refuse to let him ruin that for me. Except—I can't find my computer.

I swear I left it on my bed, but it's not there. I look under the pillow, the comforter, under the bed itself. Nowhere. That stupid fucker must have taken it to mess with me.

Leaving my room, I head down the small staircase and walk toward his bedroom. It's quiet, meaning he's not in there. I quietly open the door and slip inside. The place is even more a mess than it was the other day.

I look around, even pulling open some drawers. No computer, but there is a rather sizable bag of weed. Cade smokes pot? A familiar voice has me freezing in place.

"What do you think you're doing?"

I straighten without dropping the bag, and when he sees it in my hand, his brows furrow. I let it go and it falls back into the drawer. My heart pounds inside my chest as he grows angrier.

"I was looking for my computer," I tell him. "It's missing."

He snorts. "And what makes you think I had anything to do with that?"

"Oh, I don't know. Maybe the way you've done nothing but fuck with me lately."

Smirking like he's the actual fucking devil, he comes closer until he's unnecessarily close. "Oh beautiful, you haven't experienced anything yet."

The nickname has me swallowing hard.

"I didn't take your computer, and I haven't been fucking with you either, but I will now. You just started a war that you don't stand a chance in hell at winning."

He takes a step back and looks me up and down, biting his lip for a second and causing goosebumps to break out across my skin. There's a fire burning in his eyes, one that dares me to go against him, but I don't have the guts. He looks like he could slit my throat just for fun.

"Now, get the fuck out of my room and don't ever let me catch you in here again."

14

CADE

"ARE YOU SURE THIS IS A GOOD IDEA?" BRYCE ASKS, helping me carry the ten bags of sand up the two flights of stairs to Lennon's room. "I thought you wanted to get with her, not piss her off."

I roll my eyes. "Don't you ever fucking listen? That was before she became everything I thought she was."

A liar.

A bitch.

A traitor.

She made me think that I finally had someone on my side, only to stab me in the back with my own damn knife. I was going to just ignore her. It was fun enough seeing her work for my attention, and I had no intention of doing anything else to her but that—until she invited herself into my shower.

Seeing the way she checked me out had all sorts of thoughts running through my mind, and when she hesitated at the choice of either getting out or getting on her knees, it only got worse. Messing with Lennon has become one of my new favorite hobbies, and it's only just begun.

"Besides, this is petty compared to what I'd like to do."

Bryce bounces his brows at me. "Oh yeah? And what's that?"

I take one of the bags of sand and chuck it at him. "Get your mind out of the gutter."

"I can't help it. I live there."

Okay, that's probably the most honest thing he's said in weeks. "Whatever. Let's just get this done before she comes home."

We pull back her comforter and pour the sand on top of her sheet. She's been at dance all day. Something about needing to learn a couple master-skill moves before she leaves in a couple months. Regardless, she's bound to be exhausted by the time she comes home tonight, and this will piss her off enough to hold me over for a couple days.

Once all the sand is out of the bags, we move the comforter back into place. Sure, Lennon probably won't be the one cleaning this up, but it will make it so she has to sleep in another room for a night or two. It's an inconvenience, at best.

TEN O'CLOCK COMES AROUND, and I hear the alarm beep as Lennon finally gets home. I mute my TV and listen as she makes her way upstairs. Standing by my door, I wait for the scream, and it does not disappoint. It only takes a couple seconds before she's storming down the hallway and pounding on the door.

"Cade!"

I open the door and smile innocently. "Yes?"

Her face is red with anger. "What the fuck did you do to my bed?"

"Whatever are you talking about?" My tone is sweet. Mocking.

"Don't play coy," she sneers. "It doesn't look cute on you."

I grab her wrist and pull her into me. "Oh, yeah? And what does look cute on me?" I drop my mouth to the shell of her ear. "I bet you would. You'd look real cute on me."

Her whole body shakes, but before I can enjoy her reaction, she's shoving me away. "You're a fucking prick."

Now that makes me laugh. "I tried telling you that. You didn't want to listen."

"You wanted a war? You've got one." She steps back and licks her lips, giving me a dose of my own medicine. "Don't think I'll go down easy."

"Maybe not, but you will go down."

There's an underlying want in my words with the double meaning. Thankfully for me, my hatred of her burns hotter than my desire to watch her bounce on my cock. Don't get me wrong—I want her. I fucking hate that I do, but I do. I'm just not willing to let bygones be bygones to have her. I'd rather ruin her and then fuck her while she's broken down to nothing.

I DRIVE HOME FROM the beach, enjoying the way the wind blows through my hair with the top down. Despite Ken buying me an overpriced Shelby GT to try to bribe me for my affection, I still drive my Jeep to and from the beach every day. I haven't even gotten behind the wheel of the GT, no matter how tempting it's been. It's dirty, just like him.

The cool water of the shower runs down my body, ridding me of all the salt from the ocean. I revel in the feeling. I love nothing more than a shower after spending the day at the beach. To feel the clean water on my skin. It's soothing.

I step out and dry myself with a towel before wrapping it around my waist. If I hurry, I can probably think of a way to fuck with Lennon before she gets home from Tessa's. Colby picked her up this morning as I was leaving, and she made sure to smile sweetly at me before getting in the car—so I can only imagine what she has planned.

Walking over to my closet, I slide it open to find everything gone. All my shirts, hoodies, literally anything to cover the upper half of my body—they're all nowhere to be found. I can't help but chuckle as I pull on a pair of sweatpants.

This is how she thinks she's going to take me down? She better try harder than that.

THE SOUND OF LENNON'S voice reaches my ears. Judging by the way I can only hear one side of the conversation, I'm guessing she's on the phone. I quietly make my way closer so I can hear what she's saying.

"Ugh, I'm just so tired lately. I guess with dance and all this bullshit with Cade, I just haven't gotten much sleep."

Bullshit with Cade, huh? I step into the room, and the second she sees me, her sentence gets completely cut off. I open the fridge and pull out a bottle of water, completely aware of her staring as I chug half of it in one go. When I'm done, I wipe my mouth with the back of my hand and come up next to her.

"You know, if you wanted me to go shirtless, all you had to do was ask. I would've saved you the trouble of hiding all my shirts." I can hear Tessa chuckle in the phone, and I reach up and pull Lennon's bottom lip from in between her teeth. "By the way, that's not the only thing I'm not wearing."

She watches as I reach down and grab my crotch. As if Tessa's going into full blown hysterics brings her back into reality, she scowls at me. Her hand presses against my chest and she pushes me back until my ass hits the counter. She hangs up the phone without a single word and slides it into her back pocket.

"Your ego is a little too big, so let's get one thing straight. I'm not just out of your league. I'm not even in your stratosphere." She arches up on her tip-toes and presses a soft kiss to the underside of my jaw. "Let's be real. You've got nothing on Colby Hendrix."

That strikes a nerve, and in a single move, I spin us around until she's caged in with my hands on the counter. "Let me find out he touched you. I fucking swear, Lennon. One goddamn finger on you, and I'll break every bone in his body."

"Why?" she presses. "Whose job is it to touch me? Yours?"

"Lennon," I growl.

A smug grin spreads across her face as she comes closer, until her lips are only centimeters from mine. I should pull away, get more control of the situation since I clearly don't have much right now, but I can't.

She licks her lips and drags her finger down my neck. "Never going to happen."

With that, she breaks from my hold and saunters out of the room without looking back, leaving me to wonder what the hell just happened. *Tied score, 1-1.*

THE BENEFIT TO OUR parents being out at some charity function and my sister sleeping over a friend's house is that it gives me the chance to redeem myself. After earlier, when Lennon still managed to take the win, I need a win in my column. And after hearing her complain to Tessa about how she hasn't been sleeping lately, I know exactly how to do it.

I rummage through the shoebox that stays hidden in my closet until I find the familiar DVD. It's been at least a year since I've watched this thing, and even longer since it happened, but desperate times call for desperate measures.

Besides, after she used my jealousy against me, it's only right I do the same to her.

Glancing at the clock, I notice it's already 12:30. Judging by the way all the lights are off and the alarm is set, I know she's trying to sleep. I slip the disc into my DVD player and turn the volume all the way up.

Josslyn's obscene moans loudly fill the room. She chants my name like it's the only thing keeping her grounded as I thrust into her. Filming this wasn't even my idea, but when a girl tells you she wants to make a sex tape, you don't say no.

I watch the screen, but my dick barely stirs. Her hair is just a little too dark. Her voice a little too high pitched. My eyes fall closed, and I imagine Lennon being the one I'm fucking from behind. Just like that, I'm hard in an instant.

It's going to be a long night.

THE NEXT MORNING, LENNON comes into the kitchen, looking like something out of a zombie movie. Her eyes meet mine and she glares at me. I used my phone to track my mom's location, and didn't stop playing the sex tape until they were just about home—which also happened to be 4:30 in the morning.

"Good morning, Lennon," my mom greets her. "Do you want something for breakfast?"

"No thanks," she answers. "I just need some coffee."

I'm leaning against the counter right next to the coffee pot as she comes over. Her moves are lazy, like she doesn't have the energy to do much of anything. I reach across her and grab an apple out of the bowl.

"What's wrong? Didn't get enough sleep, *sis?*"

She narrows her eyes on me but says nothing as I take a bite of my apple and give her my best boyish grin. I almost think I won this round, until she once again flips it all upside down. After pouring her coffee into a travel mug, she heads toward the door but stops just before leaving.

"By the way, Nora, I'm pretty sure Cade has chlamydia. You may want to make sure he gets that checked out."

Tea spews out of my mother's mouth at the same time my jaw practically hits the floor, but she's not done.

"Oh, and could you tell my dad I'll be spending the night at Colby's? Thanks."

She focuses all her attention on me and winks before disappearing out of sight. My mom raises her brows at me, and I shake my head.

Cade - 1 Lennon - 2.

15

LENNON

I PACE BACK AND FORTH ACROSS THE OVERSIZED living room. Tessa and Asher's penthouse may be smaller than my house, but this room is definitely bigger than mine. I know I said I was going to be at Colby's, but that was only to piss Cade off. Instead, I came to stay at Tessa's, where I thought I'd get a full night sleep, but even when he's nowhere near me, he plagues my thoughts and makes it so I can't focus on anything at all.

"He's just so—ugh!" I whine. "He literally fucked some girl until four-thirty in the morning! She was so loud that I had no choice but to listen to it. I even tried shoving a pillow over my head but it didn't work."

"Is that why you lied and said you were sleeping at Colby's?" Tess questions. "To make him jealous?"

I smirk. "It worked yesterday."

She scrunches her face up and tilts her head from side to side. "Eh, until he went and fucked out his frustrations with someone else."

Okay, so maybe she has a point, but mentioning Colby seems to be the only thing that gets even the slightest reaction out of him. It's like he has this invisible claim on me or something. The way he looked like he was fully prepared to strangle Colby with his bare hands just for looking at me —no one should make being possessive look that hot.

"I think I need to find another boyfriend."

Tess snorts. "Is his name going to start with a 'ka' sound too? You've had Kellan, Colby, and Cade. I'm starting to notice a trend here."

I roll my eyes and cross my arms over my chest. "Ha ha. Why am I even friends with you?"

"Because I call you out on your shit, like the fact that you want your step-brother to do naughty things to you." She sticks her tongue out teasingly, and I laugh.

"You make it sound so taboo."

She shrugs. "It is, but that's what makes it so hot. Like me with Asher. The forbidden romances are always the most exciting."

I don't even bother denying it. Tessa can read me like an open book, like when she told me I had a crush on Colby. She wasn't exactly wrong, but that's not a place I let my mind go to anymore. Not after realizing that he and I are better off as friends. Don't get me wrong, the girl he ends up with will be lucky as hell, but it won't be me.

"Let's send Asher to that Italian place down the street," I pout as I plop down onto the couch. "I need comfort food."

I STAND IN THE foyer with Cade by my side as our parents make sure they have everything for their trip. Nora's parents already came this morning to pick up Molly, and now all that's left is for them to leave for their month-long cruise. A part of me was pissed that I only have a couple months left at home, and my dad is choosing to spend it out at sea with his girlfriend, but I'm more excited to have a month filled with no authority figures.

"All right. You have all the phone numbers you need if there's an emergency?" Nora asks us both.

Cade groans. "Mom, we're legal adults, not children."

She waves him off dismissively. "Don't get fresh with me, Cadence. I just worry."

"Yeah, *Cadence*," I tease, loving the way he tenses up.

"Try not to kill each other, you two," she tells us.

Cade scoffs. "Who, Lennon and me?" He drapes an arm over my shoulder. "We're the best of friends. Don't worry about us."

I plaster the best smile I can manage across my face and wave happily as they grab their suitcases and head out the door. As soon as they drive away, Cade rips his arm away and shoves me to the side. Dick.

"Now, now, Cadence. Remember what Mommy said."

His brows raise, and he looks away for a second, smiling. I'm frozen in place as he takes a step toward me and pins me to the wall.

"Call me Cadence again, and I'll make it so you can't sit down for a fucking week."

My throat goes dry at his words, and at least half of me wants to do it—call him on his bluff and see exactly what happens. He must notice the way I'm actually considering it, because his glare turns to a smirk.

"Go ahead. Do it."

I swallow harshly. It's tempting as hell, but I don't have the guts to say it. My first sexual experience of any kind should not be getting spanked by my potential stepbrother. I don't care how hot Tessa says it is; I deserve better than that.

He hums and takes a step back. "I didn't think so."

The door opens, and Bryce walks in with Jayden, each holding a case of beer. Cade does their bro-handshake with both of them and I glare.

"They've been gone three minutes and you're having a party?" I ask.

He rolls his eyes at me. "If you don't like it, Sunshine, there's the door."

I cross my arms over my chest. "This is my house. I'm not going anywhere."

"Suit yourself."

SEEING A BUNCH OF people I've never met in my life fill my home is an uncomfortable feeling. Cade didn't even go to school for senior year. How does he even know all these people?

"Put that down," I demand, grabbing the expensive vase from a random partygoer.

Tessa chuckles as I put it under the sink. "Okay, maybe you should just calm down."

"They're destroying my house," I protest.

She shakes her head. "They're not. Just relax. Everything will be fine in the morning."

Leading me through the house and into the backyard, Tessa takes me out back to sit by the pool. She grabs two beers from the cooler and hands me one. She might have a point. It's just a party. I pop open the can and take a swig.

"I guess a little fun wouldn't kill me."

Her grin widens. "Exactly. You've been killing yourself getting ready for Juilliard. Just let loose for a bit. You've earned it."

I smile and turn away, and my eyes land directly on Cade. He looks happy, throwing his head back laughing at something Bryce said. But what really catches my attention is the girl hanging on his arm. She's only wearing shorts and what barely constitutes as a bikini top. If she wasn't so young, I'd wonder if he hired hookers for tonight.

His gaze meets mine and he winks, pulling the girl closer and moving his hand to her ass. She stares up at him like he can do no wrong, and all I want to do is punch her in the face. He's doing this to get to me, and fuck if it isn't working.

"Now we just need to figure out what you're going to do about him," Tessa says while watching Cade.

I sigh. "I'm going to do what I've been doing all week. Give him a dose of his own medicine."

OKAY SO MAYBE INVITING famous NFL player Colby Hendrix to a party wasn't exactly the smartest choice. It worked, just not exactly in the way I thought that it would. I intended to hang all over Colby and make Cade jealous the same way he was doing with that girl, but instead, Colby became a magnet for every girl here. Even the one looking at Cade like he's a holy sex God ditched him the second she saw Colby from across the backyard.

Now, I'm standing here being forced to watch over a hundred girls throw themselves at my best friend. He glances at me and gives me a dimpled grin—one that makes it impossible for me to hold a grudge. When he realizes I'm not mad, he goes back to his groupies.

"See what you did?" Cade asks accusingly, appearing next to me out of nowhere.

I roll my eyes. "Aw, I'm sorry. Did Colby take away your little slut?"

Laughter bubbles out of him, and he smiles down at the ground. "Nah, he can do whatever he wants with her. You, on the other hand..."

He backs away, and I watch as he leaves without finishing that sentence. I swear, that guy has more mood swings than a pregnant woman. One minute he's ready to kill me with his bare hands, and the next he's saying things that make my whole body tingle.

Could it all be part of him messing with me? Of course, but it feels too real to be faked. At least for me it is.

Tessa comes over with a couple shots, and I sigh in relief as I see her.

"Thank God." I grab a shot and down it in one go.

She hands me the other one. "You look like you need both."

A SHOOTING PAIN RADIATES through my head as I feel all the consequences of a night full of drinking. I groan, crawling out of bed in search of some aspirin. As I walk down the stairs, a part of me expects to find a huge mess from last night, but instead, it's all in order. Thank you, Melani.

The windows in the kitchen showcase the storm brewing outside. Thunder, lightning, and pouring rain—the whole nine yards. So much for going shopping with Tessa. Knowing her, she won't want to venture out in this. Besides, watching storms from the penthouse is one of her favorite things to do. She's got the view of the world up there.

It takes a few minutes for the meds to kick in, but the pain fades a little as they do. That is, until Cade walks in. He grabs a bottle of water from the fridge then kicks it closed.

"I'm going surfing," he says, without sparing me a single glance.

Okay, so either he's deaf or just downright stupid. "I don't think that's a good idea."

He laughs dryly. "Thanks, Mom."

I jump down from the counter I was sitting on and follow him to the front door. "I'm serious. You really should stay home."

"And why's that? So I can sit here listening to your shit all day?" He opens the door and freezes when he notices a tree branch fly past our driveway.

"More like so you don't drown or get struck by lightning," I reply. "But I take it back, you should go."

His unamused eyes look back at me, and I smile sweetly. *Douche.*

THE LONGER I'M STUCK alone with Cade, the more I realize I should have just let him go surfing. Granted, he would have seen the storm without me saying anything, but maybe if I kept my mouth shut, he would have gone anyway. I was hoping he would spend the day in his room like he normally does, but he hasn't, and I refuse to be the one to leave.

"Do we have to watch this shit?" he groans.

I glance up from my phone to see *Keeping Up With The Kardashians* on TV. Honestly, I don't really like this show, but knowing Cade is this annoyed with it makes me want to start.

"Yep."

He gets up and goes to grab the remote, but I pull it away just in time. He rolls his eyes and tries to take it from me.

"Give me the remote, Lennon."

"No," I refuse.

When he lunges for it again, I do the first thing I can think of and shove it down my shirt. His brows raise and the corner of his mouth forms into a devilish smirk.

"Do you really think that's going to stop me?"

No, I don't, and that's probably one of the main reasons I did it, but there's no way in hell I'm telling him that. I shrug and do my best to cover my chest, but he goes for it anyway.

I can't help but giggle. "Quit, or I'll call for Melani." He doesn't stop. "Mel! Mel, Cade is trying to go down my shirt!"

He chuckles. "Nice try, but she left about an hour ago."

Fuck, that means we really are completely alone together.

I don't know whether that excites me or scares the living shit out of me.

I look up at Cade and notice how close he is. One leg is draped over my lap, one hand is on my wrist, and his face is only inches away from mine. The two of us both stop moving and just stare back at each other. The second he glances down at my lips, my breath hitches.

At a snail's pace, he starts to lean in—until a bolt of lightning comes slamming down and hits the backyard. I scream as thunder roars and the power goes out. Cade jumps at my reaction and falls onto the couch beside me.

"Now look what you did," I tell him.

He groans. "Shut up. Don't you have backup generators in this palace?"

We do, and they should have turned on by now. "They should kick in any second." A few more seconds pass and there isn't any sign of the lights coming back on. "Any second now."

"ALL RIGHT, THANKS DAD. Have fun, and tell Nora I said hi."

I hang up the phone and turn my attention to Cade, who is currently lighting every candle we have. "He said he'll have someone come by to check out the generators, but we have to wait until the storm passes."

"Of course," he grumbles. He pulls his phone out of his back pocket and tosses it onto the table. "And my phone is dead. This is just great."

I huff. "You're such a baby."

It's one thing to be stuck with Cade when he has something to entertain him, but with no power and a dead cellphone, I don't stand a chance. It doesn't take a rocket scientist to know that he's going to fill his time by fucking with me, and I'm not in the mood for it.

I pull my iPad from the kitchen drawer and pass it to him. "Knock yourself out."

He purses his lips for a second before opening the iPad. I swear, it's like entertaining a child with him.

The wind continues to blow harshly outside, wreaking havoc and causing destruction all over the city, if the articles I've been reading are accurate. I look out the window, and my eyes narrow at something shining on one of the tables. When I recognize the piece of jewelry, my heart stops.

"My necklace!" I shriek.

Immediately going to the back door to go get it, I'm stopped by two strong arms pulling me back. "Oh, no you don't. Have you seen it out there?"

"I need to get that necklace, Cade."

"It's just a necklace."

I fight against him until he lets me go. "It's not. It was my grandmother's. I must have taken it off last night for some reason, but I have to go get it."

Cade steps around me and opens the door. "Fine, but be fast, and careful."

A part of me is shocked. Is he actually worrying about me, after spending the last couple weeks wanting to slit my throat for sport? I shake the thoughts from my mind. Now isn't the time for this.

The wind is even worse than it looks. I brace myself against the door and muster up the courage. Once I've got a handle on my fear, I run out into the storm. Shingles from the roof are scattered across the backyard, even some landing in the pool. The trees all look like they're going to snap. It's a mess out here.

I reach the table and grab my necklace. As I go to run back, however, Cade's eyes widen.

"Watch out!"

My head turns to see what he's talking about, and I see an umbrella from one of the tables flying toward me. I don't have time to react before it smacks me in the head and knocks me to the ground.

"Lennon!" Cade screams, but I can barely hear him over the roar of the storm.

I try to get up, but everything is blurry. Cade runs out into the yard and pulls me off the ground. The two of us rush back inside, and he slams the door shut behind us.

"Are you all right?" he pants.

I wince at the pain. "I think so? It really hurts."

He comes over and grabs my chin, forcing me to look up at him. "Len, you're bleeding." He lifts me up and sits me on top of the table. "Stay here. I'll get stuff to clean it."

I'm stunned into silence, mainly because I've never seen this side of him—the side that actually gives a shit about me. I thought I saw hints of it in Malibu, but since we got back, he's been nothing but cruel. And still, I crave him.

Cade comes back with the first aid kit and immediately gets to work on my head. I hiss as he cleans it out and covers it with antiseptic.

"And you called me a baby," he teases.

I kick him in the leg. "Shut up. It really hurts."

"I bet it does. I told you not to go out there." He covers the cut with a bandage and pushes the kit to the side. "There. Good as new."

I lightly feel where it is and crinkle up my nose. "I probably look real cute now."

He laughs. "You look like you fought an umbrella and lost."

"Fantastic."

I look down at my lap and let out a long exhale, suddenly feeling self-conscious. Cade must notice the quick change in mood because he takes pity on me.

"Hey, I was kidding." He puts a hand on my cheek. "I

don't know anyone else who could make battle wounds look that good."

I raise my eyes to meet his. "You're just saying that."

Gently, he rubs his thumb back and forth. "I'm not. You and I both know you're gorgeous."

There it is again, that closeness paired with a look in his eyes that renders me defenseless. I want him. I want him more than I want to breathe. My heart pounds inside my chest as he starts to lean in, but deep down, I know this is a bad idea.

"Cade," I whisper. "We shouldn't."

He doesn't look away from my lips. "I just need to...I just...let me...."

His sentence goes unfinished as the gap between us closes and his mouth covers my own.

16

CADE

HER LIPS ARE SOFT AS THEY MOVE WITH MINE. I force them apart and lick into her mouth, loving how sweet she tastes. My free hand snakes around to her lower back, and I pull her closer. She brings her arms up to my neck. My cock is spurred to life as I realize this table is the perfect height for sex, but fuck if this isn't the time for all that.

Lennon's tongue fights for dominance—a fight she never had a chance at winning. I suck her bottom lip into my mouth and pull. The reaction I get out of her is exactly what I wanted, and she becomes putty in my hands. I slide my touch from her cheek down to her chest. Her breast fits perfectly inside my hand, and she arches her back, pushing herself further into my hold.

Her phone starts to ring, and she jerks away quickly. She covers her mouth with one hand, as if what just happened finally processed in her mind. To be honest, I'm feeling the same way. She grabs her phone and brings it to her ear, but her eyes don't leave me.

"Hey Dad," she breathes. "Okay, I'll tell him. Thanks."

I run my fingers through my hair to try and ground myself as she hangs up.

"He said that there is a way to reset the generators, and that the instructions are on the side panel."

Nodding slowly, I take a step back. "I better go do that then."

Her brows furrow. "Don't you think you should wait until the storm clears? You'll get soaked."

I shake my head. "Nah, I could use the cold shower."

Finally breaking our eye contact, I look away and head outside, trying like hell not to get carried away in what the fuck just happened.

IT ONLY TOOK A few minutes to get the generator back up and running, but of course then the power kicked back on shortly after. Thankfully, Lennon was nowhere to be found when I came back in. I don't know what I would have said to her if she was waiting for me.

I'm lying in my bed, staring up at the ceiling. Kissing her was stupid, and totally not something I planned. She's a traitor—a wolf in sheep's clothing—and I fucking caved. I shouldn't have, that much I'm sure of, but after seeing that umbrella fly into her head, something came over me. My heart dropped, and the only thing I could think of was getting her inside and safe.

The feeling of her lips on mine is burned into my brain. It's refusing to budge and torturing me with every second that passes. I wanted nothing more than to carry her upstairs and show her everything she's been missing by being with Kellan. But then her dad called, and it was like someone poured a bucket of ice water over my head.

No part of me should want her, especially not after the shit she pulled when we got back from Malibu. My focus needs to be on her demise, and not her pleasure. She's the antichrist of everything I want right now, so why the fuck can't I stop thinking about that kiss?

AVOIDING LENNON WHILE WE'RE alone in this house is easier said than done, but the massive size of it definitely helps. After she left this afternoon for dance, which I only know because I overheard her on the phone with Tessa, I called Bryce—and that's how I ended up with almost a hundred kids filling the whole downstairs.

The speaker system in the living room is intense enough to carry a beat through most of the house. Two kegs, courtesy of Jayden's brother, sit in the middle of the patio. People jump off the roof and into the pool, and a part of me considers making them sign some kind of waiver. If Ken gets sued for someone getting injured, my mom might disown me. Then again, maybe I should encourage it.

"What did I tell you?" Bryce shouts with two cups in his hands. "A party is exactly what you needed, especially in a house like this! There should be one of these every damn night while Mr. Bigshot is away."

I chuckle and roll my eyes. "Whatever you say, man."

"Seriously?" A voice sounds from behind me. I turn around to see Lennon looking at me incredulously. "A little heads-up would have been nice."

Bryce snorts and hands me a beer. "I'll just leave you to that."

Once we're alone, I square my shoulders and glare down at her. "I didn't know I needed your permission to throw a party. Oh, that's right. I don't."

My words are meant to push her away, but she's no more afraid of me than she was when we kissed. She runs her fingers through her blonde hair, and I notice how her ocean eyes sparkle with the sunset. *Fuck, focus.*

"Do you think we could talk later? About the other day." She pulls her plump bottom lip between her teeth.

I swallow. "Uh, yeah." Wait, what? That's not what I wanted to say. "If I don't have someone in my bed."

It's hardly the redemption I was looking for, but it does its job. Lennon's eyes widen, and she takes a step back.

"Seriously?"

I shrug.

"You're such a pig," she scoffs. "Just forget it. Forget the whole thing ever happened."

Oh baby, trust me. I fucking wish I could. I've been trying to do that for days, hence this party, but I can't. It haunts my dreams, my thoughts, all of it. It won't go away.

I watch as Lennon storms away from me and takes out her phone, most likely calling Tessa. Good, maybe she can get her to leave me alone. I don't need her looking all cute and testing my restraints. What I need is to hate her.

OKAY, SO TESSA DEFINITELY wasn't the right answer. After getting a call from Lennon, she decided to come to the party, and she brought Zayn Bronsyn with her. Zayn is Knox's best friend, and while there's no bad blood between him and me, we're not exactly friends either. Therefore, he has no loyalty here, and nothing against pissing me off.

I'm leaning against the outside bar, watching as Zayn flirts with Lennon. Judging by the way she keeps looking over at me, I know it's only to get under my skin, but it's fucking working. I should be enjoying this party. It's my goddamn party. And instead, my eyes stay locked on the one girl here I should want nothing to do with.

"Uh, Cade?" Jayden says hesitantly. "Some guy is drawing on the portrait above the fireplace."

Now that makes me laugh. "Is he really?"

"Yeah. Should we stop him?"

I'd prefer if they didn't. Vandalizing anything to do with Kensington Bradwell is a go in my book, but I can definitely use this to my advantage.

"Nah," I reply. "Go tell Lennon. She'll take care of it."

He looks over at where Lennon stands with Tessa and Zayn, with Zayn's arm around her. "Ah fuck, okay."

It plays out exactly as I expected. Jayden goes over to Lennon and the second he tells her what's going on, she glares at me and storms inside. Tessa follows behind, but Zayn looks at me. I nod my head toward the other side of the yard, and he starts walking over there.

The two of us meet up in the corner, away from prying eyes. He pulls out a blunt and lights it.

"Cade, right?"

"Yeah. We've met a few times, through Knox."

He inhales a long drag and holds it for a second. "That's right. Sorry, college makes it so faces all kinda blur together. What's up, man?"

"Not too much. Moved in here recently." I shake my head as he offers to share.

"Ah, yeah. Lennon was saying something about that."

"You and her. You look close," I point out the obvious. "Are you two together?"

He chuckles. "Playing coy ain't your forte, Mr. Cade."

Fuck. "Just answer the question, dick."

"Down, boy." He raises his hands up in mock defense. "Nah, she and I are both just friends with Tess. Why? She off limits?"

"Are you and I close enough to make someone off limits?"

Zayn takes another hit of his blunt. "I like to avoid drama as much as possible, so if you say she's spoken for, I'll back off. And besides, Knox seems to think you're all right, and I trust his judgment."

Now *that* I can respect. "Thanks, man."

"No problem, but just keep in mind..." He nods behind me to Tessa coming our way. "The two of them together are fire. If they want you burned, they'll make it happen."

Tessa smirks as she approaches the two of us. "And what are you two talking about?"

I narrow my eyes at her. "Oh, just your little plan of using Zayn to get a rise out of me."

She giggles and takes the blunt from Zayn. "Don't get pissy at me because it worked."

"Whatever." I look around for Lennon but don't find her. "Where's your other half?"

Tess's brows furrow. "Uh, Rhode Island?"

"Not *that* other half." I groan. "Where's Lennon?"

"Oh." She glances back at the house. "She went to her room for something, though I honestly think she went to look for you."

The thought of someone else getting their hands on her makes my blood turn to lava. That, mixed with the alcohol running through my body, has me ready to snap someone's neck just for looking at her too long. I walk away from Zayn and Tessa, completely ignoring the commentary from Tess.

It takes a few minutes to get from the back door to the staircase, but I don't see Lennon in any of the rooms downstairs. Maybe she really did go to her room.

I climb up the stairs and turn down the hallway when I see her. She's frozen outside my room, staring at something with wonder in her eyes. As I get closer, I see what she's looking at. Bryce is on my bed, fucking some girl, and Lennon is watching it happen.

The sight of her looking so turned on while she stares at them like a deer in the headlights—it does something to me that I can't explain. Pressing myself up against her back, I firmly grip her shoulders to keep her in place. She squirms against my hold, but I'm stronger than she is.

"You like that, don't you?" I murmur against her ear. "The way he slams his dick in her pussy."

"Let me go," she demands.

I push her against the doorway and grab a fist full of her hair, pulling her head back and forcing her to watch Bryce. "Imagine me doing that to you. Fucking that tight little hole of yours until you cum all over my cock."

She struggles against me like my words aren't wanted, but the way her breathing changes gives her away. I use my body to keep her in place and slide my hand down her side. When I reach between her legs, I apply the slightest bit of pressure on her clit. Even with her jeans in the way, her breath hitches.

"Keep fighting, baby," I breathe. "It only makes me harder."

An elbow flies back and gets me right in the stomach, damn near knocking the wind out of me. I release Lennon and take a step back. As she spins around, she pushes me back against the wall.

"Is that what you like? You get off on making people feel like shit?" A small hand slaps me across the face. "Don't ever fucking touch me without my permission again."

She marches away and toward her room, while I'm left with a stinging cheek, bruised ego, and massive hard-on. I might not have the upper hand when it comes to Lennon Bradwell, and that could be a major fucking problem.

IT'S WELL PAST ELEVEN by the time I wake up. I rub my hands over my face and adjust to the light before getting out of bed. The swells today are supposed to be perfect, but first, I need to talk to Lennon.

I go downstairs first, knowing she's probably been awake for a while now. However, the living room, kitchen, and dance studio are all empty. I go back up and check her room. There's no sign of her, and her bed is still perfectly made.

Jogging back to get my phone, I send her a text.

Cade: Where are you?

When I see the three little dots, indicating she's typing, the relief that runs through me is alarming, but I do my best to ignore it. Now isn't the time for feelings and honest revelations.

My phone vibrates in my hand, and her message appears.

Lennon: Colby's. Leave me alone.

Son of a bitch.

17

LENNON

I CAN'T BELIEVE THE AUDACITY OF THAT ASSHOLE. More so, I can't believe the way my body responded to him. I'd gone upstairs to leave something in Cade's room—something he could read later—and instead, I found Bryce. No part of me meant to stare, but I couldn't look away. It's like I was stuck. Couldn't move.

Cade's words echo in my mind. The way he spoke those dirty words, with his voice all gravely and seductive, I was so close to falling for it. It's like my body was struggling against him, but my subconscious wanted it. Wanted him. Then I remembered everything else.

After we kissed the other day, a part of me wondered if I had imagined it. I thought maybe I had a concussion from getting hit in the head, but the feeling of his kiss lasted long after it was gone. The way he avoided me like the damn plague told me all I needed to know. He regretted it.

Don't get me wrong, I did too—kind of. Cade is a prick—the worst kind of asshole with a bad attitude—but there's something about his broody, pissed-at-the-world demeanor that draws me to him. I can't explain it. All I know is that every time I'm around him, I'm taken over by thoughts of what it would be like to touch him. What it would be like if he touched me.

Colby comes in the room, popping open a beer and snapping me out of my thoughts. "Sorry. I didn't mean to scare you."

I shake my head. "You didn't."

"Lennon, you jumped like three feet."

Sighing, I shut off my e-reader and put it on the couch next to me. "Fine, you win."

He grins triumphantly. "I always do."

"Yeah, yeah." I wave him off.

"So, talk to me. What's got you so distracted? And don't tell me that book. You've been on the same page for at least ten minutes."

I groan and run my fingers through my hair. "Fucking Cade."

He snorts. "Fucking the faux-bro. Nice."

"Not what I meant." Or at least not yet, anyway.

Colby takes a sip of his beer and puts it on the coffee table. "Okay, okay. What about him?"

"He's just so, *ugh*! One minute he's somewhat tolerable, and the next he's a total douchebag."

He shrugs. "Maybe he just likes you."

My eyes narrow. "Or maybe he's satanic and determined to ruin my life."

"Could be that, too."

I lay my head back against the couch and watch the ceiling fan. I just wish I knew what was going on in that brain of his. I knew what Tessa's plan of using Zayn to make Cade jealous would do, but I didn't think it would cause *that* reaction. There's been a lot of banter, but nothing like that. What's worse is that a part of me liked it. God, how I liked it.

I'M LAYING ON A lounge chair by the pool while Colby swims laps for his morning workout. Tessa occupies the seat next to mine, with a pair of oversized sunglasses on her face as the sun beats down on us.

"You know, you're going to look like a raccoon if you keep those things on. Your tan lines will be atrocious."

She rips the glasses off her face. "This is why I love you. Ugh, what am I going to do when you leave me?"

I tilt my head to the side. "Probably burn down the penthouse or something Tessa-extreme."

Laughter bubbles out of her, and she splashes me with her water bottle. "Bitch."

Colby climbs out of the pool and I can't help but watch as droplets of water roll down his toned stomach. When he catches me staring, he smirks, and I flip him off. He knows he's hot. He doesn't need the ego boost.

"Take a picture, Len," Tessa tells me. "It'll last longer."

I force myself to look away and roll my eyes. "Shut up. Not everyone can be dating Asher Hawthorne."

"Maybe not, but you could be dating Colby Hendrix," she counters.

Yeah, right. "Even if he was the settling down type, I don't know if my jealousy could handle it."

Her lips purse. "Yeah, you're probably right."

I know I am. Colby has at least ten women throw themselves at him daily, even when he's just sitting home. Over the past few days, I've seen how much his phone goes off with calls and texts from numbers he never cared to save. Some of them are requests to hang out, while others are just naked pictures. I swear, when it comes to him, it's like morals go right out the window—if they ever had them at all.

Colby comes over and plops onto the end of my lounge chair. I flinch when a drop of water lands on me, which only makes him shake his hair out like a dog. I try to shield myself from the onslaught of water, but it's no use. I glare at him when he's done, and he laughs.

"What are you two talking about?" he questions.

"Oh, you know, just how Lennon wants to—"

I cut Tessa off before she can say anything else. "Suck...on a popsicle."

She smirks. "Close, but not quite."

I try to level her with a look, but she's not intimidated by me at all. Down side of her knowing me so damn well—she knows she can get away with murder. Not buying my pissed-off expression, she snickers and grabs her water bottle.

"I need a refill. I'll be back."

She goes inside and leaves Colby and I alone. He hops over to her seat and lays back, basking in the sun. I can't help but laugh.

"She's going to kill you for getting her seat all wet."

He keeps his eyes closed but scrunches up his nose. "Nah, Asher would be really mad if she murdered his best friend."

My brows raise even though he isn't looking at me. "Uh, are you forgetting how they get through their arguments? Don't give her any ideas. She might slit your throat just for the angry make-up sex."

Colby jumps up in an instant and comes back over to my seat. "Touché."

His phone starts to ring on the table. He looks at the number for a second before answering and walks away. Whoever it is, he clearly has no intentions of me hearing what it's about, not that it's any of my business. He had a system before I came in and took over his bachelor pad. We might be close, but I'm not dumb enough to expect his whole lifestyle to change just because I'm here.

If it were an option, I'd stay until my dad gets back from the cruise, or maybe even until I leave for school—but I can't. Colby's guest room is great, but I know he's been avoiding having people over and going out, to be a considerate host.

I've seen him when he goes without sex for too long, and let's just say it isn't pretty.

He hangs up the phone and puts it back on the table, acting like whatever that conversation was doesn't matter. He sits back down in front of me, and I sigh.

"I think I'm going to spend tonight at home."

His eyes widen. "Really?"

I nod. "I can't avoid my house forever, and I can't let Cade, who has only lived there for a little over a month, keep me away."

"Okay, well, if you change your mind, you know you can come right back here."

"Thanks, Colb."

"Anytime, babe."

WALKING THROUGH THE FRONT door, the last thing I expected was for Cade to come out of the kitchen wearing only a pair of sweatpants. They hang low on his hips, showing off his Adonis vee. Fuck, okay. Maybe I was better off staying at Colby's.

His eyes meet mine, and he stops. "Where have you been?"

"I told you," I say as I shut the door behind me. "I was at Colby's."

"For three days?"

"Yep."

As I go to walk by, he steps right in my way. "What were you two doing?"

Here we go with the jealous and possessive again. If I didn't find it so irritatingly hot, it would get on my nerves. I smirk deviously as I run my finger down his torso.

"Everything." I moisten my lips with my tongue. "Including lots and lots of s...crabble."

He lets out a breath, almost as if he's relieved that it isn't what he thought, and it makes me laugh.

"When you're ready to talk, and not avoid me like a scared little boy, come find me."

It looks like he wants to argue, but I don't give him a chance as I move around him and head upstairs. When I get into my room, I throw myself on my bed. Colby's house is great, but there really is no place like home. I've missed the comfort of my own room.

WHY IS IT THAT some sex scenes in movies look so real, while others are obviously fake? I swear, I think in some they actually have sex and then just lie and say they don't. Otherwise, they'll end up being classified as X-rated. It's practically softcore porn.

Thoughts of the party the other night play through my mind for the millionth time, and my center clenches around nothing. Is it wrong that I want him this bad? Who am I kidding? Of course it is. We're practically related, but my body doesn't seem to care about that. All it wants is him. His hands, his tongue, his cock.

Unable to resist anymore, I reach into my nightstand and pull out the vibrator Tessa bought me for my birthday. I haven't used it yet, but I did take it out of the packaging. Slipping under the covers, I slide the vibrator under my shorts and panties.

As soon as I turn it on, I flinch at the contact. It's intense, but feels good as I hold it against my clit. I close my eyes and press my head back into the pillow, imagining Cade being the one doing this to me. I picture his abs that are perfectly toned from surfing all the time, and the way he pulled my hair the other night and demanded control. Fuck, I shouldn't like it, but I do.

"Cade," I moan softly. "Fuck, Cade."

"This is *not* what I thought you meant by talking."

My eyes jolt open to find the devil himself leaning against my doorway, with his arms crossed over his chest and a cocky grin on his face. I quickly turn off the vibrator and toss it aside.

"Please, don't stop on my account."

I scoff. "Haven't you ever heard of knocking?"

He takes a step inside. "And miss the show? What fun would that be?"

I'm about to snap back when I see it. His cock is rock hard and straining against his sweatpants. Did *I* do that? I mean, I had to, right? What else would have made him have that reaction while standing in my room?

It could be the overwhelming number of hormones rushing through my body, or the sexual frustration that he interrupted me before I could finish, but I get a sudden urge to be confident and daring. I slip out of my bed and walk toward him. When we're chest to chest, I look up, and my eyes lock with his.

Neither one of us move, testing our own restraints, but I can tell he wants this. His pupils are blown, and his body is tense. Unable to wait any longer, I lunge forward, and our mouths collide.

He kisses me with the same intensity that I give. The grip he has on my waist might cause bruising, but I can't find it in me to care. I fucking need this.

My hands slide from around his neck to his chest, when he grabs my wrists to remove them. "Did I say you could fucking touch me?"

Normally, I'd tell him off for a comment like that, but there's something about his tone, how demanding and in control it is, that makes me want to please him. He stands in front of me, looking so goddamn sexy, with his head only tilted slightly and looking at me through hooded eyes. I give in, taking my hands and holding them behind my back.

"Fuck," he growls. "That's my girl. Now get on your knees. I want to fuck that pretty little mouth of yours."

My heart starts to race, but I do as he says. When I'm in position, I look up at him and watch as he pulls out his rock-hard cock. It's huge—bigger than the average nineteen-year-old guy—and a part of me thinks he would rip me in half if we had sex. He strokes it in his hand, with his muscles flexing at the action.

As he lines up at my mouth, I stick out my tongue and kitten-lick the tip. He exhales at the contact before slipping inside. I've never done this before, but the last thing I want is to disappoint him. Don't ask me why. He's rude, and obnoxious, and a total prick—but when he's around, I just want his attention on me and his hands on my skin.

I gag around him as he hits the back of my throat. It must feel good, because his head falls back and he lets out an animalistic moan. His fingers lace into my hair, and he starts to thrust, harder and faster. He's practically choking me with his solid length, and somehow, it's one of the hottest things I've ever experienced.

Swirling my tongue around the tip as he pulls out a little, his legs start to shake. I look up at him with his dick filling my mouth and watch him as he watches me. I grab his cock with one hand and his hip with the other, hoping not to get yelled at for touching him. I suck on what I can while jerking the rest.

When he gets close, he slaps my hand away and thrusts into the back of my throat. A sound unlike anything I've heard before leaves his mouth as he explodes down my throat. It's salty, but not bad, and I take every drop. Once he pulls out, I swallow it down.

"Fucking hell," he says as he pulls his pants back up. "Who knew you were so good at that?"

I shrug, trying not to preen at the attention, and stand back up. Cade takes his thumb and wipes a bit of cum from the corner of my lips before slipping the digit into my mouth. It's erotic and exhilarating as I suck the juice from his skin.

Before I can say anything at all, he takes a step back. I try to read his expression, but there's a mask firmly in place as he walks backward toward the door. I already know he's about to avoid me again, and fuck if that doesn't sting.

"I'm going to Bryce's," he tells me. "Don't wait up."

My jaw drops, and I watch as he leaves without so much as a glance back in my direction.

And to top it off, I'm still sexually frustrated. *Fuck my life.*

18

CADE

I FUCKED UP, *AGAIN*. I GOT CLOSE TO HER, *AGAIN*. I LET myself taste her, *again*. Only this time, it was more than just a little taste, and now I don't know how I'll resist. The way she listened when I told her not to touch me. The look in her eyes when I demanded she get on her knees. Fuck, she was so goddamn submissive.

How am I supposed to stay away now? She's trouble, bad news with a capital b, but she's so fucking alluring. Like a siren, grabbing my attention and pulling me in with no mercy. Now all I can picture is the way she looked as she choked on my cock.

I pace back and forth across Bryce's room, just like I was doing when I got here last night. Anyone with eyes can tell that I'm agitated and completely on edge. Bryce lays in his bed, watching me like I'm some kind of circus act.

"So, you let her blow you. Big deal."

My hands cover my face and I groan. "It is a big fucking deal. I'm supposed to despise her, not fool around with her."

He squints and tilts his head to the side. "Eh, you know what they say—hate sex is the best sex."

"Fuck off, Hurley. You're not helping."

My phone rings in my pocket, and I pull it out to see Jayden calling.

"Yeah?" I answer.

"Hey, man." He sounds hesitant. "Have you talked to your dad lately?"

Dread fills my stomach. "Not in a couple weeks. Why?"

"He...uh." He pauses. "He..."

"Spit it out."

Jayden sighs. "He just got kicked out of Park East Tavern for being too drunk."

I pull the phone away from my ear to look at the time. "It's eleven in the morning."

"I don't know, man. I gave him a ride home, but he's really wasted. You might want to go check on him."

Nodding, even though he can't see me, I grab my keys off Bryce's nightstand. "Yeah, I'm heading there now. Thanks for the heads up."

WALKING THROUGH THE FRONT door of my dad's house, it's hard to believe this is the same place I lived for years. Garbage is scattered everywhere, attracting bugs and creating a horrible odor. Bottles of alcohol fill two of the counters and I wonder how much he's drinking a day.

"Dad?" I call out.

"Cade?" my dad slurs from the other room. "Cade, is that you?"

He stumbles in and halfway to me, he trips. Thankfully, I act fast and catch him before his head slams against the countertop. That's the last thing I need right now—having to sit in the hospital with my drunk and concussed father.

"Dad, you're drunk."

He points to himself in a silent question and then shakes his head. "No, I'm just a little buzzed."

Keeping an arm under him for support, I walk us over to the couch and lay him down. "It's Friday. Why aren't you at work?"

"Because, work is for pussies, and *I* am not a pussy."

I look around the room and sigh when it hits me. "They fired you, didn't they?"

He scoffs. "A couple days of showing up smelling like booze and they told me I was no longer needed. Can you believe that? A bunch of buzzkills is what they are."

Jayden was right, he's really shitfaced. Even I'm having a hard time deciphering his words with how badly they're slurred. Is this what he's been doing since mom left? Drinking himself into oblivion?

"How are you going to pay your bills, old man?" I question softly.

His hand swats at the air, like it doesn't matter. "Bills, shmills."

I take a deep breath and get up from the couch, going over to where we've always kept the mail. Sure enough, past due notices are stacked high—unopened and unanswered. At this rate, everything is going to get shut off, and he'll lose the house.

"Hey, how's your mother doing?" my dad murmurs. "Is she still pretty? She was always so pretty."

My mother. Right. The woman who is off on some extravagant cruise with her rich new boyfriend, while my dad is a fucking disaster. I wonder what she would think if she saw him like this. Would she even care? Probably not. She barely even pays attention to Molly anymore, let alone me.

Dad passes out on the couch, and I spend hours cleaning up most of the mess. It's only helping a fraction of the damage, but it'll have to do for now. I write a note, telling him I'll be back tomorrow, and put it on the counter next to a bottle of water and some Advil.

The second I step outside, I pull out my phone and hit speed dial two. Bryce answers on the second ring.

"Hey, C. Everything good with Pops?"

Running my fingers through my hair, I hop into the Jeep. "Not even a little. I need to find Ken's Achilles heel, and I need to do it fast."

AFTER BRAINSTORMING FOR WHAT feels like an eternity, Bryce, Jayden, and I determine that I need a way to go through his office. However, during the day, there's staff around. The housekeeper, Melani. The chefs. Lennon. I need a distraction to keep the attention away from Ken's office. A party is the best way to do exactly that.

Jayden gets the beer while Bryce splurges on a DJ. My only assignment is to figure out how to get Lennon out of the house. She's the only one that won't stay away from the party, or from me, for that matter. If she catches me, I don't trust for a second that she'd keep that little bit of information to herself. Especially not after the shit she's already pulled.

I watch as Bryce sends a mass text to everyone in his phone, telling them about tonight and to bring all their friends. There's a good chance it'll get out of hand, but it is what it is. I need to get my hands on something that will either make my mom leave him, or something powerful enough to threaten him with and have him toss my mom to the curb. Honestly, I'd prefer the second. There's less chance for error if it's his doing.

THE HOUSE IS PACKED to the brim, and Lennon is nowhere to be found. The two of us haven't spoken since I left her room last night. If she's pissed at me, I can't say I blame her. I got what I wanted and then left her high and dry. Then again, I also can't say I care.

A DJ is set up in the corner of the backyard, but he has lights and speakers run throughout the house. We also made sure to get liquor as well as beer, just to really make sure if anyone sees me in the office, they'll be too drunk to remember it. Not that I think any of these shitheads would get involved. I just don't want to take any chances. And besides, I wouldn't complain if they puked in a vase or two.

I'm standing in the yard with Bryce and Jayden when Lennon finally appears. Her brows furrow when she sees me but she doesn't seem half as angry as I was expecting.

"Another party? I'm starting to think this is all you know how to do."

I roll my eyes and use the movement to stop myself from checking her out. "I'm sorry, *Mom*. Did I not ask if I could have a few friends over?"

She snorts. "A few? Cade, do you know even half the people here?"

"Of course, I do," I argue.

Lennon hums and turns around. "Okay, her." She points at some random chick. "What's her name?"

"Heather." Is that really her name? I have no fucking idea, but I'm going with it.

She giggles. "For a minute, I almost believed you."

Fuck, I hate how she does this shit to me—makes me wonder what it would be like to not hate her guts. The things she does to me are like nothing I've ever experienced before. For example, the other night. When I told her not to touch me, it wasn't because I didn't want her hands on me. It was because if she felt the way my heart was pounding against my ribcage, it would've given me away. The last thing I need is her thinking she has some kind of advantage.

Thoughts of how my dad was today push to the front of my mind and hit me like a ton of bricks. If I wasn't too busy being wrapped up in all things Lennon, I would've thought to check on him sooner. He might not be as bad as he is if he didn't feel so alone. But I abandoned him, just like my mom did, because I was too busy fraternizing with the enemy.

There's only one thing I can do to get back on track, if not for me than for my dad. He needs this. I have no choice but to push Lennon away. Far, far away, to where I know she'll never come crawling back.

I cross my arms over my chest and narrow my eyes at her. "You know, I liked you a lot better with my dick in your mouth," I say, louder than necessary. "At least then you weren't talking."

The hurt look that plasters across her face threatens to break me, but I hold strong. Her mouth opens and closes a couple times, like a fish out of water. She glances around the party and sees how many people are staring at her and whispering to each other. When she turns back to me, I can see the tears building in her eyes, but she holds them back.

"Oh, you mean when you came in under a minute?" She looks me up and down. "At least Kellan knew how to please a girl."

Low fucking blow. I wince slightly at her words, but I don't have a chance to respond, because she's already storming through the house and out the door. Bryce and Jayden gape at me with shock all over their faces, while I'm still stuck staring at where she just stood.

I swallow down the regret and focus on the task at hand. Lennon is gone. Now I can do what needs to be done. That's all that matters. All that can matter. I need to ruin Kensington Bradwell.

ONE OF MY FAVORITE things about surfing is how unpredictable the water can be. I've always said that my dream is to live on the beach, so I can wake up and see what the waves are like for myself. Thankfully, today's a pleasant surprise. There were only supposed to be somewhat small ones, according to the report, but as we got here, we realized they're decently sized.

I cut my board through the water, practicing tricks for the competition coming up next month. Soon, Bryce and Jayden will start helping me train. Honestly, we should have started already, but my attention has been taken up by other things.

Lennon never came home last night, though I didn't really expect her to. If she ever talks to me again, I'll be shocked. She'll come home, because she's too stubborn to let me win entirely, but I don't think she'll pay any attention to me when she does.

I spent hours searching Ken's office while the party went on right outside the door. I even bribed some nerd into helping me hack into his computer, but it all came up empty. Some would say that he's just an honest man, but no one reaches that level of success without skeletons in their closet. There has to be something. I know it. It's just really well hidden.

"If you want to win Mavericks, you're going to need to up your tricks," Bryce tells me as I paddle back to them. "I've seen the competition. It's pretty fierce."

I sit up on my board and run my fingers through the water. "I'll be ready. Don't worry. Once I find what I need on Mr. Moneybags, I can focus on training."

Jayden sighs. "How do you know there's something to find?"

"Because he's the most powerful man in North Haven. Maybe even in Northern California. There's no way in hell he's squeaky clean." Bryce and Jayden share a look, and my shoulders sag. "What?"

Bryce shrugs. "We just don't want to see you throwing away a chance at a sponsorship because you were too busy with your parents' relationship. Being invited to this competition is huge for you."

I throw my head back, groaning because they have a point. "I know, but I need this. My dad needs this."

"That's kind of why we have another idea." Bryce nudges Jayden.

"I'm listening."

Jayden smirks. "Out of all the research we've done, there's always been one constant. The one thing he seems to put above all else. Mentioned in every interview. Always comes first. Gets everything her little heart desires."

My chest tightens when I realize where he's going with this. "Lennon."

"If you're looking to get information, or even looking to hurt him, the best way to get it is to go through her. Daddy's little princess. His pride and joy."

I lay back on my board and stare up at the sky. They're right, and I can't believe I didn't see it sooner. Lennon is the best option. I just don't know if she's an option I have anymore. I'm going to have to grovel, and I fucking hate groveling.

Shit just got real.

19

LENNON

Music blares through the AirPods and into my ears, blocking out any noise around me. I sway my hips back and forth as I make something for lunch—a turkey and cheese sandwich with a pickle on the side. Being here alone, I'm in the best mood.

It took two hours last night of me convincing Colby not to go after Cade. After the way he humiliated me in front of everyone, I stormed out of the house. I needed to get as far away from him, and the party, as possible.

First, I called Tessa, but she didn't answer. Turns out she was out to dinner with Asher and didn't hear her phone. The only other person I could think to call was Colby. He came to get me in record time, but the way he was shaking showed he genuinely wanted to deck Cade in the face.

Part of me wonders if I should've let him. What Cade said was totally uncalled for, and I can't believe I gave him the power to hurt me like that. I knew he was going to be standoffish after what we did the other night, but I never expected that. It was downright cruel, and even Bryce's reaction to it showed he thought the same.

I considered staying at Colby's again, but after spending

one night there, I decided against it. This is my house, not Cade's. I'm stronger than to give him this power over me, and I won't let him take over my home. If anyone is leaving, it's going to be him.

As One Direction sings "Where Do Broken Hearts Go" into my ears, I nod my head to the beat and spin around. On the second rotation, someone catches my eye, and I let out frightened shriek. Cade leans against the doorway, watching me. I rip the pieces out of my ears and glare at him.

"Can I help you?"

He smirks and takes a step closer. "That depends. Is having you move like that against me an option?"

I put a hand up to stop him from encroaching in my personal space. "Not a fucking chance. After what you pulled last night, you're lucky I haven't set your room on fire."

"Fair enough," he chuckles. "Would an apology orgasm suffice?"

Is this dude for real? "No, asshole! I want nothing to do with you, so do both of us a favor and stay the hell away from me."

I push past him and go to walk out when he stops me.

"Lennon."

Turning around, a small piece of me hopes he's going to apologize, and not with sexual favors. Instead, he holds up my plate.

"You forgot your sandwich."

I look at it with a grimace. "Keep it. After having to look at you, I lost my appetite."

OVER THE NEXT COUPLE days, Cade does everything in his power to try and get me to talk to him, but I'm just not interested. He even goes as far as making me breakfast and leaving it on my nightstand. I didn't eat it, just on principle alone. Besides, it wouldn't surprise me if he poisoned it.

I'm getting ready for dance when I notice my bag is missing. I know I left it in the corner of my room where I always put it. My phone buzzes in my pocket—a text from Brady telling me he's on his way. *Crap*. Where the fuck is it?

It hits me like a slap in the face.

Cade.

I roll my eyes and slam the door shut behind me as I march down to his room. My fist pounds harshly against the wood. When he opens it, I'm two seconds from punching that smug grin right off his face.

"Where is it?" I ask, pushing my way inside.

His brows raise. "Oh, so you're talking to me now?"

"Cut the shit, asshole." I glance around the room and then turn back to him. "My dance bag. Where is it?"

"White duffle? Your name embroidered in rose gold on the side? Looks like it was expensive?"

I nod, waiting for him to tell me where it is but instead, he shrugs.

"Haven't seen it."

Remember when I stopped Colby from kicking his ass? Yeah, I shouldn't have done that. I should have cheered him on as he beat Cade into next Tuesday. A concussion might do him good—knock some sense into him.

I take a step toward him and use a hand to press him up against the wall. "I'm not messing around, *Cadence*."

The name is meant to piss him off, but instead, it makes him smirk. "Oh, I'm in full name trouble. You know, I've never liked that name, but it sounds kind of sexy when you say it."

"Cade!"

"Mmm, yeah." He bites his lip. "Scream it like that."

This is pointless. "Ugh! Forget it. I'll just deal without it."

I get halfway out the door when he grabs my wrist and

pulls me back. Before I can stop him, I'm pinned between him and the doorway, with his body pressed up against mine. He smells like salt air and suntan lotion, and I hate the way my body reacts to it.

"I can't figure it out," he murmurs softly.

My resolve is shaking, but I do my best to keep my composure intact. "Figure *what* out?"

"Whether you're actually angry, or just masking your desire with hate."

Honestly? It's probably an equal blend of both, but there's no way in hell I'm admitting that to him. Fool me once, shame on you. There won't be a second time. I'll make damn sure of that.

I use all my strength to push him off me. His back hits the other side of the door jamb and he doesn't care to try again. My eyes rake over his face and down to his abs that look carved from stone, doing nothing to hide the fact that I'm checking him out. Then, I bring my gaze back up to meet his.

"I guess you'll never know."

I LOOK AROUND THE studio, watching as the soon-to-be new owner notes changes they're going to make with their designer. It's surreal to me, being as I've been dancing here for years. I can't imagine what it's going to be like when this place is no longer here. When I can't come here just to let off some steam and dance my heart out.

Sure, I have the studio in my basement, but this place was always a safe haven for me. I used to love coming here with Brady and Savannah, and just having as much fun as we could. I can't even count the number of dances that have been choreographed in this room, let alone the rest.

"This sucks. Why is your mom selling it again?"

Brady shrugs while looking through his playlist. "Because she's been doing this since she was twenty-two years old. She wants to retire, and I didn't want to take it over."

"But why not? You'd be great at it. I mean, you practically run this place as it is."

He chuckles. "Maybe the grown kids, sure, but my mom gave them the groundwork as children in lessons."

Okay, I guess that makes sense. Still, it's going to suck to see this place go. If I wasn't on my way to Juilliard, I'd take it off her hands. This town needs a good dance studio, and this one was the best around. Mrs. Laurence did an amazing job at creating a happy place for everyone.

"All right, enough of the pity party," Brady announces. "I have something that will cheer you up."

I cross my arms over my chest. "I have the stepbrother from hell, and my favorite place in the world is closing. Somehow, I doubt that."

"Damn, Brady. Her lack of confidence in you is a bit disappointing." A familiar voice echoes through the room.

Brady's grin widens as I turn around and see none other than Savannah Montgomery behind me. I squeal and run into her arms. She giggles, hugging me back.

Savannah and I have always been Mrs. Laurence's favorite dancers—though I've always believed she's much better than I am. When in the same age categories, we always took silver and gold together. After she graduated last year and moved across the country to attend Juilliard, we've lost touch, and I've missed her.

"What are you doing here?"

She goes over to give Brady a hug. "Did you think I'd actually miss the closing recital of this place? I've been coming here since I was seven."

I snicker. "Okay, good point."

In all fairness, Sav and Brady have been here much longer than I have. My dad hired a private dance teacher for me, and

I learned the basics in my studio at home. However, when she no longer had anything to teach me, I begged my dad to let me come here instead. He was hesitant at first, but eventually he caved, and I got what I wanted.

"So, tell me about this stepbrother from hell," she says.

I groan loudly, making Brady laugh. "Where do I even begin?"

I SHOULDN'T BE SURPRISED when I pull up to my house and see a party going on inside. It seems all Cade knows how to do is invite people over and drink an overwhelming amount of alcohol. Savannah glances out the window from the passenger seat of Brady's Escalade.

"Uh, Len?" she asks. "Why are there like a million people at your house?"

Sighing, I unbuckle my seatbelt. "Because Cade throws a party almost every fucking day."

She looks over at Brady, and the two of them have an unspoken conversation with only eye-contact and facial expressions. With a determined nod, she unbuckles her seatbelt and Brady puts the car in park.

"What are you two doing?"

Sav takes out her phone and puts it to her ear. "Hey babe. There's a party at Lennon's, so I'm staying here for a bit. Come if you want."

Brady turns around to face me. "We can't let you face him alone. Not after the shit he pulled at the last party."

They have a point, and this may be why I love them so much. I send a quick text to Tessa, telling her to come and bring Asher and Colby if she wants, then the three of us get out of the car. If he wants to continue to throw parties, I'm going to enjoy them. Fuck him for thinking he could break me.

GRAYSON HAYWORTH DRAPES AN arm over Savannah's shoulders as he drinks his beer. It's adorable seeing them together, especially knowing their history. Everything was determined to keep them apart, but they managed to stick together in the end.

Brady, Asher, and Colby are all talking about football, leaving me and Tessa clueless with all their official terminology. I can keep up to a degree, but when they start talking plays, I'm out.

I glance over at Cade, to find him looking back at me with a dangerous glint in his eyes. It's like he's waiting for someone to make a move on me, which is bullshit. He doesn't get to humiliate me and expect to *have* me, too. I don't know who taught him how to treat a woman, but if it was his dad, I can understand why Nora left.

"I'll be right back," I tell them. "I need another drink."

Tess stops me with a hand on my arm. "Do you want me to come with you?"

I shake my head. "I've got this."

She smiles proudly as I walk away. Unsurprisingly, I only get halfway there before Cade steps in front of me. I roll my eyes and look up at him.

"What do you want?"

He tucks a strand of hair behind my ear. "I just want to talk."

I'm not sure what exactly keeps me planted in place. Maybe it's partly that I'm afraid he'll humiliate me even more if I don't hear him out, but I think it's mostly because I'm curious what he has to say. I shouldn't be, I know, but I am.

"So, talk." I put a hand on my hip and wait for him to continue.

Cade smiles down at the ground and then back up. "You're cute when you're angry."

"Ugh." I go to push past him, but he stops me.

"Okay, okay. I'm sorry. I won't hit on you anymore if that's what you want." He pauses for a second and sighs. "It's just hard not to."

I raise one brow. "Oh yeah? And why's that?"

He smirks and takes a step closer. "Because I want you. Isn't it obvious?"

"No, it's not, because someone who *wants* me wouldn't humiliate me the way you did."

A level of vulnerability comes over him. "I was scared. I wanted to push you away. It was a mistake, and I'm sorry."

The look in his eyes chips away at my wall, but I can't let him win. Not again, and especially not without having to work at it.

I pretend to give in and take a step closer. "So, you want me, huh? Want me how?"

He bites his lip. "Anything you're willing to give. Fuck, Lennon. I'm so glad you don't hate me."

"Hmm."

Running my hand up over his abs and to his chest, I place my palm on his stomach and push him back. He falls right into the pool and under the water. When he comes back up to the surface, he shakes his hair out of his face and looks up at me.

"News flash—I *do* hate you, and that's not changing. Go fuck yourself."

I walk away to get my drink, chuckling as even Bryce puts his hand out for a high-five. Cade glares at him from where he's pulling himself out of the pool, but he doesn't back down.

Yeah, he's not in control here.

I am.

20

CADE

THE CHEAP-ASS VODKA HITS MY TONGUE AND slides down my throat, burning the whole way. My gaze is focused on Lennon as she stands with her friends. She's so unfazed by me that I'm not sure I stand a chance at all.

Tonight was not my idea. I was planning to get her to talk to me the same way I have been, by being persistent while we're alone. Bryce, however, said that I should show her affection in front of the same people I humiliated her in front of. He insisted it was the best way to undo the damage I caused.

Spoiler alert: Bryce is an idiot.

The relief that flooded through my body when I thought she was going to forgive me was overwhelming. I'd like to sit here and tell myself that it's because I need her in order to get something against her dad, and I do, but no part of me believes that lie. Regardless of my motivations, most of what I said was the truth. I fucking want her.

As if her sole intention is to piss me off, Lennon plants herself in Colby's lap, and he wraps his arms around her waist. My jaw locks at the sight. It did nothing to me when I saw her hanging on Brady, but he's gay. Colby may be the one person here who could actually steal her from me, and I hate him for it.

Zayn, Knox and Delaney walk in and immediately go over to Lennon and her friends. Tessa beams when she notices her sister, and Knox greets Grayson. It's an odd sight to see, being as they're so different, but I guess he's all about changes lately. Girlfriend. Preppy best friend. Moved away from North Haven where everyone swore he would stay forever.

Lennon's confidence goes even higher as she has all her friends surrounding her, plus being in the arms of her stupid little playboy. Doesn't she realize she deserves so much better than someone whose body count is longer than a fucking phone number? No. He doesn't get to have her.

She's mine, whether she likes it or not.

AFTER GIVING THEM A little while to get comfortable, I grab a beer and head over to Knox. Him being here gives me the perfect excuse to infiltrate Lennon's little group. As expected, the second I approach, Knox smiles at me.

"What's up, man?" He gives me a bro hug.

I run my fingers through my still damp hair. "Not too much. You're back from Rhode Island?"

He nods. "Only for the week. Have to work and all that shit."

Delaney rolls her eyes. "He doesn't *have* to work, he just likes to."

"Shush, woman," he quips. "Having a sugar mama isn't my style."

Zayn laughs. "You say that, but you also had no problem taking the car she bought you a couple months ago."

He narrows his eyes on his best friend. "Fuck off."

"No, if anyone should fuck off, it's him," Lennon says, her attention pointed at me.

The right corner of my mouth raises. "Aw, what's wrong? Only you can be a part of the cool kids?"

She goes to move, but Colby tightens his grip on her. "Leave it alone, babe."

Babe. Fucking babe. The term of endearment alone has me seeing red, and it takes everything in me not to lose my shit. It was one thing, getting rid of Kellan. He fucked that relationship up all on his own. But Colby? From what I've noticed, he's her best friend, and she already knows how he is. If they get together, there won't be anything I can do to push him out of my way.

"Careful, Colby," the new blonde that Lennon showed up with today says. "Looks like you're making him jealous."

Knox chuckles. "All right, enough of this shit. Cade's good people."

"Was he good people when he told everyone he liked me better with his dick in my mouth because at least then I wasn't talking?" Lennon questions.

Knox cringes and looks over at me. "You really know how to fuck shit up, don't you?"

I shrug. "It's a hidden talent."

Lennon sighs. "Whatever. I'm not going to let my night be ruined by the likes of you." She turns to the blonde girl. "Savannah, come with me to take over the speaker system."

"Bryce might have something to say about that." I tell her.

She laughs dryly and looks me up and down. "Last time I checked, this isn't Bryce's house, and if you keep it up, it won't be yours, either."

That comment should make me happy. That's part of what I've wanted this whole time. But it doesn't.

Not even a little.

SEEING LENNON IN HER element is like watching a rose bloom. She's gorgeous, even when she isn't trying, but when she's having a good time—my God, it's mesmerizing. I could spend the entire night just watching her.

Savannah's boyfriend, who I think is named Grayson, comes over and offers me a beer. My brows furrow in confusion, not knowing what the hell he wants, but I take it anyway. He nods to where Lennon and Savannah are dancing like professionals.

"So, you and Lennon?"

I snort. "Is that what you came over here for? To talk chicks?"

He grins. "Actually, I came over here to make sure you don't fuck it up. Lennon's one of my friends, and if your intentions are anything less than pure, Knox won't stop me from coming after you."

"Is that supposed to scare me?"

"Not if you're doing nothing wrong." He glances over to where Colby is standing with Asher and watching Lennon. "I don't think I'm the only one you'd have to answer to, though."

"Who, Colby?" I size him up. "I'm not his focus. She is."

Grayson nods. "Then you should probably make sure *he* isn't *hers*."

I don't say anything, mainly because that's a legitimate fear I have. I should hate her, not care about who the hell she dates, but I can't help it. Nothing I do to keep my mind off her seems to work, and this jealousy thing is really starting to get on my damn nerves.

"Listen," he continues. "All I'm saying is I've seen the way you look at her. It's the same way I used to look at Sav. You're angry about something, and you're fighting the feelings you have for her. And take it from someone who's been there—it's not worth it. Having a girl like that on your side beats any reason for being against her by a long shot."

Knox comes over, and all speak of Lennon ceases immediately. "What are you two girls talking about?"

Grayson smiles. "Just bestowing my wisdom on young Cade here."

Knox laughs. "Dude, he's the same age as you."

"No shit?" He glances at me, and I shrug, taking a swig of my beer. "Then stop acting like a fucking child and get your girl."

EVERYONE LEAVES BY THREE in the morning, and as soon as her friends are gone, Lennon is nowhere to be seen. I lock up and make a mental note to clean up in the morning, then head upstairs. There's no way I was going to try talking to her while the party was still going on. Not when she was sober and not when she had the strength of all her friends around. She'd reject me again just for payback.

The light that filters from her room at the top of the spiral staircase tells me she's in here, and I take a deep breath before going in. She's standing at her window, looking outside, but I can tell she knows I'm here by the way she tenses.

"What do you want, Cade?" Her voice is soft—broken almost.

I take a step closer. "I just want to talk."

"You keep saying that," she sighs. "But nothing you say is anything I want to hear."

Okay, ouch. I'm about to walk out and leave her alone when I remember what Grayson said. Granted, at first his words went in one ear and out the other, but after talking to

Knox about Gray and Savannah's history, I figure maybe he's not full of shit after all.

"I'm sorry," I tell her. "From the bottom of my heart, I'm genuinely, truly, sorry, but I'm not sorry for wanting this."

She says nothing as I walk closer and press my chest against her back.

"You stand here, up in your ivory tower, untouchable to everyone—but not me. No. Mark my words. One day, I'll claim your mind, your body, your innocence. One day, you're going to be mine."

Her breath hitches, but I'm not about to push this any further. I back away and leave her to process my words, smiling because I've never been so determined. Who says I can only have one? I'm going to get the girl, and the revenge.

I SIT IN THE kitchen as Lennon grabs a bottle of water and slips it into her dance bag that I put back in her room this morning. She's yet to say anything to me, but she hasn't glared at me either, so I'll take that as a win.

As she goes to leave, she stops in the doorway for a second and looks back at me. It almost seems like she's going to say something, but instead, she exhales and walks out. I don't know how long it's going to take before she talks to me again, but I'm definitely chipping away at her walls.

Once the coast is clear, I slip into the office and shut the door behind me. The safe is predictably hidden behind a painting that hangs on the wall. I take it down and put in the code. *Lennon's Birthday.* It's not the first time I've been in here, this having been one of the places I searched, but it's the first time I'm taking something out of it.

There has to be over a hundred grand in this thing, but I can't take more than I need. Otherwise, it'll look suspicious and Ken will notice. So, instead of going crazy, I take out a small stack of hundreds and put everything back in its rightful place.

I open the door slowly, looking around before I step out. Just as I walk away from the office, Melani comes into view.

"Mr. Knight, I didn't know you were still home."

Keeping my hands behind my back so she doesn't see the money, I give her my best boyish grin. "I was just leaving. The waves are supposed to be intense today."

She nods politely. "Well, you have a good day."

I thank her and watch as she goes back to work. Mel may work for Ken, but she's not as bad as I thought. As I grab my board from the foyer, I see her tidying up the living room. Now that I think about it, she's always made sure the house looks perfect after one of my parties—because Lord knows I can't clean for shit. I get the garbage picked up, sure, but she makes it look like new again.

With my hand on the door handle, I stop. "Hey, Mel?" She looks up at me. "Thanks...for everything."

A warm smile graces her face, and I feel a little better about myself as I leave. Maybe I don't have to be so cold all the time. The only people who have done wrong here are Ken and my mom. They're the only ones who need to pay for the choices they've made. Not the staff. Not Lennon. Just them.

PULLING UP TO MY dad's, his car is sitting in the driveway. Dread washes over me as I realize he's probably shitfaced—again. I grab my wallet from the center console and head inside.

I managed to take a little over five grand from the safe, and while it won't last forever, it'll at least keep the lights on for a bit longer. Hopefully by the time all that's gone, my dad will be back on his feet, but I doubt it. Train wreck doesn't even begin to describe the state he's in.

As I walk inside, I can see everything is a mess again, but not as bad since I just cleaned it a week ago. My dad is laying on the couch, passed out with a beer still firmly in his hand. He looks like he hasn't showered in weeks, with facial hair taking over his features.

I grab the stack of bills from the counter and bring them into my room, getting to work on paying these things.

I'M JUST MAKING THE last payment when the sound of my dad throwing up catches my attention. I tell the woman on the phone to email me the confirmation number and hang up before running to go help him. He's hunched over the toilet in the main bathroom, but there's vomit all over his shirt.

"Dad, are you okay?"

He waves me off without looking my way. "I'm fine. It's a stomach bug."

That manages to piss me off. "Seriously? You're just going to fucking lie? To Molly I could understand, but me?"

His mouth opens to answer, but all that comes out is more vomit. I cringe and turn away, shielding my nose from the smell. When he's done, I help pull his shirt over his head without making a mess. It takes everything I have not to throw up myself.

I throw the clothes in the washer and start it. When I come back into the living room, my dad is already drinking again. I grab the bottle of Jack Daniels and rip it away from him.

"What the fuck, Cade?"

He reaches for it, but I pull it away again. "No. You need to get your shit together. You think this is the kind of guy Mom would want to come back to?"

My dad snarls at me. "She's not coming back. I lost her. I lost her to some Kensington Bradwell prick."

"He's her new, shiny toy. But you two have twenty years of history and two kids together. If there's a competition to be had, you'll win in the long run, but not if you don't clean yourself up and be the man she fell in love with in the first place. She could still come back."

He rolls his eyes. "There won't be somewhere for her to come back to. The house is going to get foreclosed on when I can't pay the mortgage."

"I paid it."

His brows furrow. "You what?"

I shrug. "I paid the mortgage, and the rest of the bills. From now on, I'll deal with them. I'd give you the money, but I don't trust you wouldn't spend it on alcohol."

"How the hell did you do that?"

The truth of it all sits heavily in my stomach. No child should have to steal money in order to support their father, but in a way, Ken owes this to my dad. He's part of the reason he's in this fucked-up depression.

"Don't worry about it," I tell him, patting him on the back. "It's taken care of."

I love my dad, but I can't sit here anymore. Not seeing him like this. He's not the same guy I've looked up to all my life, and I'd like to keep my image of him firmly intact, at least until he gets up on his feet.

On my way out, I grab as much alcohol as I can find and load it into my Jeep. Then, I drive away and toward the beach.

The waves are beautiful today, but I'm not here to surf. I grab the bottle of Jack from the passenger seat and walk down onto the sand.

How did everything go to such shit? A few months ago, I was surfing, without a care in the world. And now? I'm stealing money from my mom's boyfriend to pay my drunken father's bills. I left to keep an eye on Molly, but I should have stayed. Maybe he wouldn't have ended up like this.

Broken.

Alone.

Drinking to numb the pain.

I lift the liquor to my lips and take a swig. Maybe I'll find what he's been looking for at the bottom of this bottle.

21

LENNON

My eyes shoot open in a panic. The room is dark, but I can sense someone else is here. Moonlight filters through the window, and as my eyes adjust to the darkness, I see Cade standing by my bed. I rub my eyes and sit up.

"Cade?"

As he steps closer, I can smell the booze on his breath. It's strong. Overwhelming. It only takes a second for me to know he's drunk. Did he go to a party tonight instead of having one here?

Everything he said last night echoed through my mind all night long. I had trouble sleeping, and when I finally drifted off, he infiltrated my dreams. When I woke up in the morning, my dance bag was on the edge of my bed. A peace offering of sorts, I guess.

Before I left for dance, I considered talking to him, but I couldn't bring myself to do it. That night with him, the moment we shared, it was the first time I'd ever been that sexual with anyone—and now it's tainted. Any time I think about it, I remember how he used it to humiliate me. To forgive him for that would be dumb, and I don't want to be dumb.

He sits on the side of my bed but says nothing. I turn to flick on the light, and when I look back at him, I can see how bloodshot his eyes are. Something is plaguing his mind, and I shouldn't care what it is, but I do.

"What's wrong?" I whisper.

Taking a deep breath, he turns to me, and I can see just how broken he is. His pain is evident in his expression. The vulnerability in the way he looks at me is so intense, it threatens to crumble all the walls I've built against him.

He reaches forward and runs his knuckle down my cheek. "You're so pretty."

My brows furrow, wondering just how drunk he is, and how he got home. Hell, I don't even know what time it is. I'm frozen in place as he leans over and presses his forehead to mine.

"I hate that I'm so bad for you."

He goes to kiss me, but I turn my head at the last second.

"Cade," I whisper again as he pulls away, but I don't know what else to say.

"I'm sorry," he slurs. "I'm so sorry."

Before I can stop him, he's off my bed and all but running from the room. I fall back into my bed with my eyes still on the door.

What the hell was that all about, and what got him so worked up?

SAVANNAH AND I REPEAT Brady's choreography with a practiced skill. The two of us even throw in our own ideas, from a pirouette here to a jeté there. Just things that will push it the extra mile. This is the last dance we'll be doing as a part of this studio. Saying it has to be perfect is an understatement.

Dancing with Savannah has always been my favorite,

because it gives me something to strive for. The two of us push each other to be better. From what she's told me, I can expect a lot of that at Juilliard, and I can't wait for it.

Our front aerials are perfectly in sync, and we nail the last few moves of the dance. The music cuts out as I pant heavily. I don't think I've danced this hard in weeks, which is why I wish Savannah were here all the time. Luckily, she said she'll be here until it's time to go back at the end of August.

"Damn, Lennon," she says to me. "You've really improved since I left for college."

I shrug. "What can I say? Have to stay in shape for Juilliard."

Brady chuckles. "She isn't kidding. She trains every day, even on vacation."

"That's dedication," Sav replies.

"Or insanity," Brady counters.

I want to laugh with them, because Brady is right—I've always taken dance really seriously—but I can't seem to focus on anything when the music isn't playing. The way Cade looked the other night is still burned into my brain.

Normally, when I get up in the morning, Cade is already downstairs. That day, however, that wasn't the case. I even went to his room to check on him, but his door was locked. When I got home later on, he wasn't home. I haven't seen him since.

Savannah plops down on the floor next to me. "What's got you all lost in thought?"

"It's nothing."

She smiles. "Nothing? Is that Cade's middle name?"

Laying back on the floor, I sigh. "After the party, he apologized. And I don't mean some half-assed 'I'm sorry.' He sounded like he really meant it, but I wasn't ready to forgive him. Hell, I'm still not. But two nights ago, he came into my room in the middle of the night, drunk."

Brady tenses, and Savannah looks at me hesitantly. "Len..."

I shake my head. "No, no. Nothing like that."

She relaxes. "Okay, phew. Then what happened?"

"He slurred a couple things about me being pretty and how he's bad for me, and then he tried to kiss me. When I turned my head, he mumbled an apology and ran out."

Brady furrows his brows. "And you haven't seen him since then?"

"Nope. He was gone when I got back from Tessa's and hasn't been back since. I just can't get the look in his eyes out of my head."

They share a look, and Brady exhales. "It sounds like he's going through something."

"Yeah, but what?"

"I don't know, but I'd keep my distance if I were you. You don't want to get caught up in all that."

He's probably right. He usually is. But a part of me is worried about Cade. He may be an asshole, but no one deserves to be hurting. Knowing something is wrong makes an uncomfortable pit form in my stomach. Savannah must notice, because she holds me like the little sister she never had.

"Don't worry, I'm sure he'll be okay. Just focus on tonight, okay? It's Colby's birthday, right?"

I nod. "The party is tonight. Are you and Gray coming?"

"You know it." She winks at me and giggles as she gets up. "Leave it to you and Tess to end up being best friends with two NFL stars."

I snicker. "Trust me, it was all Tessa's doing."

"Somehow, that doesn't surprise me in the slightest."

I STEP OUT OF the shower, using the towel to wipe away some of the fog on the mirror. My hair is tied on top of my head, and I wrap the second towel around my torso. Colby's party is going to be filled with all the guys from the team, and while I have no intention of hooking up with anyone tonight, I should look my best. If it's anything like the parties he's thrown in the past, there will be pictures all over the magazines.

Stepping into my room, I find Cade leaning up against my bed. His eyes are dark—sinister—and my breath hitches at how exposed I am. He looks me up and down, licking his lips.

"Now, that is a sight," he growls.

As he comes toward me, I smell it. The alcohol on his breath, again. I take a step back but end up with my back against the wall. He cages me in and runs his hand up my side.

"Cade, stop," I plead.

He sighs. "Why? This is what we both want. I know it."

I press a hand to his chest to hold him back. "Because you're drunk."

"So what?"

I cock a brow. "What's wrong with you lately?"

He shakes his head. "Don't worry about it."

"I'm already worried about it!"

"Well fucking don't be," he snaps. "It's none of your goddamn business."

I lift a hand and run it over his cheek. Whether it's intentional or not, he leans into my touch. I try to study his expression, but there's something hidden in it. Something painful.

"Talk to me," I beg, and he closes his eyes. "Is this about your parents? Did something happen?"

He tenses up. "Stop."

"No, Cade. Just tell me what's up with you. I can help!"

His gaze meets mine, and I immediately wish I had kept my mouth shut. "Oh, because you were so helpful the last time?"

Okay, so maybe I deserved that. "I can't do something that will hurt my dad, but I'm sure there's another way I can help. I have to get to Colby's birthday party, but when I get home we can figure it out."

He scoffs. "Colby's birthday party. Of fucking course. Your boyfriend."

"What? Colby isn't my boyfriend."

"Stop talking. Stop fucking talking." His anger grows even further, and he punches a hole into the wall, right next to my head. "I'm so sick of hearing that name, and seeing his hands all over you. And you just eat it all up, don't you? Little fucking cock tease."

"Excuse me?" I ask, offended.

"You heard me," he snaps back.

I place both hands on his chest and push him back, not caring that the towel falls at my feet. "Get out."

Clarity fills his eyes. "Lennon."

"I said get out!"

He looks me up and down, my naked body on full display, then grips his hair before storming out of the room. A few seconds later I hear his door slam shut.

I may have been worried about him before, but not anymore. Whatever he has going on, he can deal with it on his own, because I'm done. Fuck Cade Knight and everything he stands for.

THE HOUSE IS FULL of people, from celebrities to football players. Grayson looks like he's in heaven as he circulates, chatting with so many of his idols. Of course, not to seem like a total dork, he drags Knox with him throughout the party.

"You may lose your boyfriend to an NFL player," I tell Sav.

She chuckles. "Please. I live with him. If they want to take him off my hands for a bit, I'm fine with it."

Delaney and Tessa are talking to Asher when Colby finally has a chance to pull himself away from the conversation he was having and comes over to me. I smile happily as he gives me a hug.

"Happy Birthday!"

He grins. "Thanks, babe."

Sav gives me a look, but I ignore it. "Are you having fun? Did you have a good birthday?"

Colby looks down at me and smirks. "I just turned twenty-seven. Birthdays stopped being fun after twenty-one."

"Yo, Hendrix!" Griffin shouts across the room. "The keg is in the pool."

"*In* it?" Colby asks.

Griffin nods, trying to conceal his smile. Colby looks over at Asher and nods toward the back yard, and the two of them leave to go deal with it. Meanwhile, Savannah gives me a look.

"What?" I question.

She crosses her arms over her chest. "Babe?"

"And?" I ask, dumbfounded.

She rolls her eyes. "He's totally into you!"

"He is not."

Her mouth forms into a frown. "That's a shame, because you two would look super cute together."

"Who would look cute together?" Tess appears at my side.

Savannah smiles. "Colby and Lennon."

"Oh." She waves her off. "Yeah, it's a lost cause though. I've been trying to get them together for months."

"Jesus Christ," I breathe. "We're just friends."

All three of them chuckle, not taking me the slightest bit

seriously. Even Delaney seems to be on their side, but I just don't see it. Colby is a natural flirt. He does that with everyone. It's part of his playboy charm.

Sav sighs. "Okay, then answer me this hypothetical question. Cade or Colby?"

I groan, even at the sound of Cade's name. "Neither. Cade is a prick I want nothing to do with, and Colby has no intentions of settling down. He's practically a shoe-in to be the next Hugh Hefner."

Tessa laughs. "Well, then you won't have any problem with what I think you should give him for his birthday."

Oh God. "And what's that?"

She smirks. "A lap dance."

22

CADE

I'M LYING IN MY BED, SCROLLING THROUGH pictures on social media and trying to stop torturing myself with the vision of Lennon naked. I'm starting to sober up after the beers I had at the beach with Bryce and Jayden, and now that I think of how I acted, it wasn't exactly the smartest.

All I've wanted to do is get back in her good graces, but hearing that she's spending the night with Colby set something off inside me. I hate that stupid fucker and everything he has to do with Lennon. Even knowing she's with him right now has my blood boiling.

As I'm scrolling through my phone, #HappyBirthdayColby catches my eye. There are a ton of pictures under it, and just by looking at a couple of them, I recognize the house. It's at Colby's, the same place as the graduation party we crashed.

A picture of Lennon standing with Tess, Savannah, and Delaney comes up. She looks beautiful, and my stomach churns at the thought of her being even more mad at me than she was before. I need to talk to her, and it can't wait.

I grab a shirt from the closet and pull it over my head.

Taking my keys off the nightstand, I leave my room without a second thought.

I can't lose her, especially not to him.

MUSIC FILLS THE PARTY, but I notice everyone seems focused on the same thing. Colby is sitting in a chair in the center of the room, while Lennon stands next to him, laughing. My brows furrow as I step up next to Knox.

"What's going on?" I ask.

His eyes widen. "Cade. Uh, maybe you shouldn't be watching this."

He goes to lead me away, but I rip myself from his grasp. "No. What the fuck is going on?"

He rubs the back of his neck uncomfortably. "Tess dared Lennon to give Colby a lap dance for his birthday."

My entire body tenses as "River" by Bishop Briggs starts to play through the room. Lennon is in a fit of giggles, and a part of me wonders if she's even going to do it. Knox goes to pull me away again, but I'm not having it.

"Get the fuck off me."

The sound of my voice gets Lennon's attention, and her expression changes. *Don't do it. Don't fucking do it.* I'm mentally willing her not to, but my being here alone is motivation enough for her.

As the chorus starts, she drops into his lap and starts moving her ass, showing all the skill she possesses at dance. It's sensual and erotic, and everything I wish she was doing to me, but not him. Definitely not him.

Her eyes stay locked with mine as she moves against Colby, and I take a step closer. Savannah, Delaney, and Tessa all watch me, but my gaze doesn't leave Lennon. As she leans back against him, his one hand grips her hip while the other moves to her cheek. He turns her head and goes to kiss her.

Their lips are only centimeters from each other when Lennon's eyes droop closed, but before they can connect, I grab her wrist and pull her into me.

My mouth covers hers, stealing the kiss that was meant to be Colby's, and it's like a breath of fresh air. Her lips move against my own, as if she can't help herself. Tasting her again is like heaven, and I'm instantly high off the feeling. With her lips still on mine, I push the toe of my shoe against his chair and push. Colby falls back and onto the floor while I steal the girl right in front of him.

Like she just now realized what she was doing, Lennon breaks the kiss and pushes me away. She's seething. Angrier than I've ever seen her. And it's all focused on me. She turns and storms out the front door, leaving me alone in the middle of the crowded party.

"Smooth move, asshole," Tessa says, and moves to follow Lennon, but I stop her.

"Let me. We need to have this out."

She looks hesitant but reluctantly agrees. I rush out the door, and the second I look to the side, I see her. She's frustrated, pulling at her hair and pacing back and forth. When I get close enough, she turns around and her eyes meet mine.

"You need to stop doing that," she demands, but there's a weakness to her words. "Stop showing up places. Stop kissing me. And stop doing shit to push me away! You just need to stop."

"I know."

She scoffs. "You know, but keep doing it."

"I know," I repeat. "I'm a stupid son of a bitch, and I should leave you alone, but I fucking can't." I pause for a second and take a breath. "You're like a drug to me, and I can't seem to get my fix."

She rolls her eyes. "How romantic."

Stepping closer, I smile. "Is that what you're looking for?

Romance? To be wined and dined? Swept off your feet? Because I don't think it is."

"Oh? And what is it I want?"

"Me," I answer confidently. "Someone to fight you. Someone who makes you as angry as I do. Someone who haunts your dreams and makes you quiver with want from a single look. Because the more you hate me, the more you want me."

She huffs and shakes her head. "I'm not doing this."

Moving to push past me, I grab her wrist and pull her into my chest. "Tell me I'm wrong, Lennon. Go ahead. Fight me."

Her breathing is labored as I hold her tightly against my body, and her gaze locks on mine, but she says nothing.

"See? You can't. You want me just as bad as I want you, and one day soon, I'll pop that pretty little cherry of yours. Trust me, baby. You'll be screaming my name until your throat is raw."

A glimmer of want sparkles in her eyes, and that's all the hope I need. I take a risky chance and bend down, placing a soft kiss on her lips before releasing her and stepping back. The whole time, she stays completely still.

"Enjoy the party," I tell her. "I'll see you at home."

23

LENNON

Some people come into your life that make you question everything you've ever believed in. Cade is one of those people for me. It's been three days since Colby's birthday, and I'm still a flustered mess whenever I think about it.

I should have told him he was wrong. That I didn't want him. But the words wouldn't come out. I couldn't move. Couldn't breathe. Couldn't think. He had me exactly where he wanted me, and all my secrets threatened to spill out right then and there. What can I say? That kiss caught me off guard but in all the best ways, and I hate myself for it.

Since the party, the two of us have been sharing this house with no issues. I still don't know what to say to him, so I haven't said anything at all. And oddly enough, he's respected that. He's kept his distance while still doing things that tell me I'm there.

For example, making enough breakfast for the two of us and leaving it on the counter. Or packing my dance bag for me when I'm running late and rushing out the door.

A big part of me is still so angry. The cruel things he's said and done should be enough to make me hate him for eternity, but it's hard. It's hard because when I look at him, I can see what's under that hard exterior. The guy behind the shell. The one who's hurt by his parents' divorce and just trying to do what he thinks is right.

I'm sitting on the couch in the living room, watching another episode of *Keeping Up With The Kardashians,* when Cade comes in. He says nothing as he takes the other side of the couch and pulls out his phone. Just being this close to him has me feeling some kind of way.

I move to get up when his voice stops me. "Please, don't."

Freezing in place, I look over at him.

"Don't go. Just, sit here. I'll leave you alone, and I won't say anything. I just need to be close to you. I can't explain it."

I can, because it's the same feeling I've been fighting for weeks now. The one that keeps me up at night. The one that makes me wonder if I ever knew anything at all.

Against my better judgement, I sigh and sit back down, doing everything I can not to admire the way he smiles because of it.

OKAY, WHEN YOU GROW up with a chef, it becomes blatantly obvious that you have no idea how to cook. I look down at the pan filled with burnt macaroni and cheese. How I'm going to get through college without someone doing this shit for me is a total mystery.

"What's that smell?" Cade asks, cringing as he comes in the kitchen.

I take the pan and toss the whole thing into the garbage. He snickers at me as he glances in the garbage. I roll my eyes and glare at him.

"Ha ha. So hilarious, the rich girl can't cook."

He raises his hands defensively. "Like, at all?"

I shrug. "No one was ever around to teach me."

It's the most conversation we've had in days, and I hate the way my whole body reacts to it. I watch as Cade walks around me and over to grab another box of macaroni from the pantry and a pan from the cabinet. He hands them both to me, and my brows furrow.

"You really want me to burn the whole house down, don't you?"

Chuckling, he takes them back and the doorbell rings. "You go see who that is, and I'll get this going. I'm starving."

As I walk out of the room, I can't help but smile. He's not acting like an asshole. He's not encroaching on my personal space. He's just being himself, and I happen to like that version of him.

Pulling open the door, my heart drops at who I find on the other side. Kellan stands there, holding a bouquet of pink roses, with a sheepish grin on his face.

"What the fuck are you doing here?"

The grin vanishes in an instant. "I just want to talk."

I shake my head. "You had every chance in the world to talk, while we were together. Instead, you went and fucked Skye while I slept down the fucking hall."

He winces at my tone. "I'm sorry, Lennon. I really am. I was really disappointed about not getting into Vanderbilt, and she was there."

"Seriously? That's your million dollar excuse?" I scoff.

"Len?" Cade's voice comes from down the hall. "Who's at the door?"

He comes around the corner, and the second he sees Kellan standing there, he goes ballistic. Kellan nods at him, trying to avoid a fight, but it's useless.

"What the hell do you want?" Cade sneers.

Kellan sighs. "I just came to talk to Lennon."

"Yeah, well, she doesn't want to fucking talk to you."

My ex becomes defensive. "I don't think that's for you to decide."

Cade laughs dryly and looks over at me. "Do you want to talk to this piece of shit?"

"No," I reply firmly.

He smiles at my answer. "Hear that? She doesn't want anything to do with you, so it's time to go."

Kellan rolls his eyes. "As usual, Cade Knight is calling the shots. Whatever, she was a shitty fucking girlfriend anyway."

As he goes to walk away, Cade grabs the back of his shirt and pulls him back. The two of them fall to the ground in a cluster of punches being thrown. As I watch Kellan land a particularly rough hit to Cade's lip, I shriek. The mere thought of him getting hurt is enough to bother me, but seeing it first hand is terrifying.

"Stop!" I shout, but neither of them listen.

Looking around, I find a vase that looks easy enough to replace. I grab it and lift it over my head, before slamming it down onto the ground. The porcelain shatters into a bunch of tiny pieces, but it distracts them enough for me to separate them. I pull Cade off of Kellan and push him up against the wall. He looks like he already wants to go for another round, but I won't let him.

"Cade," I try. "Cade!"

Finally, he rips his eyes away from Kellan and looks at me. His bottom lip is cut and bleeding, and it looks like his eye is already starting to bruise, but he softens under my attention.

"Stop, please. For me."

Kellan laughs from behind me, and my whole body tenses.

"Oh, isn't that cute," he quips.

"Get the hell out of here, Kellan."

Another chuckle. "Wow, Lennon. I never took you as someone who would be into incest. You must be really desperate."

Cade moves to go after him again, but I beat him to it.

"No," I roar, turning around to face my ex. "You don't get

to judge what I do. You had me. I was yours, and I intended for it to stay that way. But that wasn't enough for you. You're the one that cheated. You're the one that paraded Skye around like you were proud of the betrayal. You ruined us, not me. So fuck you. You don't get to judge me."

He looks taken back by my words before sighing and walking back out the door. Once he's gone, I turn around and focus on Cade. His lip looks bad, but I can't tell if he needs stitches with all the blood.

"Come on. We need to get that cleaned up."

I grab his hand and pull him into the nearest bathroom, thankful that he isn't fighting me on it. I take the first aid kit out from under the sink and look through it.

"Thank you," I tell him. "You didn't need to defend me like that back there."

As I move toward him with the wet gauze in my hand, he grabs my wrist and halts my movements. "No way in hell was I going to let him say those things about you. Not ever."

I look away from his intense stare. "No offense, but I think you've said worse."

He grabs my chin and forces me to look at him. "I know, and no part of me would blame you for never speaking to me again, but that douchebag doesn't deserve you. Hell, I don't either, but fuck if I don't still hope you somehow choose me anyway."

Taking my hand in his, he presses a kiss to it and then puts it back down at my side.

"You're incredible, Lennon, and any guy would be lucky as hell to have you. Me included."

I say nothing as he pushes off the counter and leaves the room. There's a kiss mark on my hand in his blood, which should gross me out, but it doesn't. Because deep down I know he's not just some guy, and he's certainly not my stepbrother.

He's Cade—the irritating, rude, arrogant guy that drives me insane on a daily basis—and he's mine.

I TOSS AND TURN in my bed, unable to fall asleep, when I finally give in. I slip out of my bed and down the stairs. The whole house is pitch black, but I know this place like the back of my hand. As I reach the familiar bedroom door, I take a deep breath.

If it's locked, I'll go back to my room knowing it wasn't meant to be, but if it's not, we're doing this. We're actually doing this.

As I twist the knob, the door opens, and butterflies fill my stomach. I creep inside and shut the door behind me. Cade's steady breathing fills the room, but just when I go to slip in bed next to him, he wakes.

"What the fuck?"

I giggle softly. "Shh. It's just me."

He sighs. "Lennon? Is everything okay?"

I get in bed, and he moves his arm out of the way for me to cuddle into his side. I lay my head on his chest and take a deep breath, inhaling his intoxicating scent.

"Yeah, everything's fine."

As I drift off to sleep, I feel him press a light kiss to the top of my head and his arm wraps around me, holding me tightly against him.

Yeah, everything's just fine.

I WAKE IN THE morning, after what was probably the most peaceful sleep I've had in awhile. It was so deep, not even a dream interrupted. My head moves up and down as my pillow breathes.

Wait a minute.

My eyes snap open as the events of last night come swarming back. Cade's room. Cade's bed. *Cade*.

"Good morning, sunshine," he chuckles.

I sit up and run my fingers through my hair. "Uh, hi."

"Sleep well?"

The tenderness of his voice eases me away from the edge. "Yeah, actually. I did."

He smiles in the way that sets me on fire inside. "Good. Get dressed."

"What? Why?"

Standing up and walking over to his closet, his torso is on full display. "We're going surfing."

I choke on air. "In case you haven't noticed, I don't know the first thing about surfing."

"No, but you do know everything about dance, which includes balance." He pulls out a shirt and puts it on, much to my dismay. "Don't think I didn't see you eyeing up my board in Malibu."

Okay, so maybe he's right. Since seeing him do it, I've always wondered what it would be like. As a kid, I used to love boogie boarding, but I never tried surfing. And learning from him might not be too bad after all.

"You won't let me get hurt?" I question.

He snickers. "It's surfing, babe. Not rock climbing."

"Right." I climb out of bed and head for the door. "I'll meet you downstairs then?"

Nodding, he bites his lip. "One more thing."

In one swift motion, he walks over to me, wraps his hand around the back of my neck, and pulls me into the kiss of a lifetime. It's soft, yet heated. Full of all the intense emotion that has built up between us over the last few weeks. Any regrets I had about coming in here last night go right out the window. This is what I want.

He is what I want.

I LAY ON MY new board and push myself up to a sitting position, just like Cade showed me. Since he didn't have an extra, we had to stop at the surf shop to grab another. I wanted a pink and white one, but when he suggested a teal one because it matched my eyes, I couldn't say no.

"Now we just sit and wait for some waves," he explains.

Honestly, I don't think I've ever seen this side of him. Caring. Compassionate. Kind. He even brought us to a beach with smaller waves so I can learn on easier water. The way he looks when he talks about surfing, the passion that comes with his words, it's mesmerizing. He really is happiest when he's in the ocean.

A round of baby waves comes, and Cade hops off his board to stand next to mine, gripping the sides of it. I lay down on my stomach and let him turn the whole thing to face the shore.

"Okay, are you ready?"

I nod, and as soon as it gets close enough, he pushes it forward.

"Now paddle!"

Doing as he says, I fall into the wave. Just as I feel it take the board, I jump up to my feet and use everything I've learned in dance to balance.

Immediately, I can see why he loves this so much. The wind in my hair. The water beneath me. The view of the beach coming closer. It's incredible.

I lose my balance after a little over thirty seconds and splash into the water, but I couldn't care less. Grabbing the board, I paddle back out to Cade and jump off.

"I did it!"

He smiles proudly and wraps me in his arms. "I knew you would."

We lock eyes as he holds me, with his hands on my back

and my legs tightly around his hips. When we're this close, nothing else matters. It's just him, and me, and the moment. He glances down at my lips, and all I want is to close the distance between us.

"I know I have a lot to make up for," he whispers. "But I'm so glad you're here, with me."

"So am I," I answer, because it's the truth.

His grin widens and he pulls me into him, connecting our lips once again. I don't think I'll ever tire of this feeling. The chills that run down my spine, even in the warm water. The butterflies that fill my stomach. I never felt like this when kissing Kellan. Not in the slightest. Kissing Cade is something else entirely.

As our tongues tangle together, I can feel as he hardens beneath me. He breaks the kiss and carefully pulls me away from him.

"Come on. You have to catch at least a few more before we head home."

I sigh. "Fine, but only if I can sleep in your room again. Your chest is so much more comfortable than my bed."

He laughs and splashes me with water. "Deal, princess."

WE END UP SPENDING the next few hours in the water. Once I started getting into the habit of when to paddle, I was able to do it entirely on my own. Needless to say, I'm officially addicted. If we didn't have a recital to get ready for, I'd spend the rest of the summer surfing.

Don't get me wrong, dancing will always be my passion, but there's something exciting about trying something new—and this was exactly what I needed.

"I still can't believe I haven't done that sooner," I say from the passenger seat as Cade drives us home.

He reaches over and laces his fingers with my own. "Just wait until you start learning tricks."

I wince. "Yeah, I might leave that one to you and the pros. If I get hurt before this recital, Brady will have my head."

Chuckling, he turns onto our street. "Good point, although I'm more afraid of Savannah than I am Brady."

"Sav is harmless."

He glances over at me. "As harmless as a lion. Wrong person and she'll bite."

I giggle into my fist. "Then you should probably avoid hurting me at all costs. I'd hate to see you get mauled."

"Already planned on it, babe."

The look he gives me, paired with the term of endearment, has me needing to remember how to breathe. I always knew there was something there between us. Something pulling us toward each other. I just never knew how good it would feel to give into it. It's like I can finally breathe again.

As we pull up to the house, our smiles fall off both our faces. Sitting in the driveway is my dad's BMW. They're back early.

I sigh. "So much for spending tonight together."

Cade is obviously bothered by their return, but he does his best to pretend he's not. "That's why doors have locks on them."

Biting his lip at the concept, he jumps out of the Jeep and grabs the boards from the back. I follow behind him as we walk toward the door when I realize something's missing.

"Hey, what did you do with the GT?" I ask.

He smirks and shrugs one shoulder. "I donated it to charity."

The way he says that, like it's no big deal, has me laughing in disbelief. Of course, he did. It wasn't that he hated the car, but the principle behind it. My dad bought that car, so he would get rid of the Jeep, with no regard to the sentimental value of it. I can't really say I blame him.

The second we step inside, I can already hear my dad on the phone from his office. Nora comes out of the kitchen and gives us each a hug.

"Oh, I've missed you two so much," she beams, kissing Cade on the cheek and making him cringe.

I try not to laugh at the look on his face. "We've missed you, too, but I thought you weren't coming home for another week?"

"There's a hurricane off the coast, so we were forced to come back early. It was beautiful, though. I'll have to show you the pictures later."

Cade rolls his eyes, and I subtly nudge him with my elbow.

"Right," he clears his throat. "That would be great, Mom."

My dad comes out of his office and focuses his attention firmly on me. "Lennon, can I see you for a second?"

Confused, my brows furrow, but I nod. "Yeah, sure."

As I'm walking away, Molly comes running down the hallway and jumps into her brother's arms. It's an adorable sight, the way he interacts with her. It's like he's a constant hard-ass to everyone, except her. And now hopefully me, too.

"Now, Lennon," my dad demands.

Cade winks at me as I shut the door, and a light blush coats my cheeks. "What's up?"

He sits down at his desk. "Where were you today?"

"Cade was teaching me how to surf. Why are you being so cold?"

Rubbing the bridge of his nose with his thumb and index finger, he sighs. "I don't want you slumming it on the beach with that kid."

I'm sorry, what? "I thought you liked Cade."

He leans back and turns his computer screen toward me.

"I did, until he threw numerous parties in my house while I was gone. Do you think the staff doesn't tell me this stuff?"

Pictures from the security cameras in the backyard stare back at me from the screen. The evidence is damning, so I don't even try to deny it. Maybe if I said it was my party, he wouldn't care as much, but it's obvious this one wasn't mine. Not with the amount of people and the multiple kegs.

"I mean it, Lennon. Stay away from him."

24

CADE

COMING HOME TO FIND OUR PARENTS BACK A FULL week early was definitely not something I expected. It's just my luck that I finally get Lennon to stand being around me, and now this happens. And to top it all off, ever since she came out of her dad's office, she's been blatantly ignoring me.

We're sitting at the dinner table, listening to my mom and Ken go on and on about their trip and how amazing it was. I move my food around my plate, but none of it seems to meet my mouth. Something about the awkward tension and the unknown of where we go from here is killing my appetite.

I look up at Lennon and realize she's doing the same thing. There's something off with her; I just don't know what. A part of me wonders if her dad knows about us somehow, but I doubt it—mainly because he hasn't flipped out on me yet, and my mom hasn't said anything like that.

Stretching out my legs under the table, I tap her shin with my foot. When her eyes finally meet mine, I give her a look, silently asking what's up. She glances at her dad to make sure he isn't paying attention. When she realizes the coast is clear, she looks back at me and shakes her head.

Fucking great.

"I'm not hungry," I tell my mom. "May I be excused?"

She frowns. "You don't want to hear about the trip?"

"I do, but not right now. I'm not feeling so hot."

As expected, she instantly goes soft and nods. "I'll bring you some soup in a little while. You should have something in your stomach."

Sparing one more look at Lennon as I get up from the table, she won't lift her head from her still full plate. Whatever her dad had to say when we got home was enough to send her running for the hills and far away from me.

HOURS PASS AND I'M still no less on edge than I was at dinner. At this point, I'm surprised there aren't track marks in the carpet from me pacing back and forth. My mom brought me soup that I only ended up flushing down the toilet. At least that way she thinks I ate it.

I don't know what's getting to me more—the fact that Lennon won't talk to me, or that I need her to talk to me in order to get any information on her dad. Everything I want right now depends on her, and I had it in my grasp, until a stupid fucking hurricane went and ruined my plans.

At least if they had come home next week, I could have been closer. Maybe then she wouldn't have been able to push me away so easily. But with us only exploring things between us for half a day? It's basically no harm, no foul at this point.

There were so many times over the last few weeks that I thought about giving up, but I hadn't. I held on because I needed to, and this should be no different. I sit up with a newfound determination. If she wants to end this before it's barely even begun, fine, but she's going to tell me that to my face.

I slowly open my door and peek out it, looking around to see if anyone is still awake. There's no sign of life from what I can see. I close the door behind me and creep down the hallway. Halfway up the spiral staircase, I can already see that Lennon's light is still on.

My knuckles rap lightly against the door, but I don't say anything. When she opens it and her eyes meet mine, they instantly soften. To my relief, she steps back and opens the door further to let me in. She runs her fingers through her hair and sighs frustratedly.

"What's going on? What happened?" I ask as I close the door.

She looks like she's on the verge of crying, but she's still holding on strong. "My dad doesn't want me around you."

I pull back. "The fuck did I do?"

"Oh, I don't know. Threw like fifteen house parties in the course of a month maybe?"

Shit. "How does he even know about those?"

"There are cameras in the backyard," she reveals.

I laugh dryly. "You couldn't have given me the heads up?"

She shrugs. "I thought they were fake. I've never seen any actual footage from them."

"So obviously they must be fake." I roll my eyes.

She crosses her arms over her chest. "Don't get smart with me."

"Well, what else do you want from me?" I ask defeatedly. "I finally get you in my arms, only for your dad to come in like a goddamn dictator and forbid you from seeing me, and I'm supposed to just be okay with it?"

By the look on her face, I can tell that she doesn't want this, but her words say otherwise. "I don't see any other choice."

"I do," I argue. "You're eighteen years old. Fuck what he says. Do what you want for once."

"It's not that easy!" Her tone is loud, but her volume is low, careful not to wake anyone up. "My dad is all I have."

I walk closer and hold her face in my hands. "He's not. You have me, Lennon. I'm right here."

A tear escapes and runs down her cheek, only for me to quickly wipe it away. I lean forward and press a soft kiss to her forehead. The only thing I'm grateful for right now is that she's not pushing me away, because I don't know if I could handle that. Not again. Not after we finally got through me almost ruining everything...twice.

"I don't know what to do," she whispers.

I nod and take a step back, letting her go. She follows me as I slip past her and over to the door.

"You're leaving?"

Instead of walking out, I put two fingers on the knob and turn the lock. "It's okay not to be sure, but I'm going to be in here, every night, holding you, until you are."

She exhales in relief and goes over to get in bed. I flick off the light, and the two of us get comfortable, with her head on my chest, right where she belongs. It doesn't take long before her breathing evens out and she's sound asleep, but I spend hours lying awake.

Fuck Kensington Bradwell for constantly trying to take things from me. First, he takes my mom from my dad, and now he's trying to keep Lennon from seeing me? No. Fuck that. Not if I have anything to say about it.

THE MORNING COMES SOONER than I'd like, and before I know it, Lennon blinks her eyes open and looks up at me. I smile down at her, trying to ease her nerves and cover up the fact that I barely got an ounce of sleep last night.

"Do you just lay there and watch me sleep?"

I chuckle and bop her on the nose. "You're cute when you're dead to the world, and at least then you don't call me a creep for staring."

She looks totally fed up with my shit, but in a good way. "Eh, you're definitely still a creep, whether I'm calling you one or not."

"Fair enough," I cave. "But if I tried getting up, I might have woken you, and I didn't want to do that."

"And you're suddenly such a gentleman, right?"

I shrug. "I have my moments."

She hears a car door close outside, and she gets up to go over to the window. When she finally looks back at me, she relaxes.

"My dad just left for work, but I think your mom's still here."

Of course, leave it to Ken to go to work today, even though technically they're still on vacation. Maybe, if I'm lucky, he's already getting sick of my mom. Or maybe he's getting sick of having her kids in his house. Obviously he doesn't think so highly of me anymore—not if he told Lennon to stay away from me.

Speaking of Lennon, she walks over and sits down on the bed next to me. "What are we going to do?"

"Whatever you want," I tell her. "If you want to listen to your dad, I'll try to make it easy for you. But if you want to give this a shot, sneak around behind their backs, I'm game for that, too."

She looks down at her lap and fiddles with the bottom of her shirt. "Do you think it could work?"

"I think if we both want it to, yeah."

"And what happens if it gets serious?" she digs further. "They're bound to find out sooner or later."

I take her chin in my grasp and turn her head to face me. "We deal with that when the time comes."

It's obvious, just by looking at her, how torn she is with this decision. Going against her dad's wishes isn't something she does often, or even at all, but she's thinking about it. If I try to push her one way right now, it's bound to backfire in my face.

"Hey," I dip my head down to meet her gaze. "You don't need to have an answer right now. Just take some time to think about it. I'm not going anywhere." I pause. "Well, other than the skate park with Bryce and Jayden."

That gets her to laugh. "Such a boy."

"Psht." I give her a cocky grin. "I'm all man."

She rolls her eyes. "Sure you are, *Cadence*. Sure you are."

I poke her in the side and watch as she squirms. Taking advantage of paying her back for using my full name, I grip her waist and proceed to tickle her until she's fighting to push me away.

"Stop, stop," she begs. "I'll pee."

I take mercy on her and bend down to press my lips to hers. It's not anything as X-rated as I'd like, but it renders her speechless. As I climb out of her bed, I wink and commit the smile she gives me to memory.

Now I'll spend the day with the guys, hoping that by the grace of God, Lennon chooses me over her dad. Everything is relying on this. Literally, everything.

No pressure.

THE SKATE PARK IS FILLED with a bunch of twelve-year-olds who think they know how to do real tricks. Personally, I would have preferred to leave after the first ten minutes, but Bryce insisted we stay. He's always been better at skateboarding than he is at surfing, which is strange because we don't do this nearly as much.

"Let me get this straight," Jayden says. "You finally got her at least somewhat where you want her, and her dad comes home and fucks it all up?"

"Just about, yeah."

"Dude, that sucks!"

Bryce finishes landing his trick and shakes his head at me. "Nah, that's just your luck."

I kick his board out from under him and laugh as he falls. "Serves you right."

Sitting down on the railing, Jayden takes the spot beside me. "Do you think there's any chance of her choosing you?"

I shrug. "I mean, I hope so, don't get me wrong. But her dad is her whole life. I'm not even sure she has a mom, because I've never heard anything about her."

"So, she would basically be choosing you over the only parent she has," he clarifies for himself. "That's rough."

"Yeah, you're telling me."

For a moment, I start to wonder if I'm doing the right thing. But then I remember the way her hair smells and the look in her eyes when she surfed her first wave, and all hesitations dissipate.

"I don't think you have anything to worry about," Bryce says confidently.

I snort. "Oh yeah, all knowing one? And why's that?"

He nods toward the entrance. "Because she's here, and she brought an entourage."

My head whips over in that direction and I couldn't hide my smile if I tried. Lennon is walking through the gate with Savannah and Delaney, while Knox and Grayson follow behind. I get up and meet her halfway. Her friends leave us alone and continue walking over to Bryce and Jayden, but her attention stays focused on me.

"What are you doing here?"

She smirks, taking the hat off my head and putting it on hers—backwards, just like I had it. "I missed you. Sue me."

Before I can say another word, she grabs my board and puts it on the ground before skating away on it. And let me be the first one to say, it has to be one of the sexiest things I've ever seen.

SNEAKING AROUND IS EASIER said than done, especially when my mom is constantly around. Trophy wife may be her desired profession, but can't she be one of those wives that goes out and spends all of her rich husband's money or something? Between her and Molly, it's been nearly impossible to get time alone with Lennon.

After the skate park and spending most of the night hanging out with everyone, the two of us went for a drive down to the beach. We sat in the sand with her head on my shoulder, and I've never felt better. Spending time with her isn't just something I want anymore. I *need* it.

It's been a couple weeks since that night, and I can tell Ken's patience with me is growing thin. It doesn't take a rocket scientist to see the way his daughter and I look at each other, but so far he doesn't have any proof. The only thing I do know is that I need to get more money for my dad, before Mr. Moneybags kicks me out and I lose my chance of getting into his office.

I sit at the kitchen island, watching my mom get everything together. She's taking Molly to get fitted for school uniforms. Apparently, Ken decided that Molly will be attending Haven Grace Prep next year. My mom, being as spineless as she is lately, had no objections to the matter, even though Molly seems less than thrilled about the idea.

Lennon left for dance an hour ago, and with my mom gone, it gives me the perfect opportunity to get in and get some more cash. Is it wrong? Of course. But do I have any other option? Not really. It's not like my mom would help him if I told her. If anything, it would just put the final nail in the coffin of their relationship.

I watch as she grabs her purse and smiles at me before walking out the door with my sister. As soon as the car pulls out of the driveway, I get to work. First, I look around and check for any signs of staff. When there isn't any, I slip into the office and quickly get into the safe. I know I can't take much, but I need enough for at least a couple months.

I get what I need and put everything back. Just as I turn to leave, however, a person standing in the doorway has me frozen in place.

"Lennon," I breathe, but the look on her face says I shouldn't say anything.

"You're stealing from my dad? Seriously?"

I take a deep breath. "I can explain."

A humorless laugh echoes out of her. "I'm sure you can. You're just Mr. Bad Choices and Explanations, aren't you?"

"No, please. Hear me out," I beg.

She shakes her head and goes to walk away. "Save it. You're not who I thought you were."

Fuck! I follow her to the stairs but stop at the bottom of them. "It's for my dad," I blurt. "Since my mom left him, he started drinking a lot to deal with the void in his life. He lost his job, and he may lose the house if I don't find a way to keep the bills paid."

She stops midway up and turns around to look at me, but it's not the kind of look I was hoping to see. A heavy sigh leaves her mouth.

"You should go," she tells me with a broken voice. "My dad will be home soon."

And there it is. The real choice she made. I was stupid for believing I stood a chance against the man who has spoiled her since the day she was born. It was one thing when she could have both—me in the darkness and him in the light. But now, when it's one against the other, her actual decision comes to light.

Without a second thought, I turn around and do exactly as she said—leave.

BRYCE SITS ON HIS bed as I throw darts at the wall. It's not doing shit to take my mind off Lennon, but the concept of chucking pointy things in general seems like it would help my frustration. It's only a matter of time before my phone rings, either by Ken telling me to come pack my shit or my mom screaming at me for having the audacity to steal from her sugar daddy.

"You didn't see the look on her face though," I say to Bryce. "She looked so devastated."

He shrugs like it's no big deal. "So you're back to square one. Not a big deal."

My brows furrow. "What do you mean?"

Looking up from his phone, he gives me an odd look. "Well, you were only getting with her to get something to hold against her dad, weren't you?"

Fuck, over the last couple weeks I'd been so wrapped up in everything Lennon, I totally forgot about why I needed to be with her in the first place. All I could focus on was the taste of her lips and the way she clung to me when no one else was around.

"Oh shit," Bryce breathes. "It wasn't."

"No," I try to recover. "No, it was."

He scoffs. "Maybe at first, but that look on your face just now told a whole different story. Well, in that case, it's better that it ended now."

What? "Why do you say that?"

"Because, it's not like she would stay with you after you destroy her dad. I mean, you can't honestly think you were going to get the best of both worlds."

I go quiet as the truthfulness to his words weighs heavily on his chest. I hadn't even thought that far through, but he's right. While I've been sitting here thinking she was the only one with a choice, I've had one, too—put my family back together, or get the girl.

"Maybe you could use some of the money you took to hire

a private investigator," Bryce says while going back to his phone, but I'm too distracted to pay him any mind.

All this time I've been wanting her to choose me over the only family she has, and I'm not sure if I'd be willing to do the same.

We were doomed from the start.

25

CADE

SURFING IS SOMETHING I ENJOY. ALWAYS HAS BEEN, always will be. But training for a competition? Yeah, not so much fun. Bryce and Jayden become bossy little pricks and take control like a couple of drill sergeants. I once considered hiring someone legitimate to help me, but this is what's worked for me since they stopped competing, and I'm a firm believer in not fixing something that isn't broken.

We took the time to drive the forty-five minutes to the same beach where the competition will be held. The waves here are intense, to the point where Jayden won't even go in the water, but that doesn't stop him from shouting trick commands from the beach.

I surf my heart out, moving my board around with a professional skill. Even while I'm so focused, my thoughts still manage to go to Lennon. The way she looked like she wanted to fight me after she caused me to break my other board. How she bought me this one, that happens to be fifty times better. She didn't even realize when I suggested the board she bought for herself that it matches mine.

"Stop daydreaming and fucking surf!" Bryce shouts.

"You're never going to win if you spend your day swooning like a girl over your stepsister."

"Fuck off, asshole," I yell back, but it only makes him laugh.

I push the thoughts away as much as I can and focus on the task at hand, because winning this competition could mean sponsorships. Sponsorships mean a professional career in surfing, and that means getting my dad back on his feet. Maybe if he has a son to be proud of, he won't be such a sorry sap.

I PULL UP TO my old house, realizing my dad's car is still in the same exact spot it was when I last saw him. Hopefully that means he just hasn't gone out to the bar recently, and not that he's somewhere inside, dead from choking on his own vomit.

As I step inside, the sound of a familiar laugh has me more confused than ever. I shut the door behind me and walk into the living room. My mouth drops open when I see Lennon sitting there, having a conversation with my somewhat sober dad in the middle of a disgusting mess.

"Uh, hey," I greet them both.

My dad lights up when he sees me. "Cade-man. Your friend here was nice enough to stop by and drop off the money you gave her." He gets up off the couch and comes over to give me a hug. "Thank you, son. You really didn't have to do that, but I promise I won't let you down."

Meeting Lennon's gaze from over my dad's shoulder, she gives me a sad smile. I pat my dad on the back and wait for him to pull away.

"Dad, do you mind if I have a minute alone with Lennon?"

He smirks knowingly and glances between the two of us before disappearing into his room. I look at Lennon and nod toward the hallway. She stands and follows behind me until we're securely behind closed doors.

"What is this? A pity present?"

Her face scrunches up angrily. "What? Is that what you think I feel for you? Pity?"

I shrug. "Isn't it?"

"No, asshole!" She looks away from me, and rolls her eyes. "Forget it. This was obviously a mistake."

Before she can get to the door, I step in front of it. "No, wait. I'm sorry, I just thought for sure you'd tell your dad about the money I stole."

"Well, I didn't," she sighs. "I thought about it, but you were only helping your father. He's innocent in all of this, and while I might not be on board with doing anything that hurts my dad, I don't agree with his choice to break up a marriage either."

Guilt simmers under the surface, brewing from every bad thought I ever had about her. I take a minute to get a hold of my thoughts and then give in, running my fingers through my hair.

"How much did you give him, anyway?"

She looks down at the ground. "Eighty grand. Enough to get him through a full year."

My jaw drops. "Lennon! You can't take that much! Your dad is going to notice." I start to panic. "Did you even leave any in there?"

Her hand comes up to rub her arm, showing she's uncomfortable. "I didn't take it from my dad. I took it from my own account."

My brows raise. "You have eighty grand just sitting in a bank account?"

She tilts her head back and forth. "Had."

I look up at the ceiling, debating whether I should kiss her or yell at her. "I know your dad is loaded, but please tell me you didn't drain your bank account."

"Don't worry about it. It's my money, and I can do what I want with it."

Just when I thought shit couldn't get any more fucked up, I've got Lennon taking all the money she has and giving it to my dad. Who even lets their girlfriend, or whatever she is, do that? Especially when their motives have been as unpure as mine have.

Why couldn't I have met her under different circumstances? Why does it have to be all or nothing with her? I clench my fist and hold it to my mouth, trying to reign in my anger but there's no use. This has become such a damn mess, I can barely see the ground I stand on.

"Come on," I tell her. "We need to leave."

She steps back, sensing my anger. "What's wrong?"

"I said come on!"

Gripping her wrist, I pull her with me through the house and out the front door. As if she knows what's best for her, she doesn't fight me on it. Instead, she gets into the car and buckles her seatbelt. I turn on the car and shove it into drive before pulling out onto the road.

With every second that passes, I grow more and more furious. There's only one person to blame for all of this. The one person who took my perfect life and flipped it upside down with her selfish choices. The one who promised to always protect my sister and me, and now leaves for month-long vacations with her rich little boyfriend. The one who turned my dad into a drunken alcoholic mess who can't seem to do anything for himself anymore.

My foot pushes the pedal to the floor, and the car speeds up. I'm already going thirty over the speed limit, but a little more won't kill me. My hands go white as I grip the steering wheel with all the strength I have.

"Cade, slow down," Lennon pleads, but I don't pay her any mind. "Cade!"

If I were to look her way, I'd probably see the fear all over her face, but I can't. I can't even bring myself to look at her, because then I might cave. I might lose the motivation to tell my mother everything I've been holding in since she dropped an atomic bomb on our family.

I drift around the corner and pull into the driveway. I'm already out of the car and at the door before Lennon even has her seatbelt unbuckled. She climbs out and runs to catch up with me, but she's not my focus here.

"Mom!" I scream as soon as I get inside. "Mom, where the fuck are you?"

Lennon tries to grab my arm. "What are you doing?"

"Finally speaking my fucking mind," I growl. "Mom!"

"Don't," she begs as she follows me around the mansion. "You're going to regret this. Just come upstairs with me and calm down."

I turn around and point at her. "You don't know what I'll regret! This is all her fault. She ruined my whole life for her own selfish gain!"

Lennon takes a step back, shocked by my tone. Just when I think she's going to run, she squares her shoulders and that same fight in her comes out.

"Well, at least you have a mother!" she shouts, pushing me back. "One that loves you! Mine walked out on me when I was three years old and never came back! So, excuse me if I don't want to stand here and watch you throw yours away."

She turns around and storms out of the room, not giving me a second to say anything back. I look around the empty kitchen and pull at my hair. It's like everything in me has been building up and I'm at a breaking point. Between seeing my dad spiral, to wanting revenge and knowing the only way to get it is by sacrificing being with Lennon. It's all a giant fucking shitshow, and I can't take it anymore.

Wherever my mom is, she's definitely not here. This place is as empty as an abandoned house, except for one room. The princess's tower.

I make my way upstairs and don't even bother knocking before barging in. Lennon barely glances my way, and it's obvious she has no desire to talk to me right now, but I don't care.

"You don't get it," I tell her.

She rolls her eyes. "What? What don't I get? That your mom fell out of love with your dad and put herself first by leaving him for someone else? That your dad handled it badly? That you can't seem to come to terms with the fact that things don't always work out the way you want them to? Tell me, Cade. What don't I get?"

I throw my hands in the air. "She ruined everything! Even you and me! I can't have the damn girl I want because of her!"

"The only reason you know the girl you want because of her!"

"Yeah, great," I scoff. "Making her the forbidden fruit I'll never be able to have is such a gift."

Her brows furrow. "What happened to 'we'll deal with that when the time comes'? What happened to that?"

"What happened is neither one of us knew the gravity of the fucking choice we were making!"

She huffs. "So, what was the last few weeks? Just something to fill your time before I leave for college?"

I groan, looking away. "Oh, don't give me that. I saw it on your face yesterday. When push came to shove, you were always going to pick your dad."

"You don't know that!"

"Then tell me I'm wrong!"

She looks like she wants to strangle me as she shakes her head and turns toward the window, leaving me completely unanswered.

"You can't," I tell her. "You can't, because you know as well as I do that he holds so much more importance than I do."

"But that doesn't mean you're not important. He's my dad,

Cade. He's the only parent I've had for as long as I can remember."

"And me?"

She laughs dryly. "You're the guy that's yelling at me after I did something nice for you."

I blow out a long exhale. "You're right, I'm sorry. But can't you see how fucked up this is that you even had to do that?"

"I was just trying to help," she says.

"Help a guy who doesn't fucking deserve it!" My blood is boiling, my teeth grinding together. "If I were to get the revenge I'm looking for, if I break our parents up just to put mine together and your dad gets hurt in the process, what then? Who would you really choose if it came down to it?"

"I don't know!" she shouts. "But clearly you have no faith in this going anywhere at all, so go! Get out!"

No part of me wants to leave, but let's be real. It's for the best, isn't it? Like Bryce so nicely pointed out last night—we never stood a chance anyway, so better it ends now.

I look at Lennon, seeing her so detached and withdrawn from me as she stares out the window. "Whatever."

My feet carry me out the door, and I slam it behind me, but as soon as the piece of wood separates us, I stop. Turning around, I grip the doorway with both hands and my head drops. I take a few deep breaths.

The door opens, and Lennon stands there with a fire in her eyes like I've never seen. I step forward and wrap her in my arms, covering her mouth with my own and kicking the door shut behind me. Her tongue tangles with mine as our hands grip and grab anything we can.

With my hands under her ass, I lift her up and pin her against the wall. A breathy moan flows out of her mouth. Just like that, I'm rock hard in record speed. Over the last couple weeks, this would be the time I back away, but no part of me plans on stopping now. Not if I'm going to lose her. Not if there's a point where she's no longer mine.

No, I'm going to take every piece of her she's willing to give.

Lennon grinds down on my clothed cock, and I groan at the contact. I move my mouth to her neck, licking and sucking at the sensitive skin. Her breathing is heavy, but in a way that tells me she's just as turned on as I am.

She pulls my shirt over my head and pushes me back. I watch in awe as she stands there, completely in control and confident while stripping down to nothing. If there was any hesitation in my mind, it's gone the second her gaze meets mine.

She wants this. *Wants me.*

In one swift move, I grab her and toss her onto the bed. My face dives down between her legs on a mission to finally taste her in the one spot I've been craving since the moment she all but tried to fight me on the beach.

My tongue grazes the bundle of nerves, and her sweet juices meet my taste buds. She gasps, gripping the bedsheets with one hand while she uses her other to lace her fingers into my hair. This girl may be a virgin, but I'm about to create a fucking monster.

I tease her clit over and over until she's quivering beneath me. As I slip one finger inside, I can already tell—this girl is going to be my fucking undoing. A single digit and she's already clenching around me.

"Take your shorts off," she demands. "And then lay on the bed."

Normally, I'm the one in control, but no part of me is about to deny her. Not here and certainly not now. I do exactly as she says and watch as she reaches into her nightstand and pulls out a condom.

I chuckle. "Where did you get that?"

She shrugs with a proud smile. "Tessa gave me a box for my birthday. I figured I may as well hold onto them."

I go to take it from her but she pulls it away.

"No, I want to do it."

My hands move to the back of my head. "Then by all means, don't let me stop you."

She rips it open and throws the wrapper on the floor before sliding it over my cock like she's practiced this a million times over. Just her touch has me threatening to explode right here and now, but I didn't get this far only to cum like a preteen.

Her one leg comes over my hips and she hovers above me, lining me up at her entrance. My gaze locks with hers, and she bites her lip before sinking down just slightly. Even just an inch is the tightest thing I've ever felt in my life. She's never been touched, and I'm nowhere near small.

"Baby," I breathe, wishing she'd go faster.

"Fuck," she murmurs and winces at the contact.

At a torturously slow speed, she starts to move, with only the tip dipping inside her but it's nowhere near enough. I need her. More than surfing. More than air. More than life. I fucking *need* her.

I grip her hips and flip us around so she's lying beneath me. "Please don't hate me for this."

In one harsh thrust, I shove myself inside of her and feel as her hymen snaps. She shrieks, but I swallow it down with a heated kiss. I don't stop to let her adjust, don't ask her how she's doing or if she's okay. I can't. My only focus is how good she feels wrapped around my dick, like she was made just for me.

It only takes a couple more movements before her heels dig into my back and she's egging me on.

"That feels so good," she moans against my lips.

I pull away just slightly and slide my hand down to where I know she's most sensitive. "You haven't felt anything yet."

The second I apply just the slightest pressure, her head lolls back and she pushes her chest forward. I bend down and suck one of her nipples into my mouth while my hand works its magic and my cock fills her entirely. I can tell by the way she starts to arch into my touch that she's getting close.

"Don't fight it, babe," I tell her. "Let it own you. Let it rip you apart. Give me everything you've got."

She screams out as her nails dig into my back, and she tightens like a vice grip around me. Her whole body is trembling as I ride her through it, finding my own high right along with her. I explode into the condom for what feels like ages until I finally collapse down on top of her. The only sound that fills the room is our labored breathing as we both recover from sexual euphoria.

"I'm sorry," I say as I pull out, realizing I may have slightly lost control.

She shakes her head. "Apologize for everything else you've done today, but do not apologize for that."

I sit beside her and look down at the way she's all splayed out. Her hair is fanned out above her head and there might even be some bruises forming on her hips, but she's got the biggest smile on her face.

"So, you don't hate me?" I ask.

Rolling her eyes, she chuckles. "Oh, I hate you. I've hated you since the day I met you. But I've tried the whole keeping my distance thing. Never worked out."

The corners of my mouth raise until I realize the predicament we're still in. I can't have both revenge and Lennon, not without her never speaking to me again. But I also don't think I'm willing to lose her. This started as a scheme—a way to get exactly what I was looking for and have a little fun in the process—but she's become so much more.

I'm fucked.

26

LENNON

THEY SAY THAT WHEN YOU LOSE YOUR VIRGINITY, you feel different. Older. Sexier. More mature. It's all true. I may not look any different, or at least I don't think I do, but I feel it. Colors are brighter. Mornings are happier. Dreams are more erotic.

"I'm telling you, I feel like everything has changed."

Tessa rolls her eyes. "It's only because you saved it for so long. Trust me. I lost my v-card at sixteen, and I didn't feel anything like that."

"Who did you lose it to?"

"Jace London." Her lip curls up in disgust.

"Seriously?"

She cringes and nods. "Not my brightest choice, but it wasn't the worst experience in the world."

"I'm just a little disappointed it wasn't me," Colby jokes. "That's about as close to commitment as I'm ever going to get."

I cock a brow. "Since when is taking someone's virginity a commitment?"

"Are you kidding? Girls get dicked and they're picking out napkin colors for the wedding by the next week."

Tessa snorts. "What kind of girls do you hook up with?"

"Crazy ones," Asher and I reply in unison.

Colby pretends to be mad as he waves us off and gets up. "Forget you guys." He heads for the ocean. "Yo, Cadeycake! Teach me how to surf."

Cade looks Colby up and down, then glances over at me. I chuckle and shake my head.

"Don't hurt him, and I'll pay you for it later," I yell.

A grin stretches across his face, and he gestures for Colby to come with him. Just before they reach the water, he turns around.

"If he drowns, I can't be held accountable."

I giggle and watch as the two of them dive into the incoming wave. Meanwhile, Tessa is staring at me with a prideful glint in her eyes.

"What?" I ask.

She puts her hands up defensively. "Nothing, it's just maybe you're right. Sex changed you."

"That's what I'm saying!"

I lean back in my chair and pull my sunglasses into place, watching as Cade shows off by making tricks with his surfboard look easy. Even if losing my virginity hasn't changed me, being with him certainly has. And I couldn't be happier.

HAVING TO PRETEND TO have nothing to do with Cade in front of our parents is one thing I really wish I didn't have to do. Figures, I can't stand him when my dad wants us to spend time together, but when all I want to do is be near him, my dad wants me as far away as humanly possible. Could my luck get any worse?

Usually, Cade sneaks into my room after everyone is in bed and sneaks out in the morning before sunrise. It allows us to spend the night together and minimizes the risk of getting caught. This morning, however, I wake up to a knock at my door and Cade still sound asleep in my bed.

My eyes shoot open, and I panic for a moment before going over to answer the door. "I'm not decent."

"Are you okay?" Nora calls back.

Fuck. I pull the door open just a crack but make sure not to let her see past me. "Yeah. I'm just waking up. Is everything okay?"

She looks unsure. "I can't find Cade. He's not in his room but his Jeep is in the driveway."

I run my fingers through my hair. "I think I heard him on the phone with Bryce yesterday, talking about being picked up before sunrise to go surfing."

"Oh," she says. "I guess that would explain why he hasn't been answering his phone."

I smile. "Yep, just probably in the water."

It looks like she's finally about to head back down the stairs and I mentally relax, but she catches me off guard at the last minute.

"Oh, you know I should probably grab your laundry for Melani while I'm up here. She's been complaining about that issue with her hip."

Before I have a chance to stop her, she comes through the door. My breath hitches as I slowly turn around, but as I look back at my bed, Cade is no longer in it.

What the fuck?

She grabs my laundry basket and leaves with a friendly smile sent my way. I grab the door and swing it closed, when the sight of Cade standing behind it scares the crap out of me.

"Oh my God," I gasp, clutching my chest and feeling as my heart pounds against my ribcage. "Don't do that!"

He chuckles and wraps me in his arms. "I'm sorry."

"We almost got caught."

"But we didn't."

"We could have."

He pulls me closer and drops down until his lips meet my own. "But, we didn't."

All the fight I had against him leaves, and all that's left is the way he makes me feel when we're alone—when there isn't someone watching to make sure we keep a certain distance or looking at us funny for seeming too close.

"I wish we didn't have to hide," I whisper.

He sighs. "Me, too."

Since the argument that led to us having sex for the first time, we haven't talked about anything that has to do with my dad. Not how he wants me to keep my distance. Not how Cade plans on getting his parents back together. We've just focused on enjoying the time we can together, no matter how little it is.

"I have to get ready for dance, but are you picking me up after?"

He nods. "I'll be there."

With another kiss and a panty-dropping smile, he goes over to the window and climbs out to where the tree rests against it. He climbs down like Tarzan, swinging from limb to limb with his muscles flexing in all the right places. Then, he walks in the front door like he just got home.

Such a menace.

THE CHOREOGRAPHY THAT SAVANNAH, Brady and I have put together is like nothing I've ever done before. Somehow, we managed to mix different styles of dance into one, and I can't wait to perform it in a few weeks at the recital. I was supposed to leave for Juilliard a couple weeks early, just to get ready and really learn the area, but Sav assured me there's no point and convinced me to stay here.

"Sav, that kick could be straighter."

She whips her head around. "Brady, *you* could be straighter."

As soon as the words leave her mouth, I am a fit of giggles and can barely concentrate on what I'm doing. Brady, however, doesn't miss a beat.

"Eh, I kind of tried that when I fake dated you for nearly half a decade. You scared me off women for life."

Savannah mocks him with her face. "Ha ha, you're such a comedian."

The song ends and all of us nail the final move. We're exhausted, that much is obvious, but the second I notice Cade standing in the doorway, I perk up. He looks like he was watching us for a while, with the way he's so casually leaning there.

"Ayo, your boyfriend's back," Sav teases.

My eyes widen as I realize she just said the "b" word and we've never talked about labels. Cade chuckles and steps up behind me.

"Your boyfriend, huh?"

I swallow hard. "I never said that. She's just...I didn't...Ugh!"

That makes him laugh. "Relax, babe. I'm kidding."

He kisses me hello, not caring who's watching. Then again, he probably knows that I tell Brady and Savannah everything, and being as I've been here every day rehearsing, they're bound to have heard it all by now.

"Ready to go?"

I nod and walk over to grab my bag. When I go to leave, Brady calls out.

"You'll be here tomorrow, right?" he asks.

"Yes," I respond. "But I won't be here—"

"Saturday, because your boyfriend has a surfing competition," he cuts me off. "Yes, we know."

I wince at that word again but mask it with a smile. Cade

drapes his arm over my shoulders and leads me out the door. When we climb into his Jeep, he gives me a strange look. I'm not sure what to make of it, so instead of overthinking it, I ask him.

"What?"

He eyes me suspiciously again. "Why do you do that?"

"Do what?" I question, and I couldn't be more confused.

"Squirm when someone says the word boyfriend."

Oh. I take a breath to ease my nerves. "We just never talk about titles, so I wasn't sure exactly how you feel about them."

He gives me a look that makes me want the ground to swallow me whole. One that makes me question if I was thinking we're becoming something that we're not. After what feels like an eternity, he starts laughing.

"My God, you're uptight today." He leans over and kisses me quickly. "You're the only girl I want anything to do with. I think that would make you my girlfriend, don't you?"

A light blush coats my cheeks. "Okay."

He puts the car in drive and pulls away, snickering at my shy reaction. "I have an appointment to get a tattoo. Do you want me to drop you off at home, or do you want to come with?"

The idea of Cade's perfect body being inked with tattoos is enough to make me want to fuck him in the backseat. He's already hot, even without any, but I've always thought they were hot.

"Is that even a question? I want to come."

His grin widens, and he makes a right instead of a left. He reaches toward me and interlaces his fingers with mine. It's such a simple gesture, but one that I don't take for granted. There aren't many times we're able to do this—none when we're at home, if we're not in my room—and I just want to enjoy it while I can.

"So, what are you going to get?" I ask him.

He rubs his thumb back and forth over my hand. "A wave on my biceps."

"Fitting."

I don't think I could pick a more Cade tattoo than that, unless of course it was a surfboard. Speaking of surfing...

"Is it going to be healed in time for competition?"

He shrugs. "Not entirely, but it'll be at the point where I can get it wet at least."

I graze my free hand over his arm. "Won't it be sore though?"

Glancing over at me, he narrows his eyes playfully. "What are you trying to say? That I'm weak?"

"You said it, not me," I tease.

If anyone else were to say that to him, he'd probably punch them or at the very least get an attitude, but with me, he just smiles even more. He pulls up to the tattoo place and parks the car.

"You know, you weren't saying that last night when I held you up and—"

The rest of his words are inaudible as I cover his mouth with my hand. My eyes widen as I look around to make sure no one is around. With the top down, anyone could hear us.

"Shut up, jerk." I swat at his chest.

He sticks his tongue out. "I'm just saying."

We climb out of the car and walk into the tattoo place, but now I've got memories of last night playing vividly in my mind. Somehow the conversation of fantasies came up, and I mentioned how I always thought the idea of having sex against the wall was hot.

Needless to say, he stripped us both down to nothing and did exactly that. The feeling of how deep he got in that position was out of this world, and my stomach is still tender from the onslaught. I may have had to spend extra time this morning covering the hickey on my neck with makeup, but it was worth it.

I LOOK AROUND THE room at all the different tattoos while the artist works on Cade. When I come across the case of belly button rings, I stop. They all look so pretty. Every color imaginable is in there—one to go with every skin color and every outfit. I turn to the mirror next to me and lift up my shirt, wondering what it would look like.

"Thinking about getting it done?" Cade asks.

I shrug. "Do you think it would look good?"

He snorts. "Seriously? Lennon, you could make a parka look hot."

The owner looks up from Cade's tattoo and over at me. "I can do it right after this if you want."

"That quickly?"

He nods. "You're over eighteen, right?"

"Yeah," I answer hesitantly.

"Then yeah, it's that easy."

Bringing my attention back to the case, a pink sparkly one catches my eye. Brady would probably kill me, since I wouldn't be able to take it out before the recital, but it would probably be healed enough by then for it not to bother me.

My eyes find Cade's, who's being nothing but supportive and allowing me to make this decision on my own.

"Will you hold my hand?"

He throws his head back, laughing. "Yes, you big baby."

As I realize what I'm about to do, I start to see why my dad thinks Cade is a bad influence on me—but man do I fucking love it.

THE SUN BEATS DOWN on us as we all sit on the beach. Surfers from all around the West Coast are here, ready to compete for the top spot. Cade claims he isn't nervous, but he's been waxing his board for the past half hour, making sure it's perfect.

Waves taller than my house come crashing toward the shore. They're so big that they have a jetski to bring the surfers out to where they need to be. They wait off to the side, on standby for anyone who wipes out and needs help being brought back to shore.

Tessa pokes at my belly button that's still sore. "I can't believe you did it."

I look over at her through my sunglasses. "It wasn't that bad."

She rolls her eyes. "Well, I know that. I have mine done. I just didn't think you had the guts."

"Oh, thanks."

Laughter bellows out of her. "Oh, hush. I didn't mean it like that. You just don't really seem like the type to do something your dad obviously wouldn't approve of."

My brows raise. "You mean like date my stepbrother?"

Her lips purse, and she tilts her head to the side. "Yeah, kind of like that. I take it back. I don't know you at all."

"You just better hope it's healed in time," Savannah tells me. "Brady isn't the only one who will kick your ass if it's not."

I give her the sweetest smile I can manage. "But then who would join you in New York?"

Grayson wraps his arm around her and pulls her in. "She doesn't need you. She has me."

"Are you kidding? She's going to be my excuse to get a break from you," Sav jokes.

As we all chuckle at their banter, I get up and walk over to Cade. He's sitting far enough away to be able to focus but close enough to where we don't all think he's avoiding us. I plop down in the sand next to him.

"All good?"

He pulls one earbud out of his ear and hands it to me, then pulls me into his lap. "I'm better now."

THREE ROUNDS LATER, CADE is in the finals. It's down to him and one other guy. My heart is in my throat as I watch the two of them paddle out. I've been to over a hundred competitions for dance, but this is the most nervous I think I've ever been. Winning this could be huge for him.

The air horn sounds, giving them the alert to start surfing. They each get one wave, and they're scored on how they do. I'd like to say that Cade has this in the bag, but I've been watching the guy he's against this whole competition. Honestly, it could go either way.

They both let the first one pass them by, but the second, the other guy takes. He paddles into the wave while Cade stays back. I watch closely as he stands up and rides it with ease. It's graceful and talented. He spins the board in a trick Bryce told me but I honestly forgot the name of. Dread fills my stomach as I worry about Cade losing.

With one last trick needing to be done, he goes to do a noseride but loses his balance and crashes hard into the water. The entire crowd hisses at the painful-looking way his board flips around. One things for sure, this water is dangerous and not somewhere you should go if you're not an experienced surfer.

It's all down to Cade now, with his competition losing major points for wiping out. He sits on his board, with his hand in the water, waiting for the perfect wave. That's one thing that has always amazed me about him—his ability to read the ocean like the back of his hand. If I didn't think he would be offended, I'd call him Moana.

My nerves build even more as he turns around and starts to paddle into a wave. It's probably one of the biggest all day, and if he wipes out on this, there's a chance he may not get out unscathed. Even the announcer sounds surprised that he's taking the wave at all.

Tessa grabs my hand as we stand next to Bryce and Jayden. Even they look nervous at the whole thing, but there's nothing we can do but trust him.

Cade catches the wave and jumps up on his board, riding it down and keeping his footing. It curls over into the perfect barrel, and he disappears out of sight.

"Barrels are tricky," Bryce murmurs. "There's no guarantee they won't break before you get out of them."

I squeeze Tessa's hand and wait with anticipation for Cade to appear out the other end. When he finally does, I can't control my screams, and neither can his friends. Everyone on the beach cheers in celebration as he masterfully hits all three of the required tricks—making him the clear champion of the competition.

"And Cade Knight officially takes the win!"

The second he gets to the shore, I run toward him. He drops his board just in time to catch me as I leap into his arms. My legs wrap around his waist, my arms around his neck. The two of us hold each other as everyone else swarms around.

I hear people saying they're from Billabong, Quicksilver, and other huge names, but right now, Cade seems to only have eyes for me. Bryce brings over the trophy and hands it to Cade with the biggest smile on his face. Cade lifts it up into the air and presses his lips to mine.

I've never been so proud.

OKAY, SO LET'S BE real for a minute. Cade is gorgeous even on his worst day. But tonight, after winning the biggest competition of his life and being offered more than five sponsorships in the matter of a few hours, he's genuinely the happiest I've ever seen him. His grin is a mile wide and hasn't seemed to leave his face since the beach.

It only took Bryce and Jayden a matter of minutes to throw together a celebration party, and Colby was even nice enough to let us have it at his house. There's something about no parents that makes it all that much better.

"Bust It Open" by Lil Wil booms through the speakers. I'm standing with Tessa and Savannah when Tess glances behind me and smiles.

"Now that's a sight."

I turn around to find Cade and Bryce, chest to chest and in each other's faces as they sing the crude lyrics to the song. Both of them sport smiles that could make any girl flustered. It's hot as hell, and something I could watch all night long.

Savannah loops her arm with my own. "I always knew the guy you'd end up with would be hot, but damn."

I chuckle. "He's all right."

MY FEET, AND MY stomach for that matter, are killing me from dance. Maybe getting my belly button pierced wasn't exactly the best idea while still having to bend in ways that stretch every part of my torso.

I walk in the house to find Cade sitting in the living room, with my Dad. Last time I checked, Cade had meetings today with some sponsors to talk details, so the fact that he's even home right now instantly has me on high alert.

"Lennon," my dad says. "Get in here."

My brows furrow as I drop my dance bag on the stairs and go to join them. "Is everything okay?"

My dad looks like he's ready to strangle someone with his bare hands. He pulls a magazine out of his back pocket and slams it down onto the coffee table. It's not one I'd ever expect him to read, but the picture on the cover has me ready to vomit on the spot. Front and center is Cade and me, with a trophy raised in the air and our lips pressed firmly together with happy smiles on our faces.

"One of you, explain. *Now*."

27

CADE

KEN PACES BACK AND FORTH IN FRONT OF US WHILE neither Lennon or I say a word. What could we say? That nothing happened? It's right there, for the whole world to see. Even my mom makes sure to stay far away from this room.

This isn't how today was supposed to go. I was supposed to spend the afternoon talking to sponsors and tonight taking Lennon out to dinner to talk to her about what we plan on doing when she leaves for New York in a couple weeks.

Instead, my mom rescheduled my meetings and hid my car keys. How fucking nice of her. Like she hasn't done enough to ruin my life already.

I glance over at Lennon. Her face is pale, paler than usual, and she looks like she's about to cry. I know we've said that when the time comes where someone finds out about us, we'd deal with it together. But now that it's actually here, I can't let her go through this.

"Sir," I force myself to be respectful. "This is my doing. Lennon said no at first, but I was persistent. I'm sorry."

Lennon's head whips my way. "What are you doing?"

Ken glares at me, mentally shooting daggers. "You seduced my daughter?"

"I wouldn't say I seduced her, but I started having feelings for her and I acted on them."

He scoffs. "This is an outrage. You two are brother and sister!"

Lennon cringes and I can't help but laugh.

"Not really," I reply. "You and my mother aren't married. Technically, Lennon and I aren't related at all."

Reaching into his pocket, he takes out his phone and tosses it to me. A picture of them celebrating with a ring on my mom's finger stares back at me, and now it's my turn to feel sick.

"Y-you're engaged?" Lennon whispers.

"We were going to share the news tonight, until I went to get coffee this morning and saw your PDA all over the front cover of a goddamn magazine." He focuses on his daughter. "How could you be so naive? What am I supposed to tell people when it gets out that Lennon Bradwell had an affair with her stepbrother?"

She drops her head again, and I instantly hate the way she cowers to him. I try to pull the attention off her and back to me.

"Don't yell at her."

His eyes lock on me. "Don't you dare try and tell me what to do."

Okay, enough of this shit. "Last time I checked, Lennon is eighteen years old and can do whatever the hell she pleases."

"Yeah?" He crosses his arms over his chest and stands tall. "Well not in my house she can't."

Fuck. "What? You're just going to kick her out?"

He chuckles humorlessly. "No. That would create even more of a scandal. You, on the other hand, are no longer welcome in my house."

"Dad, no!" Lennon shrieks but he isn't listening.

"Pack your shit, Cade," he tells me. "I want you gone within the hour."

"Dad!"

He pays her no mind as he finalizes his decision by walking out the door. As I get up and go toward my room, I find my mom at the bottom of the stairs. It's clear she's upset, but she isn't defending me.

"You're seriously just going to let him kick me out like that?"

She sighs. "You got involved with his daughter, Cade. What do you expect me to do?"

I scoff. "Oh, I don't know. Maybe be a fucking mother for once since you met him."

Pushing past her, I go upstairs to start packing my shit. I pull a couple duffle bags out of my closet and throw everything I can fit into it. All my clothes. All my surfing trophies. The picture of Bryce, Jayden, and I from when we were younger that sits on my nightstand.

"You're leaving?" Molly's voice sounds from my doorway.

My motions halt, and I look over to find her staring at me, her eyes wet with tears. I sigh heavily and walk over to her, dropping down so we're level with each other.

"Yeah," I break the news softly. "I'm going to go stay at Dad's for a bit."

A tear escapes and slips down her cheek. "Take me with you."

"I wish I could, Mollz, but you have to stay with Mom."

She wraps her arms around me tightly and begins to sob. I hold her close, just letting her cry it out. Fuck Ken for doing this to her, and fuck my mom for not doing anything about it. I can't wait until the day Molly turns eighteen. At least then, she'll be able to come with me anywhere.

Pulling away, I wipe her tears and stand up. It's hard, knowing I'm leaving my baby sister with the wolves, but what other choice do I have?

I grab the bags from my bed and go downstairs. Ken watches me from the door of his office with a nasty scowl on his face. Just as I reach the door, Lennon calls my name. I stop and turn around, finding her at the top of the stairs.

"Lennon," her father says her name as a warning.

She ignores him entirely and runs down the stairs. "Take me with you."

"Lennon!" he roars.

Turning toward him, she glares. "I wasn't talking to you."

Her gaze meets mine once again. She's waiting patiently for my answer, but the words get caught in my throat. This is it. The moment I always swore she would pick her dad. And instead, she's standing here, in front of him, picking me.

But I can't let her do that.

I can't let her give up the only family she has, when all I've wanted is to put mine back together. I know what it's like to feel like you have no one, and I won't do that to her.

"I'm sorry, but no."

At the sound of my words, all hope drains from her face. "What?"

I shake my head and look away. "I can't take you with me. You belong here. You have your entire life ahead of you, and you need your dad to be a part of it."

"Cade," she cries. "Don't do this."

"It's already done. I'm sorry."

I take a step toward her and kiss her forehead. Molly watches confused, but she seems more sad than anything. I nudge her with my elbow, since my hands are full, and give her the best grin I can manage. She opens the door for me, and I walk out of the house for the last time.

Thankfully, the top is still down from when I went surfing this morning, so I'm able to toss my bags into the back without any issue—except for the one with the trophies. That one gets a little more care.

"Wait!" Lennon shouts.

She comes running out the door, with tears soaking her face, and stands in front of me—no longer the strong hard-ass I've seen so often. No. This Lennon is different. Vulnerable. Scared.

"Len, go back inside."

"No." Her shoulders sag in defeat. "You can't leave. Not without me."

I exhale, wishing this was easier. "I can, and I am."

As I turn to get in the Jeep, she calls my name again. "I love you."

Fuck. Hearing her say those three little words isn't something I expected. Even more unexpected, is how they make me feel. It's not the first time someone has said that to me, but it's certainly the first time I've wanted to say it back.

But it doesn't change anything. She's still better off here—without me—and she's not going to accept that unless I give her a reason to.

"What do you want me to say?" I ask with an obvious attitude. "That I love you? That you mean everything to me? That I'd die without you? Come on, Len. You can't possibly believe anyone ever means that shit."

Her bottom lip quivers, making me feel like even more of an asshole. "But you...we—"

"We were never going to be anything serious."

Not being able to stand looking at how broken she looks anymore, I climb into the Jeep and shut the door. As I reverse out of the space, the car lines up right next to her. She's crying, but won't even look at me.

"I'm sorry," I murmur, and then pull out of the driveway.

I can see in the rear view mirror as Lennon follows me out of the driveway and out into the street. Molly runs out and goes to run after my car, but Lennon catches her and holds her close—the two of them breaking down together.

The pain that rips through my chest as soon as I'm out of sight is one that threatens to take me over the edge. It's raw, and real, and makes all my dad's drinking totally understandable. Hell, I'd do it too if it meant not feeling this, and I was the one to push her away. I can't imagine what it would feel like if she left me after twenty years for another guy.

I turn onto the highway and head for my dad's, hoping he's not passed out drunk on the floor when I get there. I'm not in the mood to deal with his shit today.

THE HOUSE IS EMPTY when I pull into the driveway. Even my dad's car is nowhere to be found, which probably means he's out drinking. Wonderful.

I grab my things out of the back of the car and bring them into my room. This must be a record, moving out and moving back in the matter of a couple months. I'd like to say I should have just stayed here to begin with, and a small part of me believes that, but then I wouldn't have had those few weeks with Lennon where everything was perfect.

My phone dings with an email from one of the sponsors, telling me that he had to leave California on business but that he'd like to meet when he gets back—next month. Great. Could this day get any worse?

I fall back on my bed and close my eyes, trying to remember how I felt on Saturday—when I had everything. The girl. The trophy. The future.

Now, I'm just a shithead who lost it all.

I'M SITTING ON THE couch when the door opens and my dad walks in. Every part of me expects slurring words and stumbling, but to my surprise, he's sober. Stone cold sober.

"Hey, buddy," he greets me. "What brings you here?"

"Where were you?"

"I had a job interview."

Relief floods through me. The house may still be a mess, and everything may be a total wreck, but he's not. He's okay, or at least as okay as he can be right now.

"Y-you're sober."

He looks down at the floor, obviously embarrassed. "Yeah. I haven't had a drink in a little over a week, after your girlfriend dropped off eighty grand like it was a normal thing to do."

My heart hurts at the mention of Lennon. "I just thought..."

"That I would spend it all on booze?" he finishes for me as he puts his keys on the counter. "I thought about it, and a part of me wanted to. But I hired a therapist instead."

"A therapist?" I have to keep myself from laughing at even the idea of that.

He comes over and sits down on the loveseat. "Yeah, I know, but she really helped get through to me. She helped me understand that while what your mother and I had was great, if it was still what I pictured in my head, if it was real and meant to be, she wouldn't have been able to walk away. Another guy would never have been an issue."

I can't help myself. A chuckle bubbles out at the irony of it all. "Seriously? Sounds like a crock of shit."

My dad shrugs and leans back. "It makes sense to me."

"So, you're okay with the divorce now? You agree with it?"

"Not exactly," he answers honestly. "I don't agree with it. She cheated on me for months before she finally told me she was leaving, and that's wrong. But she wasn't happy, and I want her to be happy."

I sigh, not sure if I feel relieved or ticked off. "I spent the whole summer trying to figure out a way to get the two of you back together."

"Cade," he says sadly. "I never wanted that for you. You're

nineteen. My relationship with your mother isn't your problem to fix."

"I wanted to do it for Molly. She deserves to have two parents, in the same house. Healthy, sober, and happy."

"But we wouldn't have been happy, son, and it took a little bit for me to realize that, but once I did, it all became clear."

My mind goes to Lennon. How she looks when she smiles. The way she would kiss me back in the morning before I snuck out of her room, even being half asleep. And lastly, how devastated she was as I drove away.

The familiar pain inches up again. "Did it help? The drinking?"

My dad shrugs. "For a bit. It doused the fire enough for it to be tolerable, but it never lasted." He gets up from the couch "I'm going to order a pizza. Are you staying for a bit?"

I should tell him everything that happened, but he seems like he's in such a good mood and I'd hate to ruin that. Instead, I force a smile on my face.

"Yeah, definitely."

He smiles at me and goes into the other room to order. Meanwhile, I get up, walking over to the liquor cabinet and finding a bottle of vodka tucked away in the back. I unscrew the cap and bring it to my lips.

Just to dull the pain.

28

LENNON

One of the best things about dancing is it requires your total concentration. Any distraction, any topic other than what moves you're currently doing and how you're going to follow them up, they all have no place in the studio. It's like my own personal safe haven...that is, when Brady and Savannah aren't looking at me like I'm from outer space.

I stop mid-dance and turn to face them. "Can you stop? I can't focus with the two of you whispering and looking at me like I'm going to break down without a moment's notice."

Brady turns off the music while Savannah sighs. A sad smile forms on her face.

"We're just really worried about you."

I look away, willing myself not to break. Not again. "I'm fine."

"Lennon," she presses. "You and Cade broke up, and you ran away from home to live with Colby all in the same twenty-four hours. It's all right if you're not okay."

"I said I'm fine," I snap. "Now, can we rehearse? This recital is in two weeks, and I'm not trying to look like I don't know what I'm doing."

Sav and Brady share a look, but neither of them dares to say anything else.

It's been four days since everything went to shit, and I haven't heard a single word from Cade. If I cared, I'd ask Molly if she's talked to him, but that would require being at home—something I've refused to do since my dad kicked him out.

I tried to deal with it. I tried to swallow my pride, keep my head down, and ignore the gaping hole in everything I did, but I couldn't. Only mere hours after ruining everything for me, my dad demanded we have family dinner. As I sat at the table, watching my dad and Nora interact like there wasn't a seat that shouldn't be empty, I knew I had to leave.

I went upstairs, packed a bag, and walked out the door—never looking back.

Colby was nice enough to take me in, even though I still think I'm ruining his bachelor pad. He promised me that his guest room is mine for as long as I need it, which should only be a few more weeks. I've always been excited to get to New York, but now, it's like I can't wait for it. I crave leaving this town and everything in it like never before.

I FLOP DOWN ONTO the couch, laying my head in Colby's lap. He chuckles and puts his phone down to run his fingers through my hair. After getting home from dance, I'm exhausted.

"You look like you need a nap," he tells me.

I groan. "Yeah, but I can't have one. Tessa is on her way over. I promised her a girl's night."

He tips his head, a quizzical look on his face. "And you're not going there, why?"

"Because then I'd need a ride back in the middle of the night when we've finally had enough of each other." I backtrack for a second. "Unless you need me out of the house. Did you plan on having someone over? Am I interrupting?"

He snickers and shakes his head. "Relax. You're fine. I don't have any plans."

I exhale. "Okay, good."

It's funny, because being in this position with him, we look like a couple—and there was a point in time where I kind of wished we were one, but not now. Ever since being with Cade, I learned that the feelings I have for Colby aren't of the romantic kind. He's my best friend. My protector. The older brother I never had. But he's not the guy I'm meant to be with.

After Cade left me and my shattered heart in the driveway, I knew I had two choices. I could mope around like I didn't know what to do with myself, or I could pick up the pieces and move on. Well, the first one never did anything good for anyone, and I'm not the kind to throw pity parties.

The doorbell rings, and I whine at the fact that I have to get up to answer the door. Colby's lap is comfortable, and I've always been a sucker for people playing with my hair. It rings again as I approach and I huff in exasperation.

"Jesus, Tess. I'm coming." I pull open the door. "Why are you even ringing the b—"

My words get cut off as I realize the person standing outside the door isn't Tess at all, but Cade. He sports a sheepish look on his face, and I find myself wanting to smack it right off him.

"What are you doing here?"

He flinches at my tone, only for Colby to answer for him. "I invited him."

I turn around and glare at my former best friend. "Why the fuck would you do that?"

"Can we just talk?" Cade asks. "Please?"

Colby gestures for me to go. I roll my eyes and step

outside, slamming the door behind me—just to let them both know exactly how mad I am. Cade walks down the driveway and leans against his car, but I make sure to stay at least a few feet away. Enough to keep me from falling right back into his arms.

"You look good," he tells me.

I scoff. "And you look like shit."

He purses his lips. "I feel like shit. Hell, I am shit." He takes a step forward only for me to take one back. "I should have never left you like that. I'm sorry."

"You're sorry?" I balk. "You gave me so much shit about how if push came to shove, you didn't think I'd pick you. I fucking picked you! I trusted you, took the leap, and fell flat on my face."

"I know, but I was trying to do what's best for you." His hand comes up and rubs the back of his neck. "I couldn't be the reason you lost your family. Not when I've been struggling for months about losing mine."

I fold my arms against my chest and snort. "Then what the hell was the point to all this?" My pulse is racing, and I stop to take a breath. "You know what, I don't care. You made your choice."

He looks shocked by the fact that I'm not forgiving him. Not this time. "But you said..."

"I know what I said," I snap. "But you can't possibly believe anyone ever means that shit."

With his own words spit back in his face, he puts a hand to his chest. Tessa gets out of her car and comes over, looking confused.

"Is everything okay?" she asks.

I cross my arms in front of my chest. "Yeah. Cade was just leaving."

There's nothing left to say. Not after I was willing to give up everything for him and he threw me away like garbage. He can say he was doing it for my own wellbeing all he wants, but I'm not buying it.

I turn around and walk back inside, this time being the one to leave him standing alone in a driveway.

THE RECITAL IS ONLY a week away, so rehearsals become twice as long and three times as often. The dance we're doing is complex and with it being the last one we'll ever do for this studio, it needs to be perfect.

I'm in the middle of a pirouette when someone outside the studio catches my eye. I spin around again but fall out of sync the second I realize how familiar they look. It's an older woman, a little younger than my dad, with blonde hair and blue eyes. When I realize where I know her from, my breath hitches.

"Lennon?" Savannah asks. "Is everything all right?"

I shake my head and my jaw ticks. "Oh, hell no."

Brady and Sav follow behind me as I storm out of the room and burst through the front doors. The woman's eyes widen as she sees how angry I am, but this is not the time for this shit. Not now. Not after being gone for fifteen fucking years.

"You need to leave," I demand.

She sighs. "I know, and if that's what you really want me to do, I deserve it, but I had to come see you."

I snort sarcastically. "What, now that it's convenient for you? What happened? Did your other family not love you enough? Did you fucking walk out on them, too?"

She jerks back in shock. "I didn't walk out on you. Lennon, your dad—"

"Don't! My dad is the one who took care of me my whole life! The one who held me at three years old when I cried my eyes out because Mommy wasn't coming back! Don't you dare say anything about him to me."

She winces and her eyes fill with tears, but I'm not falling for it. I step back and find comfort between Savannah and Brady. My mother nods as she realizes I want no part of her and whatever the hell caused her to come here.

"Okay, I'm sorry. I'll leave," she says. "But I really hope one day you learn the truth of why I left. You deserve that much."

"What I deserved was a mother who stayed, no matter what."

I wipe a stray tear away from my face, because she doesn't get to watch me cry. Brady leads us back inside, while Savannah holds me close. They take me into the office, where no one from the outside can see, and I finally come crumbling down. From the shit with Cade. To my dad. To now my long-lost mother appearing out of the blue.

It's all too much.

I STEP IN MY house for the first time in over a week. Everything looks the same, but it's different. It lacks the comforting feeling I always got when I was here. All the memories that fill this place from when I was a child until now, and not a single one feels significant anymore.

My dad steps out of his office, and when he sees me, his eyes soften. "Lennon, thank God." He rushes over to hug me, and for a moment, I let him. "I tried calling you over a hundred times. I was worried sick."

I shrug. "Honestly, I didn't want to talk to you. After everything that happened with Cade, I..."

He puts a hand up and stops me from talking. "It doesn't matter. You're home now."

The two of us walk into the living room and sit down. I

waste no time in dropping the same bomb that exploded on my life today.

"I saw Mom earlier."

His brows furrow. "Since when did you start calling Nora 'Mom?'"

I shake my head. "No. I saw Mom. As in, my actual mother."

His eyes widen for a moment, but he composes himself. "Well, that must have come as a shock. Where did this happen?"

"She showed up at the studio during rehearsal."

"Wow," he murmurs. "Did she say anything? Did you two talk?"

My head tilts side to side. "If you call me screaming at her talking, then sure."

He chuckles. "You always were the 'take no shit' kind of kid."

I smile, but then her words echo in my head. "She did say one thing though. Pressed on it, actually, which made it kind of strange."

"What's that?"

"She said she didn't choose to leave me, but you always said she couldn't take being a mom. That she walked out on both of us and never looked back."

My dad chokes on air and coughs for a second, clearing his throat. He tries to play it cool, but I've known this man my whole life. Judging by that reaction, there's something I don't know, and he definitely gave it away.

"Dad?"

He waves it off. "She's always had a few screws loose in the head."

"Dad."

"It's not true."

I sigh heavily, feeling my heart break. "Dad."

His head drops and he rubs his hands together, his own nervous habit. "Everything I did, I did for you."

Not this again.

I roll my eyes and stand up. "Do you know how sick I am of hearing that lately?"

"Lennon, I mean it."

"Just like you meant it when you said she walked out? Completely on her own accord, right?" I huff and shake my head. "What were you going to do if I had wanted to see her when you had that P.I. track her down?"

He cringes and won't even look me in the eye. "I knew you wouldn't."

A dry laugh echoes out of me. "Wow, you really are an asshole."

His head lifts until he's focused on me. "Now look, she may not have chosen to leave you entirely on her own, but I didn't force her out the door."

"So, what then? How'd you get her to leave me behind so you and I could live some half-full life?"

He squares his shoulders, like he needs the internal strength. "She was going to take you, and the courts were going to let her." He pauses. "She also wanted money, and they weren't going to give her that. There was a prenup in place when we married."

The truth barrels over me before he even says it. "You paid her off."

He nods once. "She took three million dollars in exchange for signing over her rights to you."

"You've got to be kidding me."

His hand reaches out for me, but I dodge it. "Lennon, you wouldn't have had the life you deserve with her. I couldn't let her do that."

"Of course, you couldn't!" I roar. "You've been controlling everything in my life since before I even knew! Dance, School, Cade."

He shakes his head. "He has nothing to do with this."

"He has everything to do with this!" I put a hand on my hip. "I'm in love with him, and you just threw him out like he was trash."

"That boy is bad news."

"*That boy* is the only one who seems to actually care about me. The rest of you use my best interest as an excuse for your own selfish gain."

I turn around and head for the door, unable to deal with any of this crap anymore. I just make it to the door when my dad tries to stop me.

"Where are you going?"

I glance back at him with disgust. "To save the one relationship that matters, if it's not too late."

IT DOESN'T TAKE A rocket scientist to figure out where Cade is. With a storm brewing off the coast, there's bound to be some intense waves, and that's everything he lives for. Colby pulls up to the beach, and my heart flutters when I see the Jeep in the parking lot. The whole thing is empty, except for two guys standing on the sand.

I jump out of the car and run as fast I can toward the shoreline. The closer I get, the more I realize that Bryce and Jayden are there, but not Cade. When Bryce sees me, confusion covers his face.

"Lennon?" he shouts over the loudness of the ocean and wind. "What are you doing here?"

"Where's Cade? I need to talk to him!"

He looks at me skeptically as he turns toward the water. When I follow where he's looking, I see him. The waves are rough—enough to scare even the best surfer—but Cade is right there in the middle of it, paddling out with all his might.

"Is he crazy?" I shriek. "These waves could kill him!"

Jayden shrugs. "I don't think he cares anymore."

No, I can't let this happen. Not without getting to talk to him first. I glance at the board on the ground and the two guys not paying attention. Before they can stop me, I grab it and run for the ocean—no matter how scary.

29

CADE

I SIT ON MY BOARD, WAITING FOR THE RIGHT WAVE to catch. One of the things about storms, is they create a killer swell. The downside, it's not exactly the safest water to surf in. It's rough, unpredictable, destructive.

A few months ago, I would've thought twice before diving into the sea when she's like this, but now, I live for the adrenaline rush. It's the only thing that makes me feel an ounce of what Lennon did. She was nothing to me, until she became everything. My light. My air. My life. If I have to live without her because it's what's best for her, then I'll do it—but it will be my own personal hell.

I turn around and go to catch a wave, when a mop of blonde hair halts my movements. At first, I think I'm seeing things. That somehow the fear and the rush mixed together to cause hallucinations. But when she dips under a wave and comes back up again, the panic sets in.

"What the fuck are you doing?" I scream at her. "This ocean could kill you!"

"Which is exactly why you shouldn't be in it!"

I shake my head. "Get out of here, Lennon. Go back to the shore."

"No," she argues back. "Not without you coming with me."

Panic takes over, and nothing she says registers. All I can focus on is that she's still here. What she's risking. What could happen. I need to get her out of here. She's not safe.

My jaw ticks and I scream at her with everything in me. "I said fucking go! Can you just listen for once in your fucking life?"

She flinches before looking at me the same way she did when I showed up at Colby's—let down and full of hate. Still, I need her to go. She doesn't belong out here. Not when she's only been surfing for a month.

She spins the board and starts to paddle back to shore, when a wave comes out of nowhere and takes her out. My heart drops as I watch it pummel her into the water. The board comes up and flies into the air, but I'm yet to see Lennon. Even Bryce and Jayden are running into the ocean to get to her.

I abandon my board and swim as fast as I can toward her. The waves threaten to toss me around but I use all my strength to stay on path. Finally, my hand grazes soft skin. I pull Lennon into my arms and push up off the bottom.

As we finally reach the top, Lennon coughs violently. She's gasping for air and holding her chest as I bring us both to shore. Once she's out of the water, she stops and bends over. Her hands are on her knees while she gets all the water out of her.

"Are you crazy?" I ask when she catches her breath. "Why would you risk going in there?"

She shoos me away. "I get it, okay? I was stupid to come here."

Seeing her go to walk away, my brows furrow. "Lennon."

"No, okay?" She turns back around. "Don't Lennon me. I know. I'm an idiot for thinking you wanted to see me. I'm sorry I ruined your storm surfing." She looks out at the water and sighs. "And another board, apparently."

I look over at the water to find both mine and Bryce's boards in pieces, but this time I don't care. Before I can tell her that, however, she keeps going.

"My whole world is falling apart, and you happen to be the only part of it I want to keep whole, but it's fine. I deserve it after how I treated you at Colby's."

"Lennon."

She raises her hands defensively. "I'm going, I'm going."

Turning to walk away, I can't help but smile at her retreating form. She only gets a couple steps away before I rush forward and grab her wrist. With one pull, I spin her around and into my arms. She opens her mouth to say something, but I don't give her a chance. I press my lips to hers for the first time in almost two weeks, and my whole body comes alive again.

The sky opens up as the storm finally arrives and rain pours down on top of us. My arms wrap around her waist, wanting to hold her close and never let her go. All I want to do, for the rest of my life, is be right here, doing exactly this.

She breaks the kiss to catch her breath and pulls her head back. "But I thought you—"

I shake my head. "You thought wrong."

Sighing in relief, she rests her forehead against mine. "No more running. No more pushing each other away. I'm tired of each of us having one foot out the door, because I'm invested in this."

Her words cause a wide grin to stretch across my face. "You know, my dad told me that when it's real, you can't walk away. It's funny because when he said it, I laughed. But now, standing here with you, I realize he was right. Because I know I should walk away. You deserve so much better than me, and I know I'm being selfish, but I can't fucking move."

"Are you saying..." Her eyes stare into mine, with nothing but hope and admiration in them.

I chuckle and look her up and down, smirking. "I love you, Lennon. You're everything to me. I'd die without you. And I mean it, completely."

She lights up like the sun and pulls me down into her, connecting our lips once again in a kiss I never want to end.

EPILOGUE

CADE

THE THEATER IS PACKED WITH PEOPLE. SOME OLD, some young, and all dressed up. I stay firmly seated between Knox and Grayson. Knox and Delaney flew in just to see Savannah and Lennon perform, making them probably two of the most supportive friends I know.

On Knox's lap is Delaney, and on the other side of him is Asher and Colby. To my left, however, are two kids I've only just met—Carter and Jace. Apparently Grayson and Savannah know them from school, but it's clear there's some tension between Knox and Carter. When they got here, he hugged Delaney hello, and it looked like Knox was ready to light him on fire.

It reaches the end of the recital and I sit up, knowing I finally get to see Lennon. She, Brady, and Savannah are the last dance of the evening, being as they're the oldest and most talented. I've always loved seeing Lennon dance, ever since I spied on her in her basement studio when I first moved into her house. The way she moves and uses her body to tell a story—it's the most beautiful thing I've ever seen.

"Dance Again" by Selena Gomez starts to play, and Lennon steps out stage right while Savannah comes out on the left. They both look gorgeous in pale pink costumes, with their blonde hair tied back. Their moves are slow at first, precise, but as the beat drops, they break into a spin with multiple rotations. The crowd starts to cheer as they stay perfectly in sync with each other.

The chorus hits, and they're all over the stage. They fly through the air like gravity doesn't exist. Savannah is talented, but my eyes stay glued to Lennon. At the end of the chorus, Brady comes out with all of them flipping at the same time. How they managed to time this so perfectly is beyond me.

Delaney and Tessa dance on their boyfriends' laps, screaming and cheering louder than anyone in here. It's like they're having the time of their lives just supporting their best friends. It makes me happy to see someone care about Lennon as much as I do. Even Colby looks proud as he watches her.

The song slows down for a moment and in turn, so do their movements. It's full of light spins and kicks that show how insanely flexible they are. They both leap toward Brady. He holds them both in the air with one arm under each. As the beat drops again, he puts them down and they both go into a front aerial.

Everyone in the audience watches in awe, and when the dance ends, a standing ovation is more than well deserved. I practically go deaf from Delaney and Tessa's screams, but my gaze is locked on Lennon. As she blows me a kiss, Grayson drapes an arm over my shoulder.

"We are two very lucky guys."

I chuckle. "That we are, man. That we are."

I HOLD MY GIRL closely in my arms while everyone surrounds her and Savannah to congratulate them on a job well done. When everyone leaves, all that's left are the people who were sitting in our row. Carter and Jace come up and give Savannah a hug, while Lennon narrows her eyes on Carter.

"Your cousin is a piece of shit," she tells him.

He huffs and starts to laugh. "I could have told you that."

I look to Grayson. "Who's his cousin?"

"Kellan."

I snort, only for Lennon to turn around and eye me up.

"Watch it," she sasses. "You're not much better."

I chuckle happily and pull her impossibly closer, kissing her just because I can.

After finding out the truth about her dad, Lennon decided she didn't want anything to do with either of her parents. For one, her mom chose money over her own daughter. And two, her dad spent her entire life lying about it. If she ever chooses to talk to either of them again, I'll support her, but I don't think that will happen for a very long time.

My mom, on the other hand, only reaches out when Molly won't stop begging her for the next time she can see me. Thankfully, she isn't spiteful and doesn't try to keep us apart. This weekend, Lennon and I are taking her to the beach so I can finally teach her how to surf.

As for the future, it's slightly up in the air. I have a meeting with Billabong next week, and if they sign me, I could be spending most of the year traveling all over the world to hundreds of incredible surfing locations. Hawaii. Australia. Maldives.

One thing I know for sure, though, is Lennon will always be the one I come back to. It may be hard, both chasing our dreams, but we've been through worse. I have no doubt in my mind that we'll make it work.

LENNON
SIX MONTHS LATER

I watch Grayson hanging the picture of Cade's last competition on the wall. Every time I tell him to tilt it one way or another, he goes way too far. The phrase "just a bit" clearly isn't in his vocabulary.

"Ugh," Savannah groans. "Let me do it."

She pushes Grayson out of the way and moves the picture perfectly into place. The three of us stand back to look at it, and I can't help but smile. He's achieved so much. After signing with Billabong, he's been traveling almost constantly and I've never seen him happier. All his dreams are coming true.

Mine on the other hand, almost didn't. After choosing Cade over my dad once and for all, he did something even lower than paying my mom to sign her rights over—he pulled my tuition. I was getting everything ready to head to New York when I got the call from the finance office asking how I planned on paying for school. Needless to say, I was devastated.

If he thought he could break me and force me into coming home, he was wrong. You see, because I happen to have friends in high places. Ones that will have my back, no matter what life throws at me. And Colby Hendrix was exactly that. The second he found out about what my dad did, he called Juilliard and paid all four years of my tuition up front. Then, despite my telling him not to, proceeded to buy a condo in the heart of the city and insisted I live in it. Needless to say, I owe Colby my life, and even Cade can appreciate that.

"I still don't understand the significance of that," Grayson says, looking over at the two pieces of broken surfboard hanging on the wall.

I smile as I remember the first time Cade and I met. When he veered out of the way just in time to avoid hitting me. I never realized he kept the broken pieces until one day when he insisted on hanging them on the wall. He said it's part of our story, and I couldn't agree more.

"It's special," I tell him.

Savannah smirks because she knows the story behind it, but for the most part, it's mine and Cade's little secret. Something that is only our own. And I'd like to keep it that way.

A knock sounds at the door and my brows furrow. "Did you guys order food or something?"

They both shake their heads. I walk over to the door and the second I open it, my jaw drops.

There stands Cade—back from Fiji and tan as hell. He's holding a bouquet of pink roses in his hand and his suitcase in the other. I throw myself into his arms and breathe in his cologne.

"You're home early!"

He laughs softly. "I couldn't stay away any longer. I missed you too much."

Long distance isn't for the weak, but Cade and I both agreed that it's only four years until I graduate, and then the two of us can see the world together. In the meantime, we have a two week rule. No matter what, we only go a maximum of two weeks of being apart, whether it takes me going to him or him coming home. Apparently, Cade can only last a week.

I step back and help him bring his things inside, before looking over at Grayson and Savannah. "Unless you two want to see a live action porno, I suggest you leave."

Grayson wiggles his eyebrows, causing Sav to smack him in the stomach. She grabs his wrist and pulls toward the exit.

"Have fun, you two."

Cade looks me up and down, licking his lips in a way he knows turns me into a puddle of mush. "Oh, trust me, we will."

CORRUPT MY MIND

My name is Zayn Bronsyn,
and I think I screwed up.

I wasn't supposed to fall,
especially not for her.
She's in a league of her own,
and I'm just her brother's scumbag friend.

The last time I saw her,
she was thirteen with braces.
Now, she's back from boarding school,
with an hourglass body that'll bring me to my knees.

If Easton finds out I hooked up with his sister,
he might actually kill me.
She's too innocent, too perfect for a guy like me,
but I can't resist bringing her into my messed up world.

Amelia Donovan might be the one to revive my blackened heart.

Corrupt My Mind
Coming September 24th

Want more Lennon and Cade?
Check out this bonus chapter.

ACKNOWLEDGMENTS

Wow. I can't believe this series is over already. It feels like just yesterday I was sitting down to write The Sinner. These characters are an addiction to write. I honestly couldn't get enough of them, except maybe Knox. He drove me nuts.

Don't worry though, because the spin off is coming in September 2020 and it features all your favorite guys—Zayn, Jace, Carter, and Bryce. I also might have a super secret surprise coming real soon. ;)

This series, and you readers, have done things for my career that I only dreamed were possible. I honestly cannot thank you enough. Turning writing some books into a full time career that can provide for my family is something I longed for but never knew if it would actually happen. Now it's my reality, and that's so surreal to me.

To my team, Christine Estevez, Christina Santos, and Mercedez Potts—you guys keep me together. Whether it's reminding me of things I need to do, asking me if I need anything, or doing all the work I don't have time for because I'm too busy writing on impossible deadlines I set for myself, you're always there. I honestly don't know what I would do without the three of you.

To Kiezha and Tiffany, thank you for making this book as perfect as possible. I appreciate both of you so much.

To Lindsey, Alley, Sam, and Kristy, thank you for pushing me to finish this and sprinting with me so that I could. Without you guys, this book probably would have been three months late. Just saying.

To Melissa and Ashley, thank you for being there to just listen to me vent and bounce ideas off of. You two are the best and I love you for that.

Lastly, thank you to my husband, who never understands I have to write and insists we go for car rides and spend time together. You're lucky you're cute.

Until next time.
(Which may be sooner than you think.)
xoxo,
Kels

ABOUT THE AUTHOR

Kelsey Clayton is an internationally selling author of Contemporary Romance novels. She lives in a small town in Delaware with her husband, two kids, and dog.

She is an avid reader of fall hard romance. She believes that books are the best escape you can find, and that if you feel a range of emotions while reading her stories - she succeeded. She loves writing and is only getting started on this life long journey.

Kelsey likes to keep things in her life simple. Her ideal night is one with sweatpants, a fluffy blanket, cheese fries, and wine. She holds her friends and family close to her heart and would do just about anything to make them happy.

Books By KELSEY CLAYTON

North Haven University

Corrupt My Mind *(Sept 2020)*

Change My Game *(Nov 2020)*

Wreck My Plans *(Jan 2021)*

Waste My Time *(Feb 2021)*

Haven Grace Prep

The Sinner

The Saint

The Rebel

The Enemy

The Sleepless November Saga

Sleepless November

Endless December

Seamless Forever

Awakened in September

Standalones

Returning to Rockport

_ _ _ _ _ _ _ (Coming Soon)

Printed in Great Britain
by Amazon

47496437R00167